CW00358133

Grasping Nettles

For Meg

Happy Birthday!

With Love & Best Wishes

for the Future

March 31st 2019

Grandad

(Arthur B.)

For my mother and father, my wife Margaret, and Richard and Clare and their families

Grasping Nettles

Tales of Tension and Triumph

Arthur Baskerville

DOWNLAND PRESS

Copyright © Arthur Baskerville 2000
First published in 2000 by Downland Press
P O Box 1777
Salisbury SP5 1UA

Distributed by Comberow Publications
3 North Street Winchcombe
Glos GL54 5LH

The right of Arthur Baskerville to be identified as the author
of the work has been asserted herein in accordance with the
Copyright, Designs and Patents Act 1988.

All rights reserved. This book is sold subject to the condition
that it shall not, by way of trade or otherwise, be lent, resold,
hired out or otherwise circulated without the publisher's prior
consent in any form of binding or cover other than that in
which it is published and without a similar condition including
this condition being imposed on the subsequent purchaser.

All of the characters in this book are fictitious and any
resemblance to actual people, living or dead, is purely
imaginary.

British Library Cataloguing in Publication Data
A catalogue record for this book is available from the British
Library

ISBN 0-9537460-0-3

Typeset by Amolibros, Watchet, Somerset
This book production has been managed by Amolibros
Printed and bound by T J International Ltd, Padstow,
Cornwall

Contents

Snap

The post arrived just as they were finishing breakfast. As soon as he heard the metallic slap of the letterbox Ernest Rowbotham drained his teacup and made for the front door. They'd come! He picked up the plastic packages, recognised his self-addressed labels, and took them back to the table, calling to his wife, who was making his sandwiches in the kitchen.

"The holiday pictures have arrived. Three of the films, anyway."

"Oh good. I hope they've come out all right."

Joan enjoyed a certain amount of interest in his pictures, especially holidays slides, because they did bring back the places so vividly, but she had no time for the technicalities of photography, and certainly did not share his obsession.

Having ripped his way into the boxes, Ernest was holding the slides up to the window one by one and squinting up at them. He snorted from time to time and a frown of dissatisfaction creased his large, coarse-featured face.

"Some of them aren't bad, but it's the usual problem—I often didn't have the right lens with me at the time. And there's one or two badly under-exposed. I'm sure that light-meter isn't giving a correct reading. We'll project them tonight, but I don't think there's anything of competition standard."

Joan sighed. She was used to this. She had spent much of their recent holiday in Cornwall waiting while Ernest took his photographs, waiting for the clouds to clear from the sun, waiting until a blemishing parked car was driven from the composition, waiting while he changed a film. She sometimes felt that she spent half her life waiting. Ernest, though, was always as excited as a small boy when he took what he thought would be a belter, a picture that really had all the ingredients to win one of the competitions of his photographic society.

Then, after the taking, came the present stage, what Joan considered to be the phase of disillusion, when the photos came back. From her experience over a lifetime as a reluctant photographer's mate, she knew that his pictures were actually pretty good. But recently she was saddened to notice his growing discontent at what he regarded as low-standard pictures. What had been acceptable before no longer satisfied him. His constant quest for improvement, for the Holy Grail of the perfect portrait, the perfect landscape, was really getting on her nerves.

She remembered the time when they were younger, when he used to take three or four films of their early foreign holidays. In those days, when they had a slide show on winter evenings, they used to marvel at how well the colours came out, at the stunning mountains and lakes; they experienced again the picnics with the children. Of course, even then Ernest was trying to improve the quality, but he enjoyed the results as much as the rest of the family. They were a record of happy times. His photographs gave him pleasure before he began the pursuit of perfection.

"You'd better keep an eye on the clock, it's nearly time you were on your way. Your sandwiches are by the car keys."

"Right-ho," replied Ernest absently. "I'm just kicking myself that I never seem to make the best use of that 135 mm fixed-focus lens—I'd have been far better off using the big zoom."

Ernest, rising sixty-five, big and ungainly, with a shock of wiry grey hair, had only a couple of months to go before he retired.

"Still, it won't be long before I'll be free on Monday mornings. The bliss of it; no work. I'll be able to set off for a walk with the camera, or, if it's wet, I can catalogue slides, get the archives and records up-to-date. It'll be marvellous. And only eight weeks to go."

That evening, after they had eaten, Ernest erected his screen and projector and put through his slides of Cornwall. Joan, as usual, thought they were all very good and didn't know what he was fussing about. They were, after all, just as the scene was; you couldn't make it something different. She didn't see why he had to be so critical. Ernest bore this for some time with his customary suppressed exasperation, though became increasingly tetchy as a result of his disappointment with the slides and his wife's inane remarks. She didn't know what she was talking about—wouldn't know a macro-zoom from a bull's foot. There were certain criteria, certain standards, and he would continue to strive for them. Being satisfied with less was not in his make-up.

When the slide show and its post-mortem were over, Joan rustled up some supper, returning to find Ernest sitting on the settee, lips pursed, eyes focussed at infinity, still immersed in a world of film speeds, emulsion characteristics and focal lengths.

"You haven't moved all this clutter," she said irritably, waving a large round arm at the projector and screen. "And I've just nearly broken my neck again over that damned extension cable."

"I thought I'd leave it up till tomorrow night and then I could sort out some slides for next week's competition."

"You and your infernal competitions! It can't stay up, because tomorrow I've got a coffee morning and we'll need all the space there is. There are other things in life as well as photography, you know."

"Not for me there isn't!" Ernest was unrepentant, but, nonetheless, after his cheese and biscuits, he packed away the projector and screen, folded up the stand and coiled up the offending cable, muttering acerbic protests.

After he had gone to work the next morning, Joan flitted around the house to tidy up, re-arrange the chairs, and make some space for her imminent coffee ladies. Though only a couple of years younger than Ernest, she was a sprightly and vivacious soul, with curly brown hair only just showing grey strands, and a liking for colourful sweaters and tweed skirts.

She stood and looked at their bedroom cupboards, filled to bursting with boxes of photographic slides; shelves packed with his archive folders of negatives and prints; half the chests of drawers in the house were jammed tight with photographic equipment. The spare bedroom upstairs, which she used to have for sewing, had recently become a shrine to photography as a studio. Joan surveyed it and groaned. Its cupboards and shelves, too, creaked with the weight of slide boxes; the place was cluttered with tripods, an enlarger, lamps on stands, until you could hardly set foot in it. The middle of the room was occupied by a large table with a light-box surrounded by piles of slides spilling in all directions, like cascading dominoes.

What on earth was to be done with it all? Joan sometimes said to him, "What's the point of keeping all these photographs? They're no use to anyone else. The children won't want them. When we're gone they'll just be thrown in the dustbin."

Ernest, naturally enough, did not see it that way. To him, each picture was an attempt at a work of art, a stroke of creativity, a unique moment of life captured forever on celluloid. Every film he took was a celebration of the art and science of photography, a triumph of his knowledge of shutter speeds and apertures and focussing, allied with chemistry and physics. On the rare occasions when he thought about it, he realised that he was driven on by a combination of pleasure in the technicalities and the constant struggle to create perfect compositions. Much like the angler, Ernest was a slave to anticipation that the next one would be better, the picture of a lifetime.

Ernest had been retired only a month before Joan had to acknowledge to herself that their new lifestyle was not working out as she had hoped. Of course, she had expected it would take a bit of time for him to adjust, and had been prepared to make allowances. She had been apprehensive of having him about the house all day—there was a limit to the number of DIY jobs, and only two rooms really needed to be decorated.

Joan had been looking forward for ages to his retirement, so that they would be able to go out for day-trips to explore the countryside, and have peaceful weekday picnics, enjoying their new freedom—the whole summer stretching ahead. But this month had not been like that. Ernest had, in effect, become a full-time photographer. True, they did have excursions into the countryside; they still trudged across the open downs, still had walks along the canal, but they were few and far between, and had become blatant photographic expeditions.

Never the nimblest athlete, even in his prime, Ernest was now so festooned about with camera bags and lenses on straps, and so often weighed down by a bulky tripod, that his former steady plod was now a shambling, nautical roll. And, of course, he perpetually stopped to take a picture, or, at least, to stoop and crane and lean this way and that as he weighed up all the possibilities, and made little calculations. Speed, however, was not in his equation, and Joan was often irritated to breaking point as she hung about and waited. Sometimes, tired of shifting from one foot to the other, or shuffling in circles, she did walk on ahead for a change of scene. But, by the time he caught her up he was in such a poisonous mood that they ended by rowing, which spoiled the day.

"I don't know why you can't have one of those simple little cameras," she said one day as they waited for a cloud to blow over, "that you just point and press—compacts don't they call them? My friends say they take very good pictures, and ever so quick."

Ernest's features, nowadays well-adapted for it, registered intense scorn.

"You mean snap-shots?" He loaded the snap with his disdain. "Idiot boxes—about what you'd expect from your friends."

Joan flared. "They're ordinary, sensible people and they take photos like most other normal people do, to remind them of relatives and parties, and holidays—memories. And they get perfectly good snaps."

"Snaps!" sneered Ernest. "That says it all. And it certainly isn't creative photography. Here, hold this lens."

One day Joan was thinking back to her anxiety that Ernest would not be able to find enough to occupy himself after retirement. She gave a bitter laugh as she saw now how naive she had been. She looked out of the kitchen window at Ernest crouching on the patio, his eye to a viewfinder, totally absorbed in setting up a still-life photo on their garden table. Since he left work he had taken to wearing a demoted, baggy, Lovat tweed suit every day, and with his untidy, portly figure, he had a Chestertonian image.

No, getting under her feet was not the problem. Making any contact with him at all was her difficulty. She had thought that, at least when he was not out on one of his solo rambles with the camera, she would have his company at home. But no, the mania he had recently developed for close-up photography and special effects meant that he spent most of his time fiddling with set-ups in the spare room studio, or out there on the patio, where he went into raptures about the quality of the light.

For years she had been used to having the bathroom commandeered periodically as a darkroom, the huge window blackout boards often leaning for weeks against the wall to be tripped over. Now, of course, he was in and out of there practically every week, and there were enamel processing dishes stacked in the window ledge and bottles of chemicals everywhere. The whole place reeked of developer and several holes had been burnt in her good carpet.

Why the hell did she put up with it? She felt hemmed in on all sides, unable to change anything. Well, how can you forbid your husband to practise photography? Did he ever feel that he was being unreasonable, she wondered? His early interest in photography had evolved during their married life from the early stages of enthusiasm to fully-fledged obsession. They were losing contact rapidly, and Joan was becoming desperate.

Ernest came in at lunch-time and ate the poached-egg-on-toast she had put in front of him without any sign of recognising what it was.

"How's it going, dear?" she inserted to engage him. "Are you getting the pictures you want?"

"Mm. Not bad. There's endless fiddling about, though. I'll have to build an optical bench before long, that'd make it easier." He sucked his teeth and slid his tongue under his top lip thoughtfully. Momentarily he reminded her of a chimpanzee.

"You know," he went on, "eggs would make a good still-life; side lighting to bring out the shell texture. I must remember that."

And that was about as close as she ever got to him. She had furnished a meal, which, in addition to fuelling his metabolism, had apparently stoked up a flame of inspiration for a still-life study. He didn't even thank me, Joan brooded. Talk about being taken for granted. She shrank further into her isolation.

The post always came later on a Saturday, so that breakfast had been cleared away and they had both filtered through the house in different directions when the letter arrived. Joan noticed the Yorkshire postmark and realised it must be from Ernest's sister.

Her first guess of his whereabouts was correct. She found him in the studio poring over slides laid out on the cold white light of his viewing box.

"Looks like a letter from Brenda and Gordon. It's unusual for them to write out of the blue."

There was not a square inch of table not covered by slides, so she dropped the envelope onto the light-box under his nose. It was the only way to guarantee his attention. Ernest glanced down through his bifocals, as his thumb irritably ragged the envelope.

"Not her writing," he said grumpily. "Might be his."

He leaned back in his chair as he read, his leathery face becoming tense, the folds of his jowls exaggerated by the cold glare from the table. He pulled at his bottom lip, lost in thought, then skidded the letter across the slides towards her.

"She's had a stroke. In a bad way by the sound of it. Gordon's asking me to go up and see her urgently."

He stared gloomily, hit hard by the news. He and his sister had been very close as children and young folk and the bond remained, even though nowadays, hundreds of miles apart, they rarely met.

"Poor Brenda, that's ever so sad," said Joan softly. "What are you going to do?"

"Go up and see her! What do you expect?" he roared.

"All right," Joan blazed. "There's no need to snap my head off! Every time I try to get a civil word out of you, you snap at me."

She leaned aggressively towards him across the table and their eyes locked. She had an overwhelming urge to strike him, to sweep all the slides from the table in an outpouring of defiance that might break the hold his obsession had over him.

"You've changed, Ernest. My God, how you've changed!" she panted. "And I don't like what you've become. You're selfish to the core." Then, anticipating the tears, she turned and retreated downstairs.

Ernest adjusted his glasses and turned his attention once more to the tiny coloured images spread before him. He needed to select three landscapes and three portraits for the next competition and it was difficult to choose. He felt sad about Brenda, but if he went up there tomorrow, he could be back well before the photographic society's meeting on Thursday.

For the rest of the day they avoided each other. Joan cooked a perfunctory meal in the evening, during much of which Ernest read the current issue of *Practical Photography*. She had thought briefly of apologising for her outburst, but then bridled with indignation as she reminded herself that he was the one who was selfish and irritable. He snapped at her even though she did everything she could to be accommodating. No, she had nothing to apologise for; in fact, to do so would only make him worse.

In the few tense exchanges of the evening he informed her that he would travel to Yorkshire next day by train, and she offered to pack a suitcase for him, wondering, even as she uttered the words, why she was so obliging. Habit, she supposed.

On the Sunday morning Ernest rose early, and by the time Joan went downstairs he had dressed, breakfasted, and was nearly ready to depart. He announced his intention to walk to the station, brushing aside her offer to drive him.

As Joan stood waiting for the kettle to boil she noticed one of his cameras and a large lens next to his case. Ernest glanced at the clock, muttered, "I must be off," and opened the suitcase. On top were three neatly folded shirts, which she had ironed the night before. He grabbed the top one, screwed it up comprehensively, and wrapped it round the camera. The others he crumpled into a roll around the zoom lens, then carefully closed the lid.

"Ernest!" she said in a low, simmering voice, her clenched fingers digging into her palms, "I went to the trouble of ironing those shirts for you last night."

He gave a little nod and a smug, contemptuous smile.

"Well, they're ideal for packing the equipment—as you know, the camera comes first." He took the case and opened the back door.

"That's the last time I'll iron shirts for you," she screamed after him, then slammed the door. The key fell out and clanged onto the floor tiles. The electric kettle bubbled furiously, belching out a cloud of steam before it clicked off.

Joan bounded up the stairs in a fury, tore open the cupboards in their bedroom, and began hauling out boxes of slides. They were labelled meticulously. She grabbed "Austria 1975", slid the tray open and emptied a cascade of plastic-mounted slides onto the floor. "Dolomites 1976" and "Cornwall 1977" followed in neat chronology. In no time she had emptied the cupboard of twenty years of photographic endeavour, and found that drifts of blue, green and grey slides, a complete history of processing by Agfa, Kodak and Fuji, had built up against her legs. She kicked them viciously about the room, shouting, "You bastard, you selfish sod," at the top of her voice.

Next she rampaged into his photographic studio, which was really the spare bedroom, and pulled open drawers, tipping their contents onto the floor and trampling on them. She swept equipment and albums off the shelves with a slash of her arm. Like a croupier she raked hundreds of loose slides across the table towards her, then flicked them at the wall with a flourish.

Breathless with rage and effort, systematically she went through the house in an orgy of retribution to search out the hiding place of anything photographic. Safe-lights, timers, developing tanks, negative albums, boxes of paper, everything was hurled onto the floor. There were piles of destruction in every room.

Then, suddenly, her violence abated. She slumped onto the floor and sat clutching her dressing gown tightly round her. She surveyed the wreckage. This had been building up for years, and it was inevitable that she would snap sometime. It was just a question of whether she snapped inside and she was the one damaged, or snapped outwardly like this to get her own back and take charge of her own life.

Her anger was now at a constructive level and she took stock of her options. God! What a mess she'd made. It would take ages to clear up. But that was neither here nor there. She was going to clear all traces of photography out of the house, out of her life. All the slides, the prints, the junk and paraphernalia were going to the council tip. She would fill boxes and bin-liners, load them into the car and take it all away. Sunday was the perfect day. Resolved, Joan had breakfast in a heady, irresponsible euphoria. She had taken a big step, she was starting a new way of life. There was no turning back.

The clearing up was every bit as laborious as she had feared. She scooped pile after pile of slides into the sacks, occasionally pausing to hold one up to the window. Views had no effect on her, but she did feel twinges of regret when she came across a shot of a family group from a holiday long gone. Ernest had been so likeable and reasonable in those days. What had changed him?

Joan had to make a decision about the print albums, but after she had flicked through a few pictures of the children as toddlers and Scouts and Brownies, realised that she must keep those of the family. In the future she would want to look at them and reminisce.

She left the photographic studio, with all its expensive equipment, till last. She had only just noticed that in her frenzy of destruction she had not actually smashed the projector or the cameras and lenses. Curious—as though by some intrinsic respect for the craftsmanship in the instruments, she had spared them. They were worth a lot of money. In that case, she would take them all to the photographic shop in town next day and sell them. She would not keep the money. Oh, no. Ernest could have a cheque for that.

It actually took three trips to the council rubbish site to get rid of it all. As she hurled the last black plastic bag down into the skip among the rubble and old fridges, she felt a crazy freedom. She stood there, grinning into space. If only Ernest could see this! Even the thought of how she would break the news to him could not cloud her elation. She still had three days to solve that.

Selling the cameras and other hi-tech hardware next day

proved easier than likely, though loading the enlarger and projector stand into the car was tricky. In the shop she explained that the equipment had been her husband's, and found it quite natural to speak of him as if he had passed on. The staff had to examine it minutely, then confer for a while and pore over catalogues, but they eventually offered her £976-53p for the lot. While the manager wrote out the cheque, she watched with satisfaction as the young assistant carried the hated equipment into a back room and out of her life.

Over the next three days Joan had plenty of time to dwell on the enormity of the step she had taken, but was determined not to lose her nerve. Did she want to live with Ernest? She now realised, and it shocked her, for she had never exposed the feeling before, that she only wanted him if he would revert to his former self, lively, good company, above all considerate and unselfish; and the first symptom that had to be cured was his obsession with photography. No longer would she put up with the grumpy, self-centred bully that he had become. Realistically, she felt there was little chance that he would change, but it was worth a try and she would offer him a last chance.

Wednesday evening came and Joan drove to the station to meet him. She stood in the entrance hall palpitating, as she spotted Ernest's burly figure shambling along the platform, swinging his case. Perhaps he would be pleased to see her, be charming and attentive, and her resolve would evaporate; then where would she be?

She need not have worried. Once the distant and automatic greetings were over, he answered her enquiries about Brenda's state in terse phrases as they walked to the car. He criticised how she had parked. He watched the nearside wing with exaggerated concern as she reversed. He sighed and shook his head theatrically as the car jerked away from the traffic lights in the wrong gear. She simmered to boiling point, but bided her time.

When they arrived home she left the car in the drive and they went straight indoors. She had planned the scene to be in the kitchen.

"Sit down, Ernest. I've something to tell you. Would you like a drink?"

"What do you mean, something to tell me?" he grumbled. "What's gone wrong? I've barely taken my coat off. What is it this time? The washing machine? The garage door? I'll have a gin-and-tonic."

He slumped down at the table, his expression gruff and suspicious.

"No, it's more fundamental." She sloshed a generous helping of gin into his glass and pushed a bottle of tonic towards him. "I'm fed up with the way you treat me. I'm fed up with your selfishness, with your obsession with photography. I'd looked forward to your retirement for company, but you've got worse—you ignore me. I've made a decision while you've been away, Ernest. If we're to stay together, you've got to give up photography totally and start being like you used to be. Kind and good company. As other men are. If not, you leave this house and go elsewhere. I shall lead my own life as I want to."

He tried to interrupt, but she pressed on. "To make it easier, I've already got rid of all your photographic stuff—everything! It's gone."

"You've what?" he exploded.

"All the slides and small junk have gone to the tip, the cameras, projector and enlarger I took to that shop in town and sold," she said with icy calm.

"I don't believe you," he blustered. "What are you on about?"

She gave him the cheque. He recognised the dealer's name and immediately lumbered upstairs to investigate. "You vindictive bitch," she heard him bellowing as he stomped from room to room. She could imagine his feelings as he discovered the scale of his loss; his shock as he saw the photographic studio returned to use as his new bedroom, the little divan bed made up, his pyjamas laid out neatly on the pillow. She heard him opening cupboard after cupboard, drawer after drawer, and swearing.

There was a pause, and then from the direction of their bedroom came a sudden smash, then another, and another. She counted about ten. It was her little collection of Royal Doulton figures; they had started with her twenty-first birthday, and had been added at various anniversaries since. The ornaments had been constant companions throughout their marriage, in every house they had lived in.

Distressed, Joan ran upstairs to see what was happening. Hurling the figures against the wall must have brought Ernest to his senses, for he was standing petulantly surveying the splintered fragments of china at his feet.

"Sorry about these," he said coldly. "It seemed to even things up." He continued to stare at them.

"Perhaps you do have a point," he went on, grudgingly. "I suppose I do go over the top a bit sometimes. But I'm not giving it up altogether—that's out of the question. Damned if I will."

"Well, that's what I said, and that's what I mean," retorted Joan, hurt at losing her precious figures.

"I could move somewhere else, and then do what the hell I like," said Ernest, defiantly. His face fell as he considered. "But that would mean selling up here, and I'd end up in a small flat in some grotty area. I'd miss the garden and the space—and I'd have to do my own shopping, and washing and ironing. Bugger that. You've got me over a barrel."

Joan wilted inwardly. That was all he saw in their relationship; a nice house and garden, home comforts, food on the table, his washing done. He could not have spelled it out more plainly if he had tried.

He gave her a long, calculating look.

"We'll give it a try, then, shall we?" Then, briskly, "I'll get the dust-pan and clear up this mess."

"No, you go and have another drink," she said, with false brightness. "It won't take me a minute to brush up."

Kneeling among her shattered ornaments, Joan swept jagged heads and arms into the pan. They had been her only treasures, but, if it had really changed her life, it would be a small price to pay. She could not help wondering, though, what freedom would have been like.

Doing Her Best

Although it was not her first job, it was a big venture into a totally different field, and consequently Alice Goodwin was filled with apprehension on this, her first morning.

She had been put on her guard even at the interview a month earlier. The younger of the two partners, Alan, had been charming and helpful, and keen to put her at ease. But the senior partner, John Moss, the real boss, who had been in the practice over thirty years, scarcely tried to hide his scepticism about women veterinary surgeons in farm animal work. He had remained churlish and doubtful, eyeing her up and down in an unspoken assessment of her physique. She could not deny that she was on the small side, but nevertheless she was fit and athletic.

Alice had already got some experience under her belt; she had spent the first two years after qualifying as a veterinary surgeon in an urban practice, working exclusively with dogs, cats, and other pets. There she had got the hang of dealing with clients, their animals and colleagues, in an environment that was friendly to women and used to them. In fact, three of the five veterinary surgeons in the practice were women, and all the nurses and receptionists were also girls.

It had been a great atmosphere to work in, with lots of fun and camaraderie, and she had thoroughly enjoyed it. Indeed, she had only left because of her long-standing desire to work with farm animals.

Alice realised that, if she was ever to break into large-animal work at all, she would have to do it now. Everyone told her that the naïve courage of youth, that reckless willingness to have a crack at anything, all too soon becomes stifled by caution and inhibition. If she left it even a few years longer, she would not have the confidence to embark on something so different. This was her big opportunity, and she had to prove to these doubters that she was up to the job.

"You think you'll be able to calve cows, then?" John Moss had queried sceptically during the interview. "And hold up Friesians' muddy feet umpteen times a day, day in, day out? It's back-breaking work."

His demeanour left her in no doubt what his views were.

She had been surprised to hear a few days later that she had got the job, and thought ruefully that somebody else had probably turned it down; coupled with the fact that there was a shortage of vets and the prospects for farm-animal work were not rosy, especially in a God-forsaken part of rural Devon such as this, where few people wanted to live anyway. No, they had probably been desperate to get somebody to share that night- and weekend-rota and a woman was better than no one at all.

Alice had been given a well-worn Peugeot to drive, still liberally coated in red mud from the previous incumbent's rounds, and was provided with a cheerful little flat in the centre of the market town, not far from the practice premises. It all seemed marvellous. There was just the minor problem of holding down the job and proving herself in the face of obvious prejudice and antagonism.

She had stocked up her car boot with all the drugs and equipment the day before, and had been introduced to the office staff, so today the new life began for real. Her stomach churned with nerves as she entered the office to be allocated the day's visits. Mr Moss and one of the secretaries were already pondering the day-book. The phone was ringing; a youngish chap walked through carrying a green rubber gown and a large box of sheep wormer.

Mr Moss was evidently trying to be welcoming in his bluff way, and had arranged a round that was not too arduous, and allowed that Alice would be slow in finding some of the remote farms, their tiny tracks easily missed among the high-banked lanes.

"Alan's got a morning of routine fertility work, so I've had to give you some of the cases that have been phoned in today. There's a sow off her food at Mr Nethercott of Conibeare Farm, then a couple of lame cows at Mr Doble's, Higher Knapp, they're quite close together; after that you can have a nice scenic drive over the hills to Mr Elworthy of Withycombe, who's got some calves coughing. That'll keep you going till lunch-time." He weighed her up dubiously. "You're sure you'll be able to manage that? You've got the maps and everything?"

"Yeah, no problem, thanks, " breezed Alice, persuading herself that it was genuine concern he was showing, not condescension.

She did the first visit easily; found the farm straight away and won the farmer over with the cheery efficiency with which she took the sow's temperature and injected it, benefiting from its dullness and immobility due to the fever. She drove off down the lane thinking, "This is the life; this is just what I have always wanted."

Mr Doble's farm at Higher Knapp was a nightmare to find. She drove round miles of lanes with not a house in sight, stopped frequently to consult her map, was confused by signposts that seemed to contradict each other, and was beginning to panic, when, as she approached for the third time a corner with a tall beech hedge on a bank, she noticed a rough track and a wooden signboard fallen on its side. "Higher Knapp Farm" it read. As she pulled up in the yard she noticed that she was half an hour late.

She put on her Wellingtons and overall, grabbed a hoof knife and a tray of bottles and syringes, and made for the dairy, where she could hear the hiss of a power-hose on the concrete. Mr Doble was obviously the type who did not believe in the courtesies of greeting you, or breaking off from what he was doing. He scowled and turned off the hose as he saw her.

"You Mr Moss's new vet? He said he'd got a woman." His lip curled. "You're 'alf an 'our late. I should've been out with the tractor."

"I'm sorry I'm late—I got a bit lost. You've got a couple of lame cows, I gather?"

"Three. I found another since I phoned. They're out in this yard."

Alice followed him through a barn full of ancient, rusting machinery, its windows thick with dust and cobwebs. Startled cats shot off into the strawed darkness. The Friesians were standing chewing in a small yard bounded by tiled, cob-walled open sheds.

"We'll get 'em into the crush one at a time. It's all back feet that's the problem—'tis foul-in-the-foot, I expect. Once you've injected 'em that'll put it right."

The metal gate of the crush clanged behind the first cow, holding its neck in a yoke, while Alice slipped a rope round the affected foot, pulled it up, and tied it to the side bar. The hoof was overgrown and badly distorted. Routine foot care was evidently not something Mr Doble bothered with. Alice began to pare away with her knife, the cow kicking and leaping about as she touched sensitive spots.

"Oh, come on, she doesn't need all that bloody fussing about—just inject her and let's get on," grumbled Mr Doble.

Alice noticed a blackened area deep in the sole and knew it had to be pared out to allow the pus to discharge if the infection were to heal. Doubled up and struggling with the jerking hoof, Alice shouted, "It's not just foul between the claws, I'm afraid, it's got infection sealed inside the foot. A sharp injury's probably started it, a stone, perhaps. Unless I open it to drain, it won't get any better."

She straightened up, wiping her sweating brow. She knew she was embarking on dangerous ground, but it had to be said. "All her hooves are very overgrown—and those other cows too. You don't do any regular trimming?"

"No. Never needed to. If we get a lame 'un, Mr Moss comes and injects it and it's better in no time."

Alice was not going to argue or make her point any further. Having finished the foot, she jabbed an injection into the cow's neck and they released it from the crush. The next cow was easy enough, but the third was much more awkward to deal with. Already frantic, the huge brute had needed a lot of persuading to enter the crush. Alice then had great difficulty securing its hind leg to the side-bar, and had to enlist Mr Doble to hold the rope. Still the cow kicked and struggled as if demented as she pared. The feet were in the same atrocious condition as the others, the horn so grossly overgrown that the cow had been unable to walk properly.

Bent double over the foot, Alice struggled to re-shape the hooves, while Mr Doble hung on to the rope, muttering and cursing as his temper frayed. Suddenly the cow bucked, the rope slipped, and his arm was kicked crunchingly against the bar. He sprang back holding his wrist.

"Shit! Bloody hell fire!" He hopped about clutching the arm to his stomach. "That wouldn't 'ave 'appened if you knew what you were bloody well doing! Inject it and let the bloody cow go!"

Alice realised that, despite the crisis, she had to carry on; she could not leave the job unfinished. So, while Mr Doble raged at her, she patiently re-tied the leg to the crush and endeavoured to pare into the foot in the short intervals when the cow was not kicking it. Within minutes she had exposed another area of deep-seated infection.

"There it is," she announced with youthful zeal, "right inside the sole. But that's only the immediate problem—all the hooves of these cows need re-shaping. We could have an on-going programme of hoof care for you that would avoid this sort of thing happening."

"Bugger that. Just another scheme for vets to make money— I can't afford vets' bills as it is. Anyway, Mr Moss has never needed any schemes. I've been with cows all my life, and I'm not going to take advice from young upstarts that know sod-all and are wet behind the ears—" He paused, adding viciously, "—and certainly not from a woman."

Alice, though seething, said nothing, but injected the cow, released it, and gathered up her things with exaggerated calm. Her back ached and her arms were stiffening rapidly, but she was determined not to display any sign. She noticed that the wrist Mr Doble was rubbing had already swollen, and it crossed her mind that, in law, she was responsible for any injury an owner sustained while assisting. It was an arguable point, but she was sure that, if he were that way inclined, Doble could use it to make trouble for her. Most farmers accepted knocks and bruises as all part of the rough existence, so she would keep her fingers crossed. She could not feel any sympathy; he was such a rude, aggressive bastard. It could not have happened to a more deserving swine.

Mr Doble had not finished. He was still grumbling as she washed in a bucket in the dairy. He followed Alice back to her car and harangued her as she changed into her shoes.

"And I'll give you some advice, young woman. Farmers round 'ere won't 'ave you telling 'em what to do. Just you remember, they know a damn sight more about cows than you'll ever know. And you can tell Mr Moss not to send you 'ere again. Won't 'ave you on the place—don't care whether it's midnight or Sundays, I won't 'ave you. They can send somebody else."

He strode off towards the farm-house, still nursing his arm.

Alice drove away trembling with annoyance, worried about the difficulties she had obviously made for herself, and thoroughly depressed to have such early confirmation of the prejudice she was to face. These primitives did not want anybody new, anybody young, and, least of all, anybody female. She tried to put it out of her mind, and it did help that the landscape up on the edge of the moor, with its windswept trees and open spaces, was so wildly beautiful and restoring.

The next visit went well; the farmer was pleasant and amenable, and certainly, if he did harbour misgivings about women vets, diplomatically hid them. Alice was cheered. She was sure that most of them would at least give her a chance, and, if she did a good job, would gain confidence and accept her. She chuckled to herself; it was probably nearly as hard for young male vets round here—if they had not known you for thirty years you still had to prove yourself. It was one drawback of the backwoods.

After lunch she found Mr Moss in the office, looking grim.

"I gather you didn't go down too well with Mr Doble," he said, frowning. "He phoned to complain. Hurt his arm, did he? He seemed to think you were fiddling about unnecessarily with the cows' feet, instead of just getting on and injecting them for foul—that's it, is it?"

"He may think so. In fact, their feet were in an appalling state, hadn't been trimmed for ages," countered Alice. "That was part of the lameness, but two of them had infection inside the sole. I'm going to follow my clinical judgement, not be told what to do by some overbearing oaf. He called us in to get professional advice. Presumably he wouldn't think he knew better than the man mending his television?"

"That's true," said Moss, fingering his moustache, "but you have to put it carefully. Some of these characters can be very touchy. They're independent folk with little contact with the wider world, and they're used to getting their way in their own domain. You were a bit unfortunate, though. He was obviously miffed that you were late, then, because you're a girl, he wasn't expecting you to be up to it, so he was just looking for a row, and the final straw was the cow kicking him. It's the classic background to a scene—it's happened to all of us."

Mr Moss did not sound entirely convincing. "And, of course, we have to remember that, in the final analysis, it's the farmers who pay the bills. If we can't persuade them to agree with our treatments, they'll take their custom elsewhere. There's only one other practice in this area, but they can easily transfer their favours."

Oh, thought Alice. So that was it. She had got herself a boss who sided with his clients to keep in with them, rather than with his professional colleagues. He who pays the piper. After every little difficulty she had, Mr Moss was going to placate the farmers by criticising her behind her back, apologising that he had had to employ a youngster, and a woman at that. She smarted at the injustice of it.

Mr Moss continued; "He also refused to have you there again. That can be very awkward in emergencies, if you're the only one on duty." He gave a sardonic smile. "Don't get barred from too many farms, or we won't be able to run a viable emergency service."

"I'll be as diplomatic as I can," replied Alice, "but after five years learning about this job, I'm going to diagnose conditions and treat them in a rational, scientific way. The days of hocus-pocus and flannel are gone. Once you get into pandering to clients' whims, when you know it's clinically wrong, you're on a slippery slope. And what's more," she added excitedly, "I won't do it. At college we had clinical and scientific integrity instilled into us, and that's what I shall practise!"

John Moss appeared taken aback, but soon responded.

"Look, Alice. Every generation of new graduates I've ever employed has come out with the same altruistic crap. It'll wear off, believe me. You'll realise eventually that life's not so simple, that you have to compromise. You've also got to remember that we're running a business; we're trying to make money from clients who've got a choice." He paused and frowned sadly. "'Course, with the young lads, we have a word in their ear over a pint, and they usually see sense. I must admit, though, that over the years, we have had the odd arrogant sod who refused to compromise his fancy ideas, and carried on with crazily heroic surgery, or persisted in doing endless, uneconomical follow-up visits to lost causes. But they've always left to go into university departments, where they could indulge their counsels of perfection with somebody else's money. This is the rough-and-tumble of farm practice, and times are hard."

Alice looked at him with concern. He seemed to her so typical of the old school, of a breed that had worked hard to build up their practices; competent, and full of rough wisdom, but implacably opposed to any change in their firmly-held opinions. He must have allowed Alan to persuade him to take her on, she thought, and now he very obviously regretted it. To win him over was going to be an uphill struggle.

❦

She spent the afternoon in the surgery doing small-animal consultations. Apart from the restricted range of equipment, and the clients' simpler expectations, the work was similar to what she had been used to in her urban practice, and she rapidly began to feel at home again. The opportunity to develop the pet-animal side of the practice was definitely there, and several times she found herself wondering if that might eventually provide a sideways move to save face. Save face? Forget it! She had come here to do predominantly farm work, and, just because of a row on Day One, she was not about to cave in.

The next couple of days passed uneventfully. Alice found her way to the farms without much trouble; the farmers, though cagey and grudging, were, on the whole, understanding, and there were no physical struggles with the animals that she could not deal with. She felt that the balance was swinging in her favour.

On the Friday afternoon Alice had just left a farm and was driving across the hills for the last visit of the day, when her mobile phone rang. She pulled off the road and jotted down the details of the case and the directions. It was an urgent call to a calving in another area.

"What breed is it? Hereford-Friesian cross? And she's been at it a long time with no progress? Hmm. You say they've had a fair pull themselves? Reception's not that good here, you keep going faint. Right, I'll set off there now. Can you get somebody else to do my last visit? Cheers."

Alice put down the phone and contemplated the view before her. The hills were bathed in mellow September sun, the little fields etched onto the landscape by the shadows of their banks and hedges, stunted on the windward side; here and there was the smudgy brown of distant bracken. What a contrast, she thought, between this scene and the struggles taking place in it; the farmers' struggles to contend with the harsh elements and make some sort of a living, her own struggle to meet the challenges of her equally rigorous job.

She had a sinking feeling inside about this calving. It just sounded ominous. These outdoor beef cattle could present some horrendously difficult births, and, unlike dairy cows, were often not noticed to be in labour until they had been straining for hours and it was too late. Still, she was confident in her ability and would do her best. But her nagging doubt continued, whether or not her best would be good enough.

Alice found Mr Hayman of Butterleigh Farm without any trouble. It was a collection of mellow old cob-walled buildings nestling at the bottom of a steep combe with oak woods at one end. Her nervousness mounted as Mr Hayman came out of the house at the sound of her car. He was elderly and stocky, his grubby green boiler suit tucked into Wellingtons. He pulled on a greasy cap as he reached her and frowned while watching her donning the long rubber calving gown. He was clearly put out that he had been sent someone new.

"You're fresh to the practice, then? I hope you can do this

job, 'cause it's a tough bugger. The two of us have had a good pull and we're getting bloody nowhere."

A huge youth in a "Keep Britain Farming" T-shirt had appeared by the car and stood, hands on hips, anticipation of some entertainment written all over his stubbly face.

Alice rooted about in the car boot for the calving ropes and plastic sleeves.

"What bull's she in-calf to?"

"Simmental," replied Mr Hayman. "Use 'em all the time now."

"When was she due? Is she about to time?" enquired Alice, closing the boot lid.

"Well, we don't know exactly, 'cause we run the bull with 'em for quite a bit. She's a heifer, too,"

Alice's heart sank further. Christ, a heifer, and a Simmental bull. This could be a tight squeeze.

They had the heifer on straw in an ancient loose-box, and it was padding about uneasily as they entered, before arching its back again to strain. One yellow-hoofed foot protruded from under its tail.

"There's only the one leg we could feel, so we pulled on that," said Mr Hayman. "I hope you're going to be able to manage," he added doubtfully. "It's a swine."

Alice ignored the slight and pulled the plastic gloves up her arms. Holding up the tail with one hand, with the other she explored deep in beyond the single leg. Using her fingers as eyes, she visualised the position of the calf as she followed its contours at the end of her reach. Christ, this was awful. Inexperienced as she was, Alice recognised straight away the problems facing her.

The calf's head was turned to the side instead of in the birth canal. The heifer had been in labour for hours, and the membranes had long since burst, so that the lubricating fluids, which would have made the birth easier, had been lost. The calf had died as a result of the delay, and the uterus had contracted down hard, and now fitted the calf as tightly as a glove. To get it out she would first have to push it back far enough to make room for the head and other front leg to be pulled into the birth canal. That would need massive strength that she doubted she possessed.

Alice grimaced as she turned to the farmer, still heaving back on the neck with her hand. She was angry that these stupid sods had made it worse by pulling and ramming the calf tighter in the wrong position. Not to mention that they were so bloody dozy that they had not noticed it was in labour.

"Head's back, I'm afraid; that was the original problem, but the calf's dead and there's no room to manipulate it."

Alice's mind raced. She knew the options in theory, but had no experience of what might succeed and what would let her down. Her credibility was at stake. She needed to get a rope onto the other front leg and hope to pull it up, and probably rope the neck as well. But it all depended on brute strength. What if she had to give up? She would lose face completely. Luckily, it was not a big cow, so at least her lack of height was not a problem.

As the time passed, Mr Hayman became increasingly impatient. He watched as Alice changed arms more often, knowing it was a sure sign she was tiring. He brought yet another bucket of clean water for her more frequent arm-washing.

"You making any progress in there, young lady?" he growled. "Don't seem to be much happening. You wanna see Mr Moss calve cows—strong as an ox, he is."

Alice became desperate. Why didn't he stop wittering? Hadn't she enough to think about, without giving him a running commentary? Did he expect a cabaret at the same time? Of course old Moss probably entertained them with jokes and shelled out calves without breaking sweat. But then, she wasn't a super-hero.

Her hands were now seizing up with fatigue after wrenching so long trapped between the calf and the pelvic bones. Her arms and shoulders throbbed and ached till she could scarcely move them. She knew she was at the end of her strength.

Alice made a final review of the possibilities; she had now been at it for an hour-and-a-half, and, apart from roping a leg, had made little progress. Would anybody else be able to get this calf out? She could not imagine it. If not, a Caesarian was the only choice; perhaps she should have done that in the first place? Now she hadn't the strength to do the operation, pretty hard work in itself, and the cow wasn't in good shape to stand it either.

Suddenly the weariness swamped her. She would have to give in. Bugger credibility. Bugger image. She just wasn't strong enough, that was all there was to it. She had to admit it. Probably a lot of men wouldn't be either, which was some consolation. After all, it was nothing to be ashamed of, though in this environment it would appear so. And she did have mental toughness. She knew that how she handled this was crucial. The word would soon get round the farms.

"I'm afraid this is beyond me, Mr Hayman. As you said, it's a real swine. I'll phone back to the practice and get them to send one of the men out—I expect they'll manage somehow. I'm sorry, but I've done my best."

It was a speech she had never thought she would make; perhaps the first time in her life that she accepted she had limitations.

"That's all right, my dear," said Mr Hayman, picking up the bucket. "They shouldn't never 'ave sent a slip of a girl on a job like this, 'tis man's work. 'Tisn't fair on you. You phone up, then 'ave a breather. I reckon you've earned one."

Alice slumped onto a bale of straw in the yard, utterly exhausted. Her arms and shoulders had stiffened, her back ached. She didn't know how long she'd sat there in a trance, but it seemed no time before a Volvo estate swung into the yard. Oh God! John Moss himself had come. This would be utter humiliation. With an effort she stirred herself and trudged over to confront him and explain as he robed up by his car boot.

"I'm sorry, but I'm stuck with this one. The head's back, she's been on a long time, the uterus has clamped down, and I just can't push the calf back to make any room. I'm afraid my hands have given out." She sounded totally dejected.

"God, you look knackered, Alice," said Moss airily, as he pushed his arms through his calving gown. "Well, we did warn you what it's like. As well as know-how and experience, it's often brute force that's necessary. Don't forget, most of the patients are a lot stronger than we are—come to that, even their uteruses are stronger than we are. You need to be hellish tough in this job."

As Alice looked at him she did feel totally inadequate. Despite his advancing years, John Moss was a big, powerfully muscular man, with huge shoulders and massive hairy arms, his biceps accentuated now by the tight, elasticated sleeves of the parturition gown.

He grabbed a large tube of lubricant and a couple of calving ropes and slammed the boot lid.

"Let's go and have a look-see."

The farmer welcomed him with obvious relief.

"Nice to see you, Mr Moss. You've done a few of these for us in your time, haven't you? This young lady's done her best, but it's just too much for her."

Alice gave him a feeble, resigned smile. Blast his condescension; though perhaps, in his way, he was only trying to be kind.

Moss did not bother with plastic sleeves, and in no time was fishing up to his armpit inside the cow.

"Well, your assessment of the malpresentation was correct," he announced approvingly, "and it's bloody tight for space. I can see your problem. It just needs strength to push it back."

The cow swung her hindquarters round as he heaved, and Mr Hayman steadied her with his hand.

"You can say what you like, George," Moss continued "but, with the best will in the world, a woman can't cope with this sort of job. And do you know, nowadays, well over half the veterinary students are girls? That's true. Absolutely ridiculous! I don't see how practices are going to manage in the future."

Moss pushed and twisted, bent and strained, and kept up a running supply of lively banter and anecdotes, to the delight of Mr Hayman. Gradually, though he slowed down. A tortuous blue vein stood out on each temple, and sweat ran into the creases on his face. He paused to take deep breaths.

"Christ, Alice, this is tight," he gasped. "And the calf's a big sod, too."

Eventually he pulled up the other front leg and finally succeeded in grappling the head out into their view. The calf was ready for the final pull for delivery. Moss stood back, his long, bloodied arms hanging loosely.

Alice could not help but admire his feat. She had imagined, stage by stage, what he was doing. Now, as never before, she could appreciate the difficulties. She had disliked him from their first meeting, viewed his old-fashioned, chauvinistic opinions with scorn and loathing. But, if nothing else, she had to respect his toughness and experience.

Moss stepped back, and, with a mock grandiose sweep of his arm, waved Alice forward to complete the delivery.

"It's all yours. You might as well have the satisfaction of finishing the job."

Helped by Mr Hayman and his lad, she hauled on the calf's front legs and soon it slid out onto the straw, a lifeless bundle of gangling legs and bloodied membranes.

When Alice turned back to Moss, she was just in time to see him staggering sideways, his head lolling down. She rushed to support him, and, together with the other two, managed to lead him out into the yard, where he stumbled onto his knees. So heavy and awkward was he that they could not prevent him rolling onto his side. He was muttering incoherently.

Alice had been a keen first-aider as a student, and recognised immediately the seriousness of the situation. Rapidly she pulled off his rubber gown, tore open his shirt, and rolled him onto his back, bent his neck into position, and began calmly, but vigorously, giving him mouth-to-mouth resuscitation.

"Quick! Go and phone for an ambulance," she shouted in between breaths. "Tell them it's very urgent—probably a coronary."

"Right-ho," replied Mr Hayman, setting off, "but they won't be very quick; 'tis a good three-quarters-of-an-hour from the hospital, even if they don't get lost!"

After a few moments' blowing, Alice remembered that external heart massage could also be vital, so she alternated her breathing efforts with massaging Moss's chest as hard as she could. She seemed to have been struggling with him for an age, but at last he gave a few massive gasps and sighs. She pressed her ear against his chest; there was a strong, though irregular, heart-beat. Soon he was breathing more steadily and opened his eyes. Looking round wildly, he flailed his arms out and tried to sit up. Alice grappled with him, but he was too heavy and strong.

Mr Hayman now ran into the yard, shouting "I got through. They're on their way!"

"Quick, give me a hand to sit him up! Can you get a couple of straw bales to prop him from behind?"

Once they had him sitting up against the bales, legs stretched out, there was nothing to do but wait for the ambulance. Alice sat on the ground beside him, and they sipped strong tea that Mr Hayman insisted on bringing.

"So what happened, then?" Moss asked her. "Did I just keel over? I felt very dizzy for a few minutes when I was wrestling with that calf."

"Yes, it looks as though you had a bit of a cardiac arrest," said Alice. There was no point in wrapping it up. If his nature was to be blunt, then he could take it blunt, too. "Brought on by the exertion of the calving. Anyway, you seem to have survived. They'll be able to monitor your ticker and keep it stabilised when they get here."

John Moss stared thoughtfully into his mug of tea and spoke to Alice as if he was talking to himself.

"I expect you think I'm a real chauvinistic old dinosaur. It's not that at all. My generation, and the ones before, had tremendous respect and admiration for women, especially for women vets; we were really very chivalrous compared with what it's like today." He looked up at Alice with a defiant twinkle in his eye. "But we know that, at times, this job on farms is too physically hard for them. It's just Nature, and you can't go against that. You've seen it yourself this week, lame cows, calvings. And I wasn't up to it today, either." He gazed across the yard and pondered. "Perhaps there are ways we could try to make it easier; re-arrange things a bit."

They heard the ambulance winding its way down into the combe and Mr Hayman re-joined them.

"Ambulance is here, Mr Moss. How are you feeling now? Cor, you're lucky to be alive. In fact, you wouldn't have been if it wasn't for this young woman giving you that kiss-of-life business. She saved your life—make no mistake about that!"

John Moss glanced at Alice with a weary grin, then at the farmer. "Yes. She's pretty good in an emergency, isn't she? Got the right spirit, and plenty of determination. She'll be a great asset to the practice."

Pigment

Giles Green had had a difficult day at work. There had been hassle galore, he had felt tired and full of aches and pains, and then, to cap it all, he had been stuck in a traffic jam, which had converted his customary half-hour's car journey home into over an hour.

Consequently, during the evening meal he had managed to be both listless and irritable, and conversation with his wife had been spasmodic. They were well into the pudding course before he had finished complaining about the traffic and the idiots who had plagued him at work. His wife, as always, took it all with bright patience. This, in itself, was praiseworthy, but was liable to exasperate him further, because it suggested that she did not fully appreciate the outrages he had suffered.

They sat on the settee and watched television for a couple of hours, sipped milky coffee, talked of doing some gardening, but decided it was too late. He had felt increasingly tired lately, and often complained to his wife of stiff muscles and cramp after pretty ordinary exercise. He pondered about taking his problems along to the doctor, but thought his condition was so vague that there would be nothing to go on, and he would be fobbed off. The thought of sitting in that dreary waiting room for an hour was the final dissuader—and that was with an appointment. An open surgery, as they called the free-for-all, did not bear thinking about.

The television programme finished and he went to spend a penny. Giles stared in horror; he was passing dark red urine! He bent and peered into the pan. There was no doubt about it, it was discoloured and reddish. Blood! Oh, my God! What does that mean? Kidneys? Bladder? Cancer? At least it wasn't painful, whatever it was. He informed his wife, with the air of a man announcing an important news-flash.

She took it with her customary calmness, certain it could not be anything serious. She did advise, though, that he ought to keep an eye open for it happening again. He would definitely do that! Damn it all, he was talking about passing blood-stained urine! There had to be a reason for that, didn't there? It had never happened in his previous forty-five years, so it was hardly the norm. She did concede he had a point, but privately felt that men make such a dramatic fuss over small biological events. She was prepared to bet that this was trivial and would put itself right.

Giles Green woke up several times during the night, and each time, as his thoughts flitted about, he eventually remembered his discovery. Potentially, it must be a bit serious. He made up his mind to make an appointment to see his doctor next day.

When he got up he made straight for the bathroom, where he was relieved to find that he had become normal again.

"It's got better, love," he shouted downstairs to his wife.

She had actually forgotten all about his problem, and was staring blankly through the kitchen window, stirring a cup of coffee. She stifled a yawn.

"Has it, dear? Jolly good. I told you it would. I'm sure it was nothing to worry about."

Over breakfast he gave up the idea of seeing the doctor.

A few days later, his trouble was again in evidence. This time it struck first thing in the morning. Had he done anything which might have caused it? While he was shaving he thought back over the previous twenty-four hours. As it had been a nice summer evening, they had gone for a cycle ride and eaten later than usual. It was certainly not a very strenuous ride, though his calf muscles did feel a bit stiff today. Apart from that, nothing out of the ordinary.

He made an appointment to see his doctor in a couple of days, which was the earliest that his own chap was available. Green, being an intelligent man, who kept himself well-informed on medical matters by means of the television documentaries and soap operas, decided it would be advisable to have a specimen of the suspect urine to take with him. Accordingly, he kept a clean jam-jar on the bathroom window-ledge. To no avail, it turned out.

He sat in the waiting room, flicking through old copies of women's magazines, barely taking in what he read, and wondering what he was going to say. Should he mention the months of tiredness and muscle-weakness? There had been a lot about this sort of thing in the media recently. Didn't they call it "yuppy-flu" or some long medical term? Well, he hadn't had 'flu for years.

At last it was his turn. Young Dr Jackson jumped up from behind his computer and shook his hand vigorously. He was an eager young man, an awful lot younger than Green. In contrast to the brigade of previous generations, who wore dark suits and cuff-links, this one belonged to the modern, informal persuasion, who sported, at best, tweed jackets and corduroys, and were more likely to be seen slopping about in shapeless pullovers.

"Morning, Mr Green. What can we do for you? I was just putting up your details on the screen. This is my new toy." He patted it proudly.

"Oh. Are you getting the hang of it all right?" replied Green.

"A few teething troubles, that's all."

Green wondered whether to make a joke about dentists, but thought better of it. There were enough distractions already.

"And how's your good lady wife, and the children? Good. Good."

Dr Jackson simply exuded youthful enthusiasm and cheeriness, and Giles Green began to doubt if he would listen long enough to take in his clinical history. To his credit, the doctor did eventually simmer down and kept the interruptions to a minimum, mainly nodding and saying, "Mm, Mm, Mm. Yes. Yes. I see. Mm. Really? Mm. Did you?" Green became so mesmerised by these punctuations that at times he found himself losing the thread.

Eventually, he had got out most of the highlights of his case, but regretted he hadn't brought a specimen. The intermittent nature of his problem obviously made it difficult. He lay on the couch and Dr Jackson examined him, but there was clearly not much to be gleaned from that. The doctor returned to his computer and began to tap a few keys, while Green tucked in his shirt.

"It's a very interesting condition, the yuppy 'flu, you know, Mr Green. I'm not saying that's what you've got. In fact, the urine problem is probably something quite different. I just wonder how that fits in with the exertion. You say you were cycling the night before one attack? You see, there are some interesting conditions in which breakdown of muscles after exercise can release muscle pigment into the urine. I think we ought to get it investigated properly. No treatment necessary just yet."

He tapped a few more keys and peered intently at the screen. "Still at the same address? Splendid. I'll get a letter off to the hospital in the next few days, and they'll send you an appointment."

Giles Green attended the out-patients' department a few weeks later. In his pocket was a jam-jar containing, finally, a specimen of the reddish-coloured urine. Gotcha, he had exclaimed, as he screwed the lid on. Now they'll be able to find out what's going on. He gave it to a nurse at Reception, and hoped they wouldn't lose it.

His session with the doctors went well. They were only half an hour late, and the two who dealt with him seemed thorough and were at least more polite than many he had seen in the past. But it did take an interminable time. He talked to them with his clothes on, then had to undress and wait in a cubicle. Then they examined him again. Later he dressed and they questioned him still more. Finally, he was given a handful of forms to take to the pathology lab and the X-ray department, at both of which he had to wait a further half-hour. The afternoon closed with another blood sample, and he made his way wearily to the car park. It had been the guts of half a day. You'd have to be pretty fit to stand it, he thought. He could see why he didn't bother to take his ailments to them. And this, he reflected, was only Phase One; Diagnosis. He was nowhere near any treatment.

Another month passed, and another brown envelope found its way onto the Greens' breakfast table. He was invited to attend another hospital as an in-patient for further investigations.

Enclosed was a data-sheet of personal effects he should take, together with a plan of the hospital. The appointment was a couple of weeks away, which gave him time to make arrangements at work. His problem remained tantalisingly intermittent, and he even had an entire week without an episode. Should he cancel the hospital visit? It was a desperate waste of time. Funnily enough, it was his wife who insisted he should go through with it.

The Unit to which he was admitted specialised in diseases of the muscles and nervous system, and, as the nurse who took down his details at the bedside explained, was equipped with the very latest in high-tech gadgetry; they had scans, probes, ultra-this, nuclear-that, computer-assisted something else. He would be in the very best of hands. If they couldn't diagnose his problem, then nobody could. Treating it might be a different matter, but they were pushing diagnostic methods into the twenty-first century. He gave the nurse his latest jar of discoloured urine with as much ceremony as if it were vintage port, which, indeed, it resembled. There was no need to undress yet, so he ambled about the ward waiting for lunch, which was due anytime.

He could not fathom out why so few of the beds were occupied, about six of the twenty-four, judging by the fruit and books on the lockers. Three beds contained patients, evidenced by long mounds in the bedding and drip-stands with tubing leading under the sheets. It was one of those sooty, brick Victorian buildings and the ward had palatially high ceilings, a large, ornate fireplace with mantelpiece at one end, and sash windows that rattled continually in the wind. Perhaps the spare beds were for a big new intake like himself?

He heard a trolley rattle along the corridor outside and followed the noise until he found the ward's dining-room. The other ambulant inmates were standing by the table, in dressing-gowns and pyjamas. They greeted him with that grim good-humour peculiar to hospitals and prisoner-of-war camps. They exchanged lively banter with the dinner-lady and sat down. Giles Green looked at the plates. The medical technology might be state-of-the-art, but the food hadn't changed since his last stay in hospital many years before. Art-of-the-State was more like it: macaroni cheese, congealed and almost cold, followed by spotted dick covered in petrified custard.

Over the next four days he had various tests carried out on him; electrical recordings taken from his muscles, endless blood samples and X-rays, and he was even scanned by magnetic resonance in a huge machine like a tumble-dryer. The time dragged. He read a bit, chatted to the other patients, one of whom was a milkman. Doctors rarely visited him, or, indeed, any of them. It was the ward that Time forgot. Some of the patients were allowed home at weekends, returning on Monday mornings as if to a job. It was an incredibly laid-back place, though obviously they had some of the top men in the field, and the hospital had a national reputation. Green could not help wondering why there was all this fuss about a shortage of beds in the Health Service—three-quarters of the beds in this ward were empty for his entire stay. Perhaps it was so specialised that they couldn't find enough patients? He was puzzled and bored, and only occasionally was there any light relief, usually provided by his fellows' badinage.

Towards the end of the week there was another flurry of investigative activity; he did some exercises in Physiology to test his muscle fatigue; they connected his muscles to wires and stimulated them with electric shocks and recorded the responses on a screen; a garrulous young doctor tied up his arm until he could no longer feel it and took blood samples every few minutes; and still his urine remained stubbornly normal. The biochemistry department had not been able to identify the pigment which had discoloured his sample. All they could say was that it was not the stuff out of the muscle, nor was it haemoglobin from the blood. They were baffled.

On the Friday, he received word via the nursing sister that the consultant was intending to review his case that day, so that he could be discharged at the weekend. In due course the great man and his retinue appeared and gathered round his bed. For a great man, thought Giles Green, he does look rather young; under forty certainly. Must be a real hot-shot. Still, it was much better to be in the hands of somebody like that, who's up in all the modern methods and has a brilliant mind, than to be stuck with some weary old fossil near retirement, who doesn't understand the new techniques.

The young consultant was undeniably polished; the dark grey suit was impeccable, the tie had just the right suggestion of dash, the manner towards his juniors a fine balance between haughty superiority and one-of-the-boys-in-the-pub friendliness. He had obviously identified Green as Homo reasonably-intelligentia, and switched effortlessly into the appropriate mode of frankness and informality.

He outlined their findings so far, all of which were negative. He did acknowledge that there were a few values on his blood which were just outside the normal range, but were probably not significant. All the scans, the tracings, the X-rays, the yards of print-outs, didn't add up to anything you could hang your hat on.

"What about the discoloured urine?" asked Green. "Is that serious? What's the reason for it?" He only narrowly avoided addressing him as sir.

"Well, the analyses show it isn't blood or haemoglobin, nor is it myoglobin from the muscles. We're at a loss, frankly. The other tests show that your kidneys are working normally, so I don't feel there's anything to worry about. You can go home today, and we'll see you again in six months. Before you go, I've arranged for you to see Dr Champion in another department. He has a lot of experience in this type of case. I've sent your notes to him already. Goodbye."

The entourage assembled itself into marching formation and moved off to another bed, stethoscopes swinging, white coats rustling, shoes squeaking on the polished floor.

After lunch Green packed his things, said farewell to the inmates, took a last look at the ward, and set off to his appointment. He was dying to go home, and this seemed a further imposition after a week which had tried his patience to the extreme. And for nothing, what was more, he fumed. He sat in a dingy corridor outside the doctor's room for twenty-five minutes after the appointed time. At last he was summoned.

Dr Champion was sitting at a large old desk in a wood-panelled study lined with books. He was white-haired, red-faced, plump and elderly, and held a cigar in one hand. Smoke curled up into his face and he squinted over half-moon spectacles. His pin-stripe suit had a waistcoat with a watch-chain, and he sported a colourful bow-tie. He indicated a chair for Green, who thought, "Oh God, a dinosaur, what a waste of time!"

"Hello Mr Green. I've been reading your notes. I gather the tests haven't discovered much? I tend to be a bit sceptical about all this machinery and those endless lab tests. Useful in the proper place, of course, but rather overdone nowadays."

He leafed through the notes, from time to time taking a long pull on his cigar. He leaned forward.

"Tell me. Do you ever eat beetroot?"

Green was surprised by the supreme irrelevance of the remark. The old buffer was obviously an eccentric.

"Yes, I do, actually. I'm very fond of it. We grow lots of it in the garden and boil it. We eat it either cold with salad, or hot as a vegetable. But I don't see the, er…connection."

"Well, I think you'll find that's the cause of your discoloured urine. It doesn't do any harm; it's simply that some people don't possess an enzyme that breaks down the pigment in beetroot. You're probably one of them. There's a simple experiment you can carry out when you get home. Eat three or four good-sized beetroot, freshly boiled, and then have a close look at your urine about four hours later. I'd put money on it."

He leaned back in his chair, drew on his cigar, blew out a cloud of smoke, and his eyes twinkled.

"Not a very high-tech solution, I'm afraid—but then, it's not a very high-tech problem. A very old one, in fact. But it's the sort of thing some of the youngsters overlook. The art of medicine rather than the science."

He chortled as he placed his cigar in the ash-tray.

"Let us know the result of your experiment. Oh, and you might tell your GP, too. Goodbye. Thank you for coming."

Giles Green was staggered. Five days in hospital undergoing tests! At God knows what cost to the Health Service.

As soon as he arrived home and had recounted his adventures to his wife, he went into the garden and pulled some beetroot. They boiled them up in the pressure cooker and had some with a salad and an omelette for the evening meal. Then they took the dog for a walk, watched television, and waited until the appointed time. At ten o'clock, armed with his jam-jar, he marched off to the lavatory.

"Eureka!" his wife heard him shout.

Looks Could Kill

In the middle of the night I was awakened by a scratching noise. Already apprehensive of my situation in this lonely place, I lay craning my head in an attempt to locate its direction. There it was again, scratch, scrape. It seemed to be coming from near the door, as if someone was carefully working on the lock.

The scratching stopped, and I must have gone back to sleep. I had no idea of the time that had passed, but I awoke again to the same scratch, scratch from across the room. I clawed for the light switch, snapped it on, and sat up, tense with expectation. This time the noise was from the direction of my suitcase.

I leapt out of the high, ornate old bed and made for the case. As I did so, a large brown mouse wriggled out of it, dived onto the floor, and scuttled along close to the skirting-board, where it disappeared into a small hole near the door.

After all that, it was only a mouse. But my fears were not completely dispelled. This was an eerie place. Here I was, apparently the only guest in a remote French chateau hotel, in the hands of a solitary and distinctly creepy owner. I had not liked the way he had weighed me up on my arrival the evening before, his intense gaze, his piercing blue eyes. And he looked tough and athletic; you would not fight him off easily.

He had been pleasant enough with his welcome; had brought a cup of coffee, carried my case up to my room, and told me some of the history of the chateau and his ancestors. But there was a menace about him that put me on edge; a certain mocking twinkle in his eyes. His mouth might have a supercilious smile, but I felt that his brain was probably calculating, disdainful.

I examined my suitcase. The mouse must have been attracted to it by a packet of shortbread biscuits that I carried for early morning consumption, in case of breakfast being served late. It was a zipped, canvas valise, and the mouse had chewed through the zip's attachments, completely derailing it. In effect, the case was ruined. The creature had then rampaged through the contents, shredding the lining and eating a large hole in a woollen pullover. It must have only started on the biscuits, for more than half remained.

I climbed back into bed and surveyed the scene. It was a magnificent bedroom, furnished in eighteenth-century style, though the little chateau was much older. When the patron had brought me up the stone staircase to this top floor, he had expounded its charms.

"I think you will like this room. It has a splendid view across the gardens and faces south. It also has a certain…ambience." He glanced at me sharply. "I do not know how you say in English. To me it is…sympathique. These are my relatives and ancestors on the walls."

He indicated several large, gilt-framed paintings.

The ancestors now gazed down at me, all seeming to be looking directly at the bed. I imagined the events that must have taken place here over the centuries; love-making, births, illness, deaths, quarrels, perhaps violence. An owl screeched in the surrounding woods. I looked at my watch. It was three o'clock. Weary, rather than sleepy, I put out the light and gradually my mind let go and I drifted off.

I was washed and dressed by eight o'clock and had ample time before breakfast for an exploratory stroll. The gardens had fallen into neglect, but in their pomp must have been elaborate. A lichened stone fountain on the lawn dribbled forlornly.

I was joined by a huge, rough-haired dog that looked like a cross between a mastiff and a German Shepherd. He probably wanted company, but the way he kept close to my side, I felt I was being chaperoned. The lawn at the front of the house ended in a ha-ha, beyond which was a field of sheep. The great hound and I meandered together round the side, where a long, high stone wall sheltered a colourful herbaceous border, alive with butterflies on the michaelmas daisies. At the far end of the garden was the chateau's chapel, almost hidden by rampant hydrangea bushes. Surrounding everything were the menacing, dark woods of oak and sweet-chestnut. Pigeons cooed insistently, but there was no other sound, the nearest lane being half-a-mile away. I stood and admired the chateau, its carved, grey stone gables caught now by shafts of early sunshine. I could have sworn I saw a face watching me from one of the windows, but it quickly disappeared as I turned for a better look. Still guarded closely by the dog, I wandered back indoors.

Opening off the grand entrance hall, with its antlers and weapons on the walls, was the library, a high, beamed room, shelved from floor to ceiling. All the available space was crammed with books; rows of dusty leather-bound volumes, recent large art works, every conceivable type of book. I browsed along the shelves and was struck by the number of volumes on the occult and the supernatural. There were many on eastern religions, mysticism, and reincarnation. I noticed an extensive section concerning French history, aristocratic families, the Revolution, and even the guillotine.

In the background now I could hear the clatter of plates and cutlery, and willingly interrupted my tour to go in search of food. My table in the dining room was laid and the patron materialised as soon as he heard my footsteps.

"Good morning, Monsieur. I hope you have slept well?"

"Good morning. As a matter of fact, I had a terrible night. You'll hardly believe it, but I was awakened time and again by a mouse which got into my suitcase. Incidentally, it's ruined the case, and a pullover into the bargain. I wish you'd get rid of it. Did you know you have mice?"

"Well, of course, in a chateau as old as this, it is inevitable that there will occasionally be a mouse. But I did not realise there were any in your room. After breakfast I will look into the matter with you."

Later, when I showed him the shredded canvas of the case zip, and the frayed hole in the pullover, he did not seem at all apologetic, but was obviously excited by a desire to catch the mouse. His interest was aroused as a hunter's might be when told of nearby quarry.

"I have the ideal mouse-trap for this situation," he said. "Come with me to the workshop."

Part of the vast cellar was laid out with benches, tools and lathes, superbly equipped for woodwork and metalwork. He led me over to a bench.

"What about that?" His eyes sparkled. "Isn't that the most marvellous trap you have ever seen?" He stepped back, arms spread wide.

I was horrified. There before us was a perfect scale model of a guillotine in polished wood and shining metal, about a foot high. The blade was thick and heavy, but appeared to have a razor edge, like a microtome. I did not know what to say.

"Did you make it yourself?" was all I could manage.

"Of course; making such models is my hobby. I have several similar guillotines. This one is for mice and rats, but over here I have one for magpies, they are such a nuisance in the garden; also another for squirrels."

He indicated a table in the corner. Each model was slightly different, obviously exquisitely designed for the specific victims. A much more substantial one stood at the end of the row.

"What on earth is this for?" I exclaimed, uneasily.

"Ah, that is my cat model. We are sometimes troubled by stray cats, so I put this one out in the woods."

"How do they all work? Presumably you bait them just in front of the blade?"

"Correct. In the case of mice, a piece of cheese on that little platform. When the animal reaches forward it touches this tiny trigger, which releases the cord holding the blade. Voila! The blade falls. Chop! Its head is off!"

He was now highly excited and his eyes blazed. He walked along the row of machines, stroking them fondly.

"I made each one myself. They are true likenesses of real guillotines. I have made their study a great interest of mine for many years. It was a brilliant invention. Brilliant!" He paused and frowned. "Of course, some of my ancestors perished on the guillotine. Very sad. I feel it still. However, we can exact retribution, even now." He glared at me defiantly.

I was edgy, and reminded him that our immediate problem was just a mouse in my room.

"We will put this mouse model in your room tonight, and it will do the trick." He made a chopping motion at the back of his neck. "But first I will demonstrate its efficiency. Excuse me one moment."

He disappeared up the steps, returning seconds later with a carrot. This he poked carefully under the blade and touched the spring. There was a crunching thud, so sudden and violent that I started, even though I had been expecting it. The tip of the carrot lay severed in the tiny basket. He roared with laughter. I was relieved to go back upstairs and prepare for my day's outing in the car. We parted, agreeing to set up the trap after dinner that night.

Over the evening meal, despite the elegant surroundings, my discomfort mounted. The patron appeared to be both chef and waiter, and was the only soul in evidence. Any other staff must have gone off duty, and there were no signs that he had a wife or family. No other guests had appeared. We seemed to be alone; two men marooned together in this ancient chateau amidst a sea of woodland.

I was sufficiently worried to be wary of drugged food, and I confined myself to a half bottle of wine, which I watched him uncork. At the end of the meal it caused me no regret to refuse his offer of a complimentary brandy, though several times he tried to insist. I was taking no risks and felt menaced by his obvious fitness and prowling strength. There was something about him of a lion, rippling with subdued power, waiting to pounce; and always that amused, mocking expression in his eyes, eyes that seemed to rivet my attention. I sat for a while with a refill of coffee, and tried to concentrate on my book. Eventually he came in to clear the table.

"If you're ready, we can set the trap now, Monsieur. Perhaps we could use a piece of your biscuit as bait, as the mouse seems to like it."

He stood for a few moments weighing me up, as if making a calculation. Then suddenly, coming to himself, he turned and went off to get the trap.

We decided that the best location would be near the door, close to the mouse-hole. I produced a knob of shortbread and he bent down to position it and set the blade. He was completely absorbed, a master craftsman, a zealot, at work.

"There we are! Madame Guillotine! Tonight, chop! No mouse."

He moved closer to me, his eyes twinkling, teasing, though at the same time somehow threatening. I was frightened and involuntarily recoiled. He gave a condescending smirk.

"I see you are apprehensive. Do not worry. It will be quite painless. The mouse," he emphasised the word, "will not feel a thing. I wish you good night." He hovered for a moment before backing through the door.

His footsteps echoed along the corridor and immediately I locked the door, glad that he had gone. I read for the best part of an hour before putting out the light. I had a disturbed sleep, filled with fragmented dreams, frequently tossing and turning.

A mighty crash broke in on my consciousness. I switched on the bedside lamp and leaned towards the foot of the bed. The guillotine had gone off. I sprang out of bed to examine it. The blade had dropped and the mouse's head lay in the little basket. The stump of the neck oozed blood and the hind legs twitched spasmodically. There was a loud knocking on the door.

"It is me, Monsieur. May I come in?" shouted the patron from the corridor. As I unlocked the door I wondered with horror how he had heard the noise and reached my room so quickly. Had he been lurking outside? He rushed in and crouched over the guillotine in his colourful silk dressing-gown. He extracted the mouse triumphantly, holding up the head between a thumb and forefinger, swinging the body by its tail with the other hand.

"Another of those revolutionary swine gets a taste of his own medicine," he bellowed, then, no doubt noticing my baffled look, leaned towards me and confided; "They came back as mice, you know, most of them. Except for the ringleaders, they became rats. But this model can deal with rats, too; oh yes. And now I will leave you to return to bed."

He put the guillotine under his arm, and, with the mouse's corpse still in his hand, swept out into the passage shouting good night.

I locked the door again. Sleep was out of the question, so I dressed, poured a glass of water and settled down in the armchair to try to read and keep watch for the rest of the night. In my agitated state, I was afraid that he might make an assault on the door. With his talk of revolutionaries reincarnated as mice he was clearly deranged and anything might happen.

I dozed fitfully throughout the night. At last I saw the first beams of dawn through the stone mullions, and stood at the window watching as the forest's shadows withdrew and the dewy lawn gradually came into sight. The silence seemed to sing in my ears.

Breakfast-time arrived as a huge relief. At half-past seven I made my way downstairs and smelled a welcoming aroma of coffee hanging in the air. A radio was gabbling on indistinctly from the direction of the kitchen. I had no sooner taken up my place in the dining-room than the ornately carved door was flung open and the patron came in carrying a coffee-pot.

"Good morning, Monsieur. This time you must have slept better, I am sure, for no mouse."

He beamed, the first time I had seen him smile a real, human smile.

"Yes, there were no disturbances at all, thank you. I had a good night," I lied.

Now he was effusively chatty, charming, in fact. Gone was that air of watchful menace, where I had imagined he was eyeing me so closely, as if estimating my height and weight. He was wearing a casual shirt and jeans, and, with his short dark hair and muscular torso and arms, today looked much younger. He was a difficult man to age; he could have been anywhere between thirty-five and forty-five, but was evidently active and sporty—I had noticed riding-boots and a squash racquet in the hall.

He talked animatedly of sights worth seeing in the neighbouring towns, and was knowledgeable about the history of the area, and its art galleries. He said he was an enthusiastic photographer.

"Are you expecting any other guests?" I ventured, feeling that at least a few extra people would put me more at ease.

"Not tonight, I'm afraid. I should have had a family from Paris, but unfortunately they had to cancel. From September it is very quiet here—but there are compensations." He smiled knowingly.

He gave no hint of what the compensations might be. If he was really in the hotel business to make money, then guests were essential. Perhaps he had other irons in the fire? Was this a cover for something else?

I had a good breakfast, punctuated by chats with the patron as he solicitously brought in each course. The food was excellent, and I began to relax and revel in the sheer grace and opulence of my surroundings. Had the holiday brochure not said that it would be like living in a chateau?

I was revising my opinions. During the night I had decided to cut short my visit, and simply leave, never mind the lost money. I would be glad just to get away from the place. But now, looking round, it certainly was splendid, and my fears had probably been exaggerated, brought on by being tired after the journey, and having a bad night as a result of the mouse. I was probably imagining his menacing looks and misjudging the whole situation. The mouse, after all, was not the patron's fault—he was not to know that my suitcase would be attacked.

On the other hand, that business with the model guillotine, and his strange excitement at killing the mouse, was distinctly peculiar. Eccentric, to say the least. This morning, for some reason, he was a different person, lively, charming, normal in every way. It was as if killing the mouse had put him on a high. Damn it, I thought, I'll stay. I've only one more night, anyway. Nothing else can happen, surely?

I set off as planned after breakfast, and spent the day exploring the nearby town. In the late afternoon a squall came on, and, having got thoroughly wet, I decided to return earlier than I had intended to the chateau. I drove in low gear along the track in the chestnut woods, here and there swerving to avoid deep pot-holes. Some of the trees had already turned colour and a few leaves twirled down onto the bonnet.

In the soft light the chateau in its clearing looked tranquil, its ancient carved stone gables like raised eyebrows trying to peep over the woods that hemmed it in. It looked a secretive place.

As I walked to the front door, the big dog sloped up to join me, its long, rough tail waving a lively greeting, though the beast eyed me suspiciously. It looked like a dog with a very untrustworthy temperament. And it was a frighteningly dangerous size. I noticed now that the patron's Renault was not in the garage under the trees; he was evidently still out, perhaps shopping for provisions for the evening meal.

I let myself in, and, after drying and changing, walked down to the library. Not a soul was about anywhere. I found the shelf of books about the guillotine. It was a macabre collection; many of them were rubbed, leather-bound volumes from the early nineteenth century, others turn-of-the-century tomes with gilt-lettered spines, virtually text-books, full of diagrams of the construction and operational details.

I thought about his fiendish models and wondered if the cellar was open, so that I could take another look at them.

The huge, studded oak door stood ajar. I found the light switch and was surprised at how much larger the cellar was than I thought when he showed me his collection. It was like a crypt, the ceiling supported by ancient round stone pillars. The workshop section was only a small part, and, as I penetrated further, I came across an area laid out as a photographic studio, with several sets of lamps on stands, as well as modelling chairs and couches.

A tall, wooden wardrobe, elaborately carved but riddled with woodworm holes, stood against the wall. It was locked, but as I rattled half-heartedly at the knob, the door suddenly gave and swung open. There were shelves and drawers, and the floor was covered by a jumble of shoes, all of different styles. There was something odd about this pile.

It was some moments before it struck me; the shoes were of different sizes, some dainty, others large and clumsy. They could not possibly belong to the same person. On the shelf at my eye level stood a brown unlabelled bottle full of tablets; there were some coils of thin nylon rope, and, in a dark corner, a metal object. I pulled it forward. Handcuffs! I froze. What malevolence had I uncovered?

Tingling now with nerves, but drawn on by curiosity, I looked in a drawer. There were up to a dozen wrist-watches of various types, leather wallets, and an assortment of men's jewellery— chain bracelets, gold pendants, ear-rings. This was a cache of other people's possessions. Was the patron a thief, then? A pickpocket? It did not seem very likely. He did not look the type. But it was the shoes that frightened me most.

With increasing dread I pulled out another drawer. There were several plastic packets containing locks of hair; blond, black, brown, straight, wavy hair. Underneath was a brown envelope. Out of it slid a pile of photographs of youngish men in different theatrical costumes, obviously taken here in the studio. Even more curious were a few of painted scenery-sets like those at the seaside, in which you put your head through a hole and appear as one of the characters in the comic tableau. The pictures involved two different cartoon tableaux; one of eighteenth-century aristocratic hunters with weapons and dogs, the other a humorous guillotine scene. I caught my breath; yet again the guillotine theme. The characters were painted life-size, and the hole for the subject's head was exactly on the guillotine's block, with a shiny blade painted above it.

Trembling with fear, I hastily rammed the photos back and closed the drawer. The creaking wardrobe door held tight when I shut it. Perhaps my search would not be detected.

I peered into the dim recess beyond the next pillar. Surely that was the guillotine tableau against the wall? I took a closer look. Made like standard scenery, its semi-comic characters had been painted with flair. As I examined the hole for the subject's head, I noticed with alarm that the bottom edge had been reinforced with a second layer of thin board, and, in fact, showed signs of wear. Terrible thoughts formed as my mind raced. Could he really be using this device as a proper guillotine?

There was no blade—surely this was just a jokey photographic tableau? I glanced about me at the roof. Running between the pillars was a long stone supporting pier, and draped along it a pelmet of faded red velvet a couple of feet deep. On tiptoe I could just reach to lift it. Underneath was a monstrous steel blade, like a giant axe, nearly three feet wide and held by a thick wire cable which ran the length of the pier and continued down the back of the pillar. The photo-tableau could obviously be pushed into position under the blade, and the whole fiendish machine was then operated by a lever concealed behind the stone column. There was now no doubt in my mind; this was a real, working guillotine.

But how in the wide world did my host persuade his victims to put their heads in? An excess of wine at dinner? Liberal amounts of complimentary brandy? I recalled the bottle of tablets in the wardrobe, perhaps sedatives to be slipped into food, or something to induce a reckless, unsuspecting euphoria. There were endless possibilities.

I had seen enough, and was desperate to leave the cellar before the patron returned. I walked about the garden aimlessly, my mind trying to come to terms with what I had seen. I must leave at once—had I time to grab my things from upstairs? As I stood there hesitating, a car made its way through the trees. It was my host. My chance had gone. I was trapped. As soon as he had parked he came across to me. He was wearing riding-boots and carrying a helmet and a short whip.

"Sorry I am late back," he said. "Horses are never to time. I will prepare the meal immediately. Would you care for an aperitif, perhaps in the library? I will put on the heating."

"That would be very welcome, thank you," I replied, trying to act naturally. "I got quite wet this afternoon, and it's going chilly now."

I sat in the library holding a glossy art magazine and cautiously sipping a glass of pastis, as I endeavoured to formulate a plan of action. It was almost dark outside and the ornate lights reflected in the great sash windows. The dog pottered in and sat on the floor beside me. He was insistent on a bit of affection, and from time to time hooked a massive paw onto my knee to gain my attention.

In little more than half an hour Monsieur came to announce that the food was served. It was a sumptuous meal, but I ate sparingly, constantly alert for any strange flavour of drugs, and pleaded a slight stomach upset for my poor appetite and abstention from wine. When I had finished he brought a pot of coffee and some chocolate mints.

"May I join you?" he asked, smiling charmingly. "It is, after all, your last night."

"Please do. Yes, I have to return home tomorrow. My little holiday is at an end, unfortunately."

We drank the coffee and chatted amiably. He seemed to be working hard to entertain me. I felt slightly more relaxed, though watchful of his every move. The dog sat close to me, its colossal muzzle resting on my leg, its sad brown eyes looking imploringly whenever I unwrapped a mint.

As we talked I became conscious of my attention focussing more and more on the patron's face, being held by his riveting, piercing gaze. He droned on in a soft monotone, about holidays, about different regions of France, and all the time I felt more lulled. I was vaguely aware that he was exerting a definite influence over me, forcing me to watch his eyes, which he never averted, the source of this strange power. Even though I sensed that I was losing my control, that I was being slowly subordinated to his will, I was powerless to resist it. I was held prisoner by his penetrating, intense eyes.

Suddenly, I felt a clawed thump in my lap. The dog had jumped up and was standing with his front paws on my leg, trying to lick my face. The hypnotic spell was broken. I surfaced again.

The patron went berserk, leapt up, bellowing something in French at the dog, seized it by the collar, and dragged it across the room to the kitchen door, thumping its head and ribs mercilessly as he went.

I rushed after them into the kitchen, distressed at the plight of the poor dog, which was now yelping in pain and snarling in defiance. It was dawning on me that its intervention had broken the devilish hypnosis which would have been the end of me.

With both hands he had now lifted the dog high off the ground by its collar, and stood, red with rage, shouting at it. It hung there, gasping and choking, its hind legs jerking. He was doing his best to strangle it for having thwarted him. Unthinkingly, I clasped my arms round the dog's chest to support its weight.

"Let go, you savage, you'll kill it."

Immediately he released his grip, snatched up a meat cleaver lying on the chopping board, and came at me with it raised to strike. Staggering under the animal's weight, with a massive effort I hurled the dog at him, hitting him in the chest. As soon as it landed on the ground, the creature leapt at him with a terrifying snarl. The patron struck at it with the cleaver and his free arm, but the blows were brushed aside as the frenzied animal threw itself at its prey.

In no time he was forced to the floor by the dog's sheer weight and power. Long, bleeding tears appeared in the flesh of his flailing arms as he frantically tried to ward it off. He had no chance; the hound had tasted blood and was not to be denied. Snarling and slavering, it ripped at his face and throat, blood pouring from the wounds and soaking his shirt. There was nothing I could do to save him.

I closed the kitchen door and went into the hall, where I remembered seeing a telephone. Shaking with reaction, I called the gendarmerie. In one ear I could hear the distant, repeated purr of the ringing tone, in the other was the muffled snarling and tearing from the kitchen.

Forties' Children

Ronnie sat on the edge of the kerb, his feet in the gutter, and rolled a pebble between the iron bars of the grid. It splashed and echoed so satisfactorily that he couldn't help pushing another along with the frayed welt of his shoe, watching as that, too, plopped down below. He looked up the road for any sign of his friends, but nothing stirred. The line of plane trees on each side threw deep shadows across the pavement, but his grid was in the full glare of the sun.

A few yards farther along there was a pile of droppings left by the milkman's horse earlier in the morning. Flies buzzed and landed. For some reason, old Mr West hadn't yet been out to shovel it up for his garden. Ronnie and his pals weren't very keen on old West, because he shouted at them if they went near his allotment, and kept their ball if it landed in his garden. Cantankerous, he'd heard his mother call him.

Ronnie stretched forward on his chest and peered down into the grid. By tilting his head he could just see the sun glinting off the water. What were drains for, anyway, he wondered idly? His friend's sister had said you caught infantile paralysis from playing near grids. And from swimming baths. That was why they'd closed the baths now. Just at the time of the school holidays, as well. That was one of the treats if you didn't go away.

What was he going to do today? Where was everybody? Was there no-one to play with? It was hot and sweaty. When he sat up his shirt was covered in dust and gravel and his bare knees were pitted from lying on the rough road. He would walk round to look for Jimmy. He hadn't gone away on holiday yet, he was sure.

Jimmy's house was on a corner. It was large and mock-Tudor, with a long garden and dense laurel bushes down one side, where they often lost their cricket ball. He struggled with the gate, which stuck, and sauntered up to the front door. He knocked on the dark green panel until his knuckles hurt, and was about to go away, when Jimmy's mother opened the door, drying her hands on a towel.

"Is Jimmy in, please? Can he come out to play?"

"They're all in the shed at the back, Ronnie. Just go round the side gate."

Ronnie trudged off. He was pleased he'd found them, but felt a bit left out that they were assembled here without letting him know. Just like Jimmy, had to be organising everything. Secrets. The shed door was open and as he approached Jimmy spotted him.

"Here's Ron, boys. Are we going to let him join in?" He consulted the interior. "Yeah, all right, but you've got to do what we tell you."

"What you doin' then?" enquired Ronnie.

"Planning. Aren't we, boys? 'Sgonna be a raid."

"What on?"

"Shall we tell him?" Jimmy sought a rubber-stamping from his committee.

"Come inside and close the door, then we'll tell you."

Ronnie was found a space to sit on an upturned box next to the lawnmower.

"You know Ma Jenkins's pond?"

"Yeah. What about it?"

"Have you ever seen them big carp in it?" asked Jimmy, his eyes wide with excitement.

"'Course I 'ave, but they're goldfish," replied Ronnie.

"There's goldfish as well, but the big ones are carp. My brother said so."

Ronnie now realised the adventure that was afoot. Like the others, he had often squinted through knot-holes in Ma Jenkins's fence and seen great, dark fish nosing about between the water lilies, caught his breath as one turned and the sun flashed on its golden, scaly side. It was a lovely garden; huge, mysterious, and the bottom end, where the lily pond was, had long since been let to go wild, so that overgrown shrubs trailed across the paths, and moss and weeds sprouted from cracks in the stones. It was a temptingly long distance from the house, too, nearly the length of the village football field. If you kept quiet, it might be possible to fish in the pond without anybody knowing you were there. He'd never got any farther than wistfully dreaming. What if you were caught? It might be prison, or one of those homes for bad boys his parents mentioned when he was especially naughty.

"We're planning a fishing raid to catch one," said Jimmy.

"So, how you going to do it, then?" Ronnie couldn't see how the insuperable difficulties were to be got over by the gang's planning.

"I'm going to be the leader, and I've worked out what we'll do," took over Jimmy. "I need all of you to help, and the important bit is we do it very early in the morning, before they're up."

Ronnie's resentment flared. Jimmy would have to be the leader. Just because he lived in a big house and his dad was a businessman, and he was bossy. He felt even more put out because he was the keenest on fishing among them, stood for hours by the pond in the field watching his little red float while fishing for perch, and read about angling in a book he'd been given as a birthday present. He was the fisherman of the gang, so why was this expedition being planned by Jimmy and the others, who had no real interest in fishing? He smarted under a sense of injustice. They were keener on bikes and cricket and football, so why didn't they stick to that, instead of taking over his territory?

"Yeah," continued Jimmy, "we're going to do it very early, climb the fence, you lot helping me over from the outside and handing me the rod and line when I'm in the garden. Then I have a go at getting the bait between the lilies." He looked round smugly. "It should be dead easy."

"There's a lot of lilies, and what about that willow tree at one side of it? You might get tangled up in that," suggested one of the others.

"No I won't, you'll see. There's plenty of clear water. Anyway, we'll have to make the raid soon, 'cos we're going on holiday in two weeks' time."

"I think we can all climb over and fish," ventured another.

"'Course we can't, stupid. You'd make too much noise. We'll need a good rod and some line, though. I've only got that little toy thing that's not much cop. I'll borrow yours, Ronnie, that cane one."

Ronnie flushed. His fishing rod had been a Christmas present from his father and mother the year before, and was his pride and joy. It was of beautiful yellow cane, shining with varnish and with bright red binding to the rod rings. He often took it out of its bag in his bedroom just to look at it, admire it, stroke it, imagine it catching for him some monster perch under the trees of the farm pond. He would hold it by its smooth cork handle, and pretend he'd hooked a fish and would play it all round the bedroom, finally imagining landing the great slippery green and gold specimen in the corner by his bed. How could he bear to lend his rod to anyone, least of all Jimmy, and for a crazy prank like this? No, he wouldn't. Why should he? For some reason he felt hot tears welling up, but managed to blink them back, hoping that in the shadows at the back of the shed his confusion wouldn't be noticed.

"No, you can't," he found himself saying. "It's the only one I've got, and it was a present."

"Oh, a present, was it? I know, it was from mummy and daddy! Isn't he soft?"

Jimmy sidled across the shed and confronted him.

"Well, how'd you like it if you came into the garden with me, and we could take turns at fishing?"

A sense of his importance sneaked through Ronnie, and against a nagging doubt he conceded. After all, he'd be there to protect his rod and line, and he'd be in the forefront of the adventure. If it came off, they'd be talking about his exploits for months.

"Oh, all right, then. But I've got to go in and fish as well."

"'Course you can." Jimmy's wheedling gave way to the tough planner. "That's fixed, then. We'll use his rod and line."

After a time they tired of the stuffiness of the garden shed and bundled out into the fresh air. They kicked a ball about listlessly until Jimmy's older sister, Ann, came out with a friend and her yappy terrier, which persisted in nosing the ball onto the flower beds. They all sprawled out on the lawn, too hot to be energetic.

"What are you lot up to?" said Ann, mustering as much condescension as a two-year age gap allowed.

"Nothing," said Jimmy, his look swearing the gang to secrecy. "We're just hanging about. There's not much to do when it's as hot as this, and the swimming pool's closed because of the infantile p'ralysis."

"Mummy says a few more people have got it in the town this week, so it'll be closed all summer. And anyway," Ann added, "it's not called infantile paralysis. The proper name's polio."

Jimmy sat up aggressively. "It's not the same thing, is it? Why'd you have two names for something? Doesn't make sense."

"Well, clever clogs, infantile means children get it, and mummy told me the other day that Mrs Smith at the end of the avenue had caught it, and she's not a child, is she? So there! Her arm's gone paralysed; just hangs limp by her side, Mr Smith said. And he called it polio."

"Don't they put people in iron lungs?" put in Ronnie, making a heap of dandelions on the grass.

"That's when they can't breathe," Ann confirmed knowledgeably. "But then they often die, because they're completely paralysed."

They all fell silent, plucking moodily at daisy heads on the lawn. Ronnie chewed a blade of grass and tried to visualise what being paralysed was like. Once, when playing football on a bone-hard frosty morning, he had fallen heavily on his back, and for a few moments had been unable to move, shout or cry, and the sense of panic was still vivid within him. Was being paralysed like that, only for ever? A shiver of terror struck him.

"Well, let's hope none of us catches it," said Ann, standing up and shaking back her plaits. "I'm taking Tiny for a walk."

When they'd gone, the boys agreed to continue private planning of the fishing expedition, and to meet again next day to finalise the details. Ronnie was pleased that he was to play such an important part, but felt uneasy about using his fishing rod. He was well aware that Jimmy had allowed him to join in simply to use his rod. Later, when he was alone in his room, he got the rod out of its bag to admire it again. Its varnish gleamed, the red binding glowed. It was smashing, there was no other word for it. He swelled with pride when he thought how it would feature in the gang's next adventure.

The following day found him again sitting by his grid, flicking pebbles into the depths, when Jimmy and the others came into sight chasing a tennis ball along the pavement.

"Hiya, Ron. We'd better do some more planning."

They sat down by him, Jimmy tying a shoe-lace as an aid to concentration.

"What about Friday morning, very early? It's easy for me to get out, 'cos my dad goes out specially early on Fridays."

The others considered the prospects for slipping away from their families. Ronnie picked at a scab on his knee. Nobody wanted to appear not to be master of his own destiny, and they agreed without working out the practicalities. They'd manage somehow. They arranged to meet in the field behind Ma Jenkins's garden at seven o'clock on the Friday. Ronnie would bring his rod and line and some bread for bait, and the others would come along so that there would be adequate manpower to get Jimmy and Ronnie over the fence.

On the Friday morning there was a trace of mist over the field as the boys met. The grass was wet and silvery, smearing the toe-caps of their Wellingtons. It was colder than they'd expected and their shivering was enhanced by nervousness. This was the big day! They tip-toed along by the garden fence, Ronnie carrying his rod in its bag, his coat pockets bulging with the reel and a chunk of white loaf. Jimmy, sporting a corduroy windjammer and sucking a barley-sugar, was hissing instructions to all and sundry.

"Keep down, men. They'll see you."

They arrived at the nearest point to the pond. Ronnie got out his rod, pushed the two sections together, put on the reel, and threaded the line through the rings. He pulled a hook from a crumpled cellophane packet and knelt in the wet grass to tie it on.

"Right. We're ready," whispered Jimmy. "Give us a shove up."

Ronnie and Jimmy scrambled up the fence, holding onto the top while two of the others made backs for their flailing feet. They dropped heavily on the other side, and were handed the rod and line, the hook swinging precariously back and forth before Ronnie finally grabbed it. He rolled a clump of bread onto it and they were ready. The two of them now moved stealthily towards the end of the pond. The sun was higher now and glinted from the surface of the water between the lily pads. Clouds of midges danced up and down.

Without realising that it was happening, Ronnie found that Jimmy had somehow taken the rod out of his hands.

"I'll have first go, then it'll be your turn."

Ronnie fumed, he felt a blind rage to fight Jimmy for it; he was just as strong, just as tough a battler. But his common-sense surfaced in time, and he knew that a squabble now would ruin the whole expedition. He'd fight him later.

Jimmy cast the line onto the water, and they watched as the white dot of bread sank and disappeared. They waited a few minutes for the carp to find it. Still nothing.

"I'll try over there," said Jimmy, pointing to a circle of dark water fringed by shiny green lilies. He flicked the line out, but it overshot, and the bait was lost to view in the thick mass of leaves.

"Aw, hell." He tugged until the rod bent double, but the vegetation held firm.

"Let me have a go," implored Ronnie, panicking in case his tackle was damaged.

Jimmy handed over the rod willingly. Ronnie tried everything he knew; he tugged from another angle, he lowered the rod and pulled straight, as he'd read in his fishing book. No effect. Should he pull and pull until something broke, or cut the line with his penknife?

Just then he heard a rumbling noise from the direction of the house. It was coming nearer. He looked over his shoulder, and, at that moment, Ma Jenkins's gardener emerged from the bushes pushing a wheelbarrow.

"Oi! What the 'ell are you doing? Get out o' there, you young devils."

Ronnie dropped his rod, noticing with a pang as it sank the red binding reflected through the water. His beautiful rod. But now there was no time to linger. He sprinted as quickly as his too-large Wellies would let him, round the end of the pond, by an overhanging rose, and then onto a few yards of open grass. Now he could see that Jimmy, with a few moments' start, was at the fence and already beginning to stretch out his hands for the top. Behind him he could hear the gardener's heavy footsteps.

"Come 'ere, you young buggers!"

Jimmy got one leg over, then fell across the fence-top and disappeared from view. Ronnie felt his heart pounding until it seemed to choke him. He gasped for breath, but kept his legs striding forward as he did when playing football. He clattered against the wooden panelling, thinking as he did so of shouting for help to his friends. As soon as the idea flashed into his mind he realised it was no use, and would waste vital breath.

His fingers now scrabbled at the top rail, Wellington toes scraping to grip enough to lift him. The gardener must be only a couple of yards behind; he could hear the rustle of his coat and corduroy trousers as he stumbled along. Ronnie pushed up with his arms till the muscles ached . He was level with the top. He lifted his leg high and threw himself outwards. The thump as he landed made him gasp, but immediately he scrambled up and started running across the field. In the distance he could see other small figures, their black Wellingtons rhythmically rising and falling. He'd made it, but he'd left behind his lovely rod that his mum and dad had given him. He wouldn't be able to get it back. It was gone for good, and all for a stupid raid to catch one of Ma Jenkins's fish. Now he wouldn't be able to fish any more. His tears half-blinded him and he sniffed and sobbed as he ran. It was all Jimmy's fault. Why did he take any notice of him? He'd get revenge somehow.

A few days later, Ronnie and the gang called for Jimmy, but his mother told them he was ill in bed and wouldn't be able to come out for a day or two.

"He's got a headache and he's running a temperature," she said. "I'll tell him you came."

They waited until the two days were up, then called again. As they approached the house they could see that Jimmy's bedroom curtains were drawn.

"He can't still be in bed, surely?" protested Ronnie. "Not at this time in the morning."

Jimmy's mother explained that the doctor had been to see him, and that, because of the fever and headache, she had to keep the curtains drawn. "The light hurts his eyes, you see, boys."

"Well, please tell him we called, and we hope he gets better soon." They trailed off and stopped to play on the pavement by the grid.

"It's taking him a long time to get better. Do y'know, we've only seen him once since the raid on Ma Jenkins's pond?" Ronnie pointed out.

"That was a smashin' raid. Pity about that gardener," piped up one of the others. "If he hadn't come, you'd've caught some fish, dead easy."

The next day, Ronnie was dawdling on an errand for his mother, which took him past Jimmy's, and he noticed that the curtains no longer covered his window. He must be better, he thought, so went and knocked on the front door. Jimmy's mother seemed upset.

"I'm afraid they've taken him to hospital, love. They think it might be polio. Tell your mum we'll let her know how he is."

"Yes, Mrs."

Ronnie was too horror-struck to say more, and stumbled away down the road trying to imagine Jimmy's plight. His only experience of hospital had been when he'd had his tonsils out, and he still dreaded the thought of the echoing tiled corridors, the white coats, the terrifying smells of antiseptics and anaesthetics, the rumbling trolleys, the screens round the bed, the tight sheets; above all the loneliness of being far from home, away from his mum and dad, his bedroom and his toys. Poor Jimmy, if he was suffering all that. He felt a surge of sympathy, and was sorry about the grudge he'd been nursing over the fishing rod.

Later, when he told the gang, they were all affected by a collective horror, which ignited their imagination. Jimmy would get better, wouldn't he? At tea-time, among all the families, Jimmy's illness was the main topic of conversation. As Ronnie and the others lay in their beds that night, each wondered what was happening to Jimmy, each pictured him lying motionless in a shiny, silent ward, and fretted that they, too, might go down with it.

The shock to Ronnie next day when his mother broke the sad news left him numbed and tearful. He took his favourite stick and went and sat by his grid, poking stones between the bars with it, wondering where Jimmy was now. Despite Jimmy's bossiness, they'd been friends as long as he could remember, and he would miss him. He wouldn't hate anybody for being bossy again, really he wouldn't.

Hearts, Minds and Bowels

Alfred watched as his wife crouched in front of the microwave oven. What the hell was she doing now? She'd never got the hang of the thing, despite his painstaking explanations. He shook his head in resignation as he saw Doris peer at the control panel, muttering to herself as she uncertainly poked at the touch pads.

It was odds-on that the vegetables would be undercooked; whether they had runner beans or broccoli, carrots or leeks, they'd be the same, just about raw, and if there was one thing he couldn't abide, it was raw vegetables. They did his bowels no good at all. When you got to their age you had to take care of yourself, and what you ate was vitally important. That and keeping warm, of course, and not overdoing things. There again, Doris didn't see eye to eye with him. She just wouldn't take care of herself properly.

"I can't be bothered with all that nonsense," she would say, when he read her a snippet from one of his health magazines. "If folks are going to get ill, they'll get ill, and you can mollycoddle yourself too much, in my opinion. You've got to die sometime."

"Aye," Alfred would reply, "but not yet."

Despite their different philosophies, Alfred and Doris had rubbed along in marriage for over fifty years with few major crises, he wiry and pernickety, she plump and easy-going. Alfred liked to know how things worked, to fiddle and fuss at odd jobs until he got it right. If he was putting up a shelf, or hanging a picture, it had to be just so, and he would mess about long after Doris had told him it would do.

"Stupid man, I don't know why he makes such a fuss," she would complain. "It'll be all the same in a hundred years."

Doris was now setting the kitchen table for lunch. A pan was boiling over on the stove. Alfred lifted the lid and saw that the potatoes were disintegrating and clouding the water.

"As usual," he grumbled into the steam, "spuds done to a pulp."

"Come out of the way and leave them to me. They'll be perfectly all right. Don't pester."

Alfred sat down at the table in a gesture of desertion, staring sullenly into the garden. The microwave pinged. Doris limped slowly across to it and Alfred, though he had his back to her, regarded her in his mind's eye. Long gone now were all traces of the lively, teasing girl he'd married. The unruly brown hair was white, straight and sparse. Gone, too, was her shapely, active, muscular figure, replaced now by an ungainly body that was lop-sided; wasted arm muscles, knobbly hands, bulbous hips, one leg fatter than the other. And, of course, it was very much her own fault; she'd let herself go, wouldn't take enough exercise, wouldn't stop eating puddings and chocolates, just never controlled her weight. He'd warned her times without number, but she didn't take any notice.

He heard her lame foot drag across the lino, and, as usual, it irritated him. He didn't understand why, because it should have made him feel sorry for her.

She dished the food out onto the plates, and put his meal in front of him. As he expected, potatoes like sludge, runner beans and carrots practically raw. He munched pointedly on a forkful of beans with exaggerated effort and distaste, before pushing the rest to the edge of the plate, as beyond the pale.

Doris affected not to notice, though provoked till she was trembling with suppressed anger. How much more could she take of this niggling, cantankerous old stick, for whom every little inconvenience in his well-ordered life was a major catastrophe? Had she not sacrificed her entire life to serving his every whim, his food fads, his preciseness, his sense of order that must not on any account be disturbed? She had been able to cope when they were younger and he was still attractive and lively; indeed, though it was hard to believe now, he had been witty and good company. But where now was the man she'd married? Where, in that tense, sinewy carcass, was the athletic, debonair young man she'd thought such a good catch?

He had no real notion of the pain she suffered with her crippling arthritis, of the struggle she had to breathe on hot nights, of the frustration of not being able to walk about easily. When her despair made her feel like giving in to everything, he was no help at all, insisting that you simply had to pull yourself together, fight it, battle away against life's difficulties. A fat lot he knew about life's difficulties. Never had a day's real illness in his life, and, as for pain and inconvenience, well, if he got so much as a sniffle he retreated to bed, mollycoddling himself with lozenges, inhalers and gargles.

Doris found it strange; she'd loved him so much once and yet now, without ever putting her finger on a time or a reason, or even realising it was happening, she'd come to dislike him. So many little things got on her nerves; how he coughed drove her to screaming pitch at times, even the way he turned the pages of the newspaper, with an infuriating precision that she'd witnessed for fifty-five years. She noticed his wrinkled hands and scrawny frame with a pang of sadness, remembering how fine and muscular he'd been in his youth. She was still fond of him, in a way, but more and more she realised that what she was actually attached to was the memory of that other man of years ago, not the self-centred, ungrateful creature he'd become.

Doris cleared away their plates and filled the kettle. After lunch they always had a cup of tea in the sitting room, often dozing off in their armchairs. Alfred was still in a huff about the cooking when he stretched himself out. He watched as Doris brought in a tray with the tea. Watched as she stumbled over the edge of the rug, as she'd done a hundred times before. Watched her hand shaking as she poured his tea. In spite of himself, he hated all these signs of senility, aware that he, too, showed them. Instead of feeling sorry for Doris, he began to hate her.

She hadn't been sitting down many minutes before she fell asleep, head back on the chair, mouth open. The way her cheeks caved in reminded him so much of a corpse that his loathing grew. Did he really have to go on living with this old bat who irritated him so much? He thought about her ailments; the arthritis, the heart trouble, the failing lungs, her stomach problems. Something out of that lot ought to finish her off soon. But she kept on ticking, and might for quite a while yet. Would his patience stand it? Could he, for that matter, help things along? The thought caught him unawares and he put it from his mind, ashamed.

To make sure the feeling was well and truly banished by some activity, Alfred got up and took the tray back to the kitchen. The rattling cups and saucers woke Doris, who hobbled to join him, but he brushed past her and went into the garden.

The next morning Alfred was in his tool shed tinkering at odd jobs. Breakfast had been the usual catalogue of dithering senility. He had put the bread into the toaster and gone to fetch the milk from the doorstep, returning to find that Doris had switched it on again and burnt the toast to charcoal. Smoke filled the kitchen. She was pathetic in her apologies, which only made him more annoyed. He had then fussed over washing the dishes, until in her exasperation to speed up the drying she had dropped and broken a cup. This had plunged her into a tearful despair and she limped away to make the beds.

Now, in the shed, he surveyed the row of shiny chisels, the various hammers and saws. There were certainly times when he felt like hitting her with something, but he would undoubtedly be found out, and he was terrified at the thought of being in prison. And then again, despite his annoyance, he couldn't quite bring himself to think of hurting her. He sat on his stool by the workbench and fiddled with the secateurs. Suddenly it came to him. Of course! Her heart tablets. The doctor had always strictly impressed on her that she mustn't take more than the prescribed dose; any more could be very dangerous, he'd said. That was it! If he could just slip some extra ones into her, somehow, that might do the trick. She had such a big bottle of them she'd never notice if a few were missing. Death would be due to natural heart failure, and because she was on the drug already, its detection wouldn't be of any significance.

Alfred paced about the shed in great excitement. By God, this was the solution, and the perfect crime into the bargain. He sat down again to consider the details. She took one of the white tablets each night and morning, along with umpteen others. She often got so confused she didn't know what she'd taken. However, he couldn't rely on switching them, because the others were of different colours. The thing to do was put an extra couple a day into her tea or food. Surely, in two or three days, that would overload her heart so that it would simply pack up in a way that would seem quite natural? Nothing dramatic. It wouldn't be painful for her and the chances were that she'd have gone like that anyway, eventually. His hands were trembling with emotion. He'd get a supply of tablets out of the bottle this very morning.

Doris sat on her bed and sobbed until she could scarcely get her breath. She felt put upon and resented Alfred's endless criticism, his niggling tyranny. She was wearied by the constant pain racking her limbs, by the sleepless nights when she couldn't breathe, yet daren't switch on the light in case it wakened him. She often felt she'd be better off out of it all, and many a time had wondered how she could go about it. Now she stared at her bedside table, with its collection of pill bottles, glasses and inhalers. The big brown bottle of heart tablets caught her eye. Why didn't she just stop taking her heart pills, and fade out naturally? That wouldn't be suicide, would it? The doctor had informed her sternly many times that she had to keep taking medication for her heart failure, otherwise her heart would just stop, and that would be that. In her bleak desperation the idea appealed more and more. She would stop taking them from today. Alfred wouldn't notice, because she took several others, anyway.

For two days Alfred managed very easily to slip a white tablet into her morning and evening cup of tea, stirring it in with quiet satisfaction. Her watched her closely, but observed no change. It was now Saturday, and for their evening meal they usually had something a bit special, generally pieces of chicken or chops. Today, however, Doris had been re-organising her little deep freezer, and had discovered a single leg of chicken that had got overlooked. That, she thought, would be a nice treat for Alfred, and she could make do with a scrap of cod that needed to be used up.

Doris decided to cook the chicken leg in the microwave and boil the vegetables in pans. That should please him. He won't be able to moan about them being underdone.

Together they laid the table, and Alfred was so delighted with the way his scheme with the heart tablets was progressing, that he took the unusual step of opening a bottle of cheap Spanish wine. Not only was it a sly toast to his success, but he felt sure it couldn't be good for Doris's dicky heart, and might just tip the balance.

Doris served up the food, they sipped the wine, and Alfred began his dissection of the chicken leg. He had been eating for some moments when he suddenly peered at his plate, scowling.

"Hells bells! This is raw! Look—it's all bloody."

Doris gave a token glance towards his plate.

"Stop fussing, man. There's nothing wrong with it. It'll do you no harm at all. Get it eaten."

Alfred poked suspiciously, taking morsels adjacent to the red flesh, but finished most of it.

"Well, at least the veg is done properly this time," he announced. "You can't beat boiling things in pans."

After the washing-up they looked at the television, Alfred keeping a calculating eye on his wife for signs of the overdose working. How would it show? Would she just collapse on the floor? Or complain of pains in the chest? Be out of breath? He didn't know what to expect. She seemed completely normal. It was obviously going to take another day or two.

On the Sunday evening, it was Alfred who felt distinctly unwell. They'd spent a quiet day, no undue exertion, nothing out of the ordinary to eat, but he had a growing feeling of nausea and a bit of a headache. He developed a frightening diarrhoea and severe abdominal pains. As the evening wore on he became shivery, and the headache increased. He was then sick several times, which finally decided them to send for the doctor. When he arrived, Alfred was obviously running a temperature and quite ill. The doctor lost no time in summoning an ambulance and having him admitted to hospital.

Doris sat by him in the ambulance and held his hand. He was subdued and seemed pathetically frightened, talking only with difficulty.

"You know, Doris, it's just dawned on me. I bet I caught something from that chicken yesterday. I told you at the time it was red raw near the bone. And you didn't have any, and you're all right. You do feel all right, do you?" he added, wondering furtively about the progress of the overdose.

"Yes. Right as rain." She squeezed his hand. "And we'll get you put right, too, love. The doctors will have you well again in no time, you'll see."

At the hospital they were parted unceremoniously, when he was trundled away on a trolley, and she was shown into a waiting-room of shiny cream walls, red plastic chairs and piles of old magazines. She gave her name at Reception to let them know who she was with, and then hobbled across the polished floor to a seat. She had little idea of how long she'd waited, but at last her gloomy thoughts were interrupted by a nurse coming to take her to see Alfred.

When she saw his bed she panicked. He was flat out and scarcely visible above the sheets, and there were tubes and wires everywhere. She approached cautiously, as though she might disturb the intricate equipment. Bending over him she whispered; "Alfred, love, can you hear me? How are you feeling now? What do they think's the matter?"

He rolled his head towards her, sweat glistening on his brow.

"Some sort of infection, probably. I feel awful. I'm going to be here a few days."

"They'll have you fit again soon, Alf, love," she blurted out, her lip trembling.

She tried to hold his hand, but seeing the catheter in the purple vein on the back, thought better of it. The nurse came back and led her away, explaining that Alfred was seriously ill and would be receiving intensive treatment for a few days. A car was arranged to take her home.

The house was eerie and lonely. It was the first time for many years that they'd been apart. As she got ready for bed, she noticed the bottle of heart tablets. She'd been off them for three days now and hadn't noticed any ill effects. Funny, that. Was she to carry on with her plan? Well, she couldn't now, with Alfred ill. He'd need her when he came out of hospital. He'd looked so frail lying there, her heart had simply gone out to him, despite everything. He wasn't so bad to live with, really. She still loved him, and they still needed each other, and there was something to live for. She got a glass of water and started again with her heart tablets.

❦

Over the next few days, Alfred had plenty of time to think. Initially, he'd flitted in and out of delirium, having disturbing dreams, even when he thought he was awake. As he improved and became stronger, he could concentrate better and gather his thoughts. He'd nearly been a goner, there was no doubt about that. If it hadn't been for all the drips and antibiotics and whatnot, he'd be dead. The memory of his fears prompted him to assess his recent life with Doris. However frustrating Doris was at times, he really was still very fond of her. He'd been deeply touched by her concern and obvious affection each time she'd visited him; and, after all, was it fair that he should be annoyed by her disabilities? Surely, she was the one who suffered and needed his comfort and support?

When he thought of his plan to give her an overdose of heart tablets, he squirmed with guilt and remorse. For all her failings and quirks, she was a good soul, and devoted to him. And he still loved her. A lifetime of marriage and sharing together had to count for something. They had rubbed along pretty well, and these final years were precisely when they had to make a special effort to recognise each other's good points and overlook the bad. After all, she had just as much cause to complain about his funny ways. In sickness and in health they'd promised, hadn't they?

Doris visited him again the afternoon before he was due to come home. He was now sitting up in bed, in his own blue-striped pyjamas, and considerably brighter.

"I think hospital suits you, Alfred," she said. "You're a better colour and you've got a twinkle in your eye again. You really are feeling better?"

He clasped her hands on the counterpane.

"Not just better, love, different as well," he said awkwardly. "You know, it's a funny thing when it takes a dose of food-poisoning to bring us close again. Liquefies the guts and melts the heart at the same time, I suppose you could say."

Doris beamed happily. That was more like the Alfred she used to know.

A Scientist's Discovery

In a remote basement room of the university the white-coated Dr Sykes moved slowly along the row of cages, pausing at each one to study the occupant carefully, sometimes bending to have a closer look. Each monkey reacted in a similar way as he approached, jumping back onto its metal platform and gazing at him intently before looking away, often continuing to eat a piece of carrot clutched in its hand. A few bared their teeth menacingly, then hurled themselves at the bars of the cage, where they remained hanging, eyeing him warily. There were twenty rhesus monkeys in this windowless, claustrophobic room, all in individual cages round the walls.

One of the last animals for inspection provided him with special interest. He observed it for several minutes and was really excited to see that it was showing signs of nervous disease. Although its range of movement was very restricted by the small size of its cage, it had an obvious tremor of the head and neck, and didn't seem to be using one arm fully. Dr Sykes found that really encouraging. He looked closely at the label bearing the experimental details. Yes, it was in the group that had received the highest dose of the drug. And it was several weeks since the dosing began, so it would be about the correct time for symptoms to be appearing.

Fantastic! Now it was vital to make sure that the animal didn't die before they could electively kill it and carry out a post-mortem while it was still fresh to provide good pathology. A tricky decision; the disease needed to be sufficiently advanced for the brain damage to show up in the microscopy, but not so severe that there was a risk of the monkey dying. However, that was a detail; the exciting fact was that he had succeeded in reproducing the disease, which had never previously been done. If he and the team got cracking, with a bit of luck and hard work he could probably get a publication out in the next few months. That would further enhance the reputation of his research group, and help them to pull in more funds from the medical organisations which supported their work.

Sykes stood with his hands in the pockets of his lab coat and contemplated the monkey. Now he was assailed by his usual conflict. Despite his elation at having achieved his objective, and the intrinsic scientific interest of his task, it pained him to see an afflicted animal. In fact, he frequently worried about the moral justification for this aspect of his work. Yes, indirectly, and perhaps in the very long-term, he could argue that it would benefit human beings. But it was tenuous stuff, and he knew that; like everybody else, he avoided thinking too deeply and just got on with the job. He sighed. He'd been here before, many times. There really was no answer to it. Perhaps, subconsciously, he did realise that in this constant suppression his doubts didn't go away, but were building up inexorably into something that one day would explode to the surface.

He snapped back to harsh reality and began to run through in his mind how the different aspects of the work could be divided up for publication. First, there was the straightforward description of the pathological changes in the brain and spinal cord, and the effects of different doses of the drug—his junior colleagues, Frank and Geoff, could probably handle that. Then there would be a special study in more detail using the electron microscope; in fact, that would make a separate paper in another journal. And they could always repeat the experiment in another group of monkeys and carry out some physiological and behavioural monitoring, which would produce even more publications. Marvellous! This was what research was all about! Gripped by euphoria, his thoughts raced ahead. He would certainly have preliminary results which he could present at that international symposium in Colorado next summer. He'd always wanted to visit Colorado.

Encouraged and stimulated by his success, and once again submerging his doubts, Sykes left the Animal Facility. Whistling cheerfully, the greying, rangy scientist bounded up the stairs and headed towards his laboratory on the top floor of the institute. It was time for lunch.

Sykes queued at the food counter in the university refectory, bought a cheese-and-tomato roll and a cup of coffee, and joined a group of colleagues at a table in a no-smoking area.

"I've just been looking at those animals again, Geoff. One of them's got some inco-ordination. He's definitely affected. We're in business, old son. We have lift-off."

"Colorado, here we come, eh?" replied Geoff, who was in his early thirties, podgy, red-faced and prematurely balding.

"My thoughts exactly. We should have some preliminary stuff by then. When do the abstracts have to be in by? February, isn't it? Shouldn't be a problem. The main thing is we'll beat Bettelheim and his American group to it; they'll be really peeved."

"How many animals are affected so far? " asked Geoff, rooting with a large pink hand in his bag of crisps.

"One moderately and a couple of others showing milder signs. As well as their heads trembling, they seem to lose power and control in their hands. I noticed one fall when it was careering round its cage the other day, and sometimes they drop food," replied Sykes.

Dr Barnard, an owlishly bespectacled biochemist in the department, who was not involved in animal experiments, could restrain himself no longer.

"My God, you're a callous lot. It's a depressing experience having lunch here. You'd think that in a university common-room there'd be some high-minded discussion about the finer things in life. But no. Instead we get Sykes positively enthusing over having fatally crippled some monkeys, and all of you cynically plotting the next paper as a ticket to a freebie jamboree, and a stepping-stone in your precious careers."

"Harsh words, Barney," returned the object of his attack, "but we're enthusiasts for our subject, just as you are for yours. Unfortunately, ours involves doing things to animals, which can't be avoided. Yours doesn't. What would you rather we discussed, then, in this intellectual hot-house? Most people in the university seem to talk about football or sex. I suspect that many of them are only television spectators at both. Shall we discuss the reasons for Liverpool's recent lack of success?"

"Oh, sod off. You know perfectly well what I mean," retorted Barnard, an ardent armchair Liverpool supporter, who had not seen them in the flesh for three decades.

Sykes suddenly noticed it was two o'clock, and picked up his cup and plate. He nodded to Geoff and Frank as he stood up.

"Perhaps we'd better have a quick get-together at the end of the afternoon to sort out that everything's ready for doing this monkey. Might even be tomorrow. You've got all the fixatives and what-not for the perfusion?"

He made his way along the maze of corridors to his office. There was always good-humoured banter with Barnard. He was a decent, easy-going spud, who was fortunate not to have to use animals in his research. Barnard also, of course, wasn't exactly a ball of fire when it came to getting research completed or papers published. He certainly wasn't driven, thought Sykes, in the way he himself was, by a burning desire to find out new things. No sooner was one paper written than data for another was being amassed. In the rat-race of today's research, papers published equalled success and fame, and that equated to a cheque in the bank at the end of the month.

There were a number of fellows like Barnard, who were inclined to wonder philosophically what it was all about; why they were doing this and that. Sykes himself was usually so wrapped up in rushing about that he didn't often stop to examine the why or the wherefore. He didn't consider himself insensitive or lacking imagination; it was simply that he never seemed to have the time to dwell on consequences or reasons. As a young scientist with a career to develop and a fascination for his subject, he had been a willing recruit. Now, he'd been harnessed to his treadmill for so long that it had become a habit. He rarely lifted his eyes from the wheel.

Later that afternoon, a technician came to tell him that his monkey was now much worse. Sykes had another look at it and decided that he ought to check it again that evening; he certainly daren't risk leaving it until the next morning. If it died overnight he would lose some marvellous material. Decomposition would have set in and the brain would be useless for their studies.

He cursed to himself as he realised the inconvenience of having to drive home and back again. Most of all, he dreaded the thought of going into the animal rooms alone at night; it gave him the creeps. As he had discovered on previous occasions, it exposed his vulnerable conscience. There was more time to contemplate the full horror of what he was doing. At night the reality was starker than in the busy, working day, when his reservations were easily submerged.

He returned at half-past nine. The building was deserted, apart from a couple of security men in the foyer. The Animal block was in darkness and he blundered about trying to find the light switches. At least he had remembered his plastic card-key, which allowed him into his laboratory suite. The corridors were dark and silent. He peered through the window of the animal room. Before they noticed him, his monkeys were sitting silently in their cages, but as he opened the door they were startled and sprang about, screeching and shaking the bars. The rattling echoed round the room, then subsided as they watched him suspiciously.

This was a totally different place at night, he thought. Eerie and menacing. These poor little blighters must be even more bored than during the day. Fifteen hours every day of this penetrating nocturnal loneliness, seven days a week, three hundred and sixty-five a year. It was unimaginable.

There was an empty cage by one wall, and he peered into it. It was below his own height and only a few feet wide and deep, with solid metal sides and back. He opened the door, put his head inside, and tried to imagine being forced to live in such oppressive confinement. He'd go mad. Anybody would. This was sheer cruelty, worse even than the smallest solitary prison cell. It wasn't just the experiments that were repulsive; in fact, they usually didn't last long and often weren't painful. What really upset him was the confinement. He turned round. Many small faces were pressed against the bars, their sad eyes following him.

Sykes walked across to the affected monkey. It was now unable to stand, and lay on the floor of its cage. It twitched frequently, but raised its head pitifully and made feeble paddling movements with its arms as he opened the cage door. Its large brown eyes fixed on him, reproached him. The pathetic state of this creature was more than he could bear. He was suddenly overwhelmed by revulsion at what he had brought about.

Ashamed and filled with disgust, he leaned back against a table, his heart aching with compassion. At long last he had been caught unawares. The festering guilt had burst to the surface. How could he have been doing this so unfeelingly for so long? Slowly he realised that the wound to his conscience and emotions was so deep that it would not heal.

He became angry, and found himself shouting aloud; "I know very well that everybody will say it's sentimental and anthropomorphic. I know all the arguments and how they justify it. Don't give me that bloody crap any more. There's no justification for this. None!" He thumped the table, startling some of the monkeys, which leapt about in their cages. "We have no right to do this. Under any circumstances. Do we gain any worthwhile knowledge from experiments? Precious little that can't be predicted from an armchair. Why do we do it then? Because we've become terminally insensitive, that's why. We no longer see it for what it is, we do it to advance our careers. To satisfy our curiosity, for some piddling paper in a scientific journal, for more research funds, we'll subject these poor buggers to years of hellish confinement and a lingering, miserable illness. You inhumane swine, Sykes," he shouted. "You despicable bastard. How could you? How could you?"

In his agony he glared round the room and felt a tremendous urge to open all the cage doors and release every monkey to freedom, but, even in his frenzy, there was still a shred of practical sense, and he realised that it wouldn't help them. Instead, he walked over to the paralysed animal. Trembling, he bent and stroked its head, and through his tears he saw again its reproachful eyes.

"I'm afraid there's no way I can make amends to you now, little one," he said aloud. "Please forgive me. But I will make you a promise. You haven't suffered in vain. Thanks to you, I shall never again do experiments on animals."

He turned out the lights, and, like a sleep-walker, made his way back through the gloomy corridors to his office. For a long time he sat slumped in the chair, lost in tortured introspection. Questioning. Agonising. It might be that at some later date he would be able to analyse his feelings and motives. All that mattered to him now was that he had taken a decision.

A few days later it was a subject for gossip throughout the university. Sykes had resigned.

After The Storm

he trouble was, I had miscalculated. I thought I could judge from the map the size of these remote New Zealand communities. This one was printed in large letters, and, as it seemed the only place for miles, I had assumed it would at least be a village serving a fair few folk, with stores, a garage and somewhere to stay. Not a bit of it. Sure, the roadside sign was there to confirm that I'd arrived, but instead of an increasing straggle of houses and a centre, I'd passed just one long wooden shack with a shop front and petrol pump, a few dilapidated old bungalows with verandahs, and a tiny school.

A hundred yards farther on I reached a field with rugby posts and sheep grazing it, and realised that I'd run out of all there was. Ahead I could make out a clump of cabbage trees bending in the howling wind, and beyond them the shore. The hills loomed dark and menacing in the low cloud. To return the way I'd come wasn't an option; it had been three hours of tricky driving on an unsealed track through mountains and bush, with scarcely a farmstead.

I enquired about accommodation at the store-cum-post-office. The owner was cheerful. There was a sheep farm not far up the track that took in travellers and sometimes did riding and farm holidays. They'd see you right. There was a storm on the way, so best to get off the road and lie low for a day or so till it blew itself out. It seemed good advice as I wrestled with the car door, the rising wind shrieking in the telephone wires.

I found the farm easily from his directions, despite the fading light. The shabby wooden house and outbuildings stood among tall evergreen shrubs and trees and seemed deserted. Rainwater gushed and frothed from the downspouts. A few bedraggled hens huddled under the verandah. My knock echoed through the house without reply.

I splashed across to the yard, from where I could see a shearing shed clad in faded red corrugated iron. There were signs of life at last. A couple of dozen sheep poured out of the back into a pen, a crouching black-and-white collie snapping at their heels. They were followed by a tall, sun-tanned figure in a black vest and shorts, wiping his brow with the back of his arm.

"Hello there." I shouted into the gale. "You seem to be hard at it. I'm looking for a night's lodging. Do you have any?

"Yeeah, we do. There's a couple of characters in the huts already, been with us a few days, but I reckon we can manage another." He put out his hand. "My name's Mike Mackenzie."

He eyed me up and down, amusement jostling with distaste. "It's not what you'd call fancy accommodation, but it'll do you. Out here there's bugger-all else. And there's a storm coming up. You'd better come in and keep dry."

In the shearing shed it was hard to find somewhere to stand where I wasn't in the way. Four sets of electric clippers dangled from the roof by black cables, each positioned by a shute and a pen of sheep. They were clipping the soiled wool from the animals' crutches, and the screech of the shears and the bleating made conversation difficult. Mackenzie shouted to me and pointed to the nearest shearer bent over his sheep.

"This time o' year we're just dagging, but we've a hell of a lot to do—about five hundred a day."

He took a swig from a tin of beer on the bench. He was about forty, dark-haired, and a typical Kiwi farmer, tough, athletic, hard-working and blunt.

"Where you from, England?"

I nodded.

"I thought you were a Pom."

Immediately he launched into a diatribe on the European Union and its cosseted farmers, and on Britain for joining. At that moment a motor bike roared up outside and a tall blond girl in the vest and shorts uniform clumped up the steps. She stroked back her soaking hair, took off one rubber boot and shook out the water onto the floorboards. The farmer glanced at me, a twinkle in his eyes.

"'Course, I have to be careful what I say about Europe when Helga here's around. She's got some quaint old ideas, coming from Germany. Haven't you, Hel?"

She stood close to him and stared back, proud, teasing, a confident insolence about her which struck me immediately.

"No, not quaint ideas. Just a longer and more civilised tradition."

She giggled. Rain glistened on her face and bronzed arms and legs, reminding me of those advertisements in which a lavish beauty in a swimming costume walks from the waves. Helga was just such a girl. She was working for a year on the farm to learn about agriculture, and, of course, to have some adventure. In this backside of nowhere, though, there wouldn't be much high life. It would have been more suitable for a recluse.

Their banter continued. They were obviously very well acquainted. I wandered off to watch the shearers as they bent and clipped, straightening only to push each sheep down the shute and drag another from the pen. The mounds of wool grew, and the whole shed reeked of sheep, muck and sweat.

At last it was time to down tools. The shearers flipped open a few beer-cans and stood easing their backs and mopping their faces. Mackenzie and Helga had gathered up the soiled wool into sacks and now he called me over.

"We'll take you back to the house on the bike. The missus should've finished the horses by now. She'll fix you up with a berth and some tucker."

I perched precariously on the back of the four-wheel motor bike as we bumped and splashed to the house. In the kitchen I was introduced to Jean Mackenzie. She had curly fair hair and a round, pretty face, though careworn for her age, which was probably late thirties. She had taken off her riding boots, but was still wearing jodhpurs, and was rifling through cupboards assembling ingredients to prepare the evening meal.

"You're welcome to eat with us if you like," she said. "There's a couple of shearers who live in, and another two travellers staying. I can as easy cook for eight as for seven."

I thanked her, and she asked Helga, with tense coolness, to show me the hut I was to sleep in.

It was primitive in the extreme, virtually a garden shed, with a broken windowpane and a faded curtain swinging in the draught. There was just room for the little bed against one wall, my bag taking up most of the floor. Helga assured me I would be comfortable, pointing out that she had a similar hut a few yards away in the bushes. She spoke good English, and bubbled with self-confidence, her blue eyes provocative, teasing.

The evening meal was an uncomfortable affair. On the face of it, with eight of us round the big pine table, it should have made for a jolly occasion, but there was a marked tension amongst us that poisoned the atmosphere. One of the shearers, a surly, red-headed fellow called Craig, said little, but glared at Mike from time to time with obvious dislike. The other travellers turned out to be a lean Australian with a pony-tail and drooping moustache, and a rotund, grey-bearded Dutchman on a cycle trek.

Jean Mackenzie had obviously made a special effort to smarten up; she had changed into a patterned shirt with a denim skirt, and had gone to some trouble with understated make-up. Her efforts, however, drew a dismissive response from Helga, who sneered, "My! We're being shown up by the lady of the house tonight!"

Jean's suppressed anger almost visibly reached boiling-point, and for the rest of the meal the taut lines of her face, the steely glare in her eyes, hinted at the tumult beneath her forced politeness.

The only people who were relaxed and enjoying themselves were Mike and Helga, who sat together and kept up a duet of conversation about sheep, politics and Poms. No-one rose to the bait except me. As the newcomer, I was expected to keep an end up, but Helga, self-opinionated, dominated the discussion. The shearers occasionally growled some earthy comment, and the visitors chipped in more as the beer flowed. Jean Mackenzie seemed distant and preoccupied. When we'd finished eating she took some plates into the kitchen, appealing for volunteer dish-washers.

She returned to clear the table in time to see Mike and Helga hastily disentangling their hands. She gave me a look of searing desperation before turning away with an armful of plates.

I passed a disturbed night, wakened frequently by claps of thunder, my shed and the shrubbery lit up by sheets of lightning. Once I was sure I heard a door slam in the wind. Time and again I found myself going over the events at dinner, fearful of the forces building up in the family.

It was after seven o'clock the next morning when I went over to the house for breakfast. The storm had blown itself out, but there were puddles everywhere. One of the resident shearers was alone cooking a fry-up, the Mackenzies, Helga and Craig having gone to the shearing shed early to make a start. I didn't spend long eating and set off to watch them at work. As I crossed the yard, Jean came running from the shed in obvious distress.

"There's been a terrible accident," she wailed, turning and pointing back. "Mike and Helga have been electrocuted—they're dead."

She looked at me distraught, her features creased with anguish, though tearless.

"Somehow the clippers were live," she gasped. "I'm going back to phone for the doctor and the police." She ran away towards the house.

When I reached the shed I noticed through a window that Craig was working with a screwdriver on the wiring of one of the clipper's control units. On the floor by him were several bodies. By the time I had walked round to the door he was standing surveying them, smoking a cigarette.

"It's a bad job, mate. Did she tell you what happened? Clippers were live, mate. Some kinda 'lectrical fault. We'd better leave everything just as it is till the police get here."

Beneath two of the dangling clippers lay a dead sheep, and across one was the sprawled body of Mike, on the other that of Helga. I bent closer. There was no sign of life. We waited in awkward silence, and I wondered how much I would tell the police.

Cordial

onsieur Chevalier finally finished cutting the long laurel hedge. He threw down the shears irritably and mopped his brow with a grimy handkerchief. How he hated hedge-cutting! Especially when there was a deadline like this. The trouble was, this summer there had been a deadline for everything, what with having to get the house and garden spruced up for the wedding in three weeks' time.

It was midday, swelteringly hot, and he decided that, having achieved one of his wife's objectives for the day, he would go and sit down with a glass of his home-made cider before lunch. He made his way across to the old barn, selected a bottle from the shelf, twisted off the wired cork, and sat down on an upturned barrel. Here in the coolness among the cobwebs was refuge, and he often sat happily for hours, if left in peace.

He watched the froth subside in his glass and his thoughts turned, inevitably, to the wedding. Their remaining unmarried daughter had suddenly decided, after years of living with the fellow, that she would get married. That was fair enough, but why did there have to be so much fuss, such preparation, such a spectacle laid on? That was what wearied him.

Monsieur Chevalier sipped and contemplated in the quiet gloom of the barn. This damned wedding seemed to have taken over Madame's existence completely. Ever since they had been married, she had never been able to sit still for five minutes; that was just her personality. He conceded that it was a useful trait, and had been the driving force behind bringing up their five children and running the household as well. Five children, plus himself and a big farmhouse, he mused, had taken a lot of managing.

Unfortunately, since the children had grown up and left home, all Madame's formidable organisational talents had been focussed on him. Since he had effectively retired from running the farm and was around more, he was an easy target. However, he felt that he had learned a trick or two, and had become quite adept at delaying or avoiding her tasks and deflecting the nagging. Tall, fit, still handsome, though weather-beaten and grey-haired, the twinkle often to be seen in Monsieur's eye, and the charm he beamed effortlessly on female guests, suggested that there were compensations.

He heard Madame's voice approaching from the direction of the garden. "Hervé! Hervé! Where are you?" she barked.

It was time to take pre-emptive action. He jumped up and stood at his workbench and pretended to mend a broken toaster, which had been gathering dust for some days, in a feeble attempt to appear busy.

"Hervé! Where are you?" Her voice became shrill.

"I'm in here, chérie. I've finished the hedge and a few other jobs, and now I'm having a go at the toaster." He indicated it with the screwdriver.

Madame Chevalier sized up the situation at a glance.

"And the cider, I see. Can't you leave that stuff alone?"

She stood silhouetted in the doorway, holding a large bowl of raspberries she had just picked from the fruit cage. She was a small, compact, formidable woman with short grey hair and a determined expression—a bundle of energy.

"There's no point in fiddling about with that now," she snorted dismissively. "We've got more urgent things. You still haven't put out the geraniums in the front beds; they won't be flowering in time if you don't do it soon. And Mr and Mrs Russell will be here tomorrow. You haven't forgotten, have you?"

Forgotten? How could he? As if this confounded wedding wasn't trouble enough, their daughter was marrying a foreigner—an Englishman, of all things. Still, he supposed, it could be worse. After all, they had friends whose daughter had married an American.

Monsieur was only too aware that the following afternoon they were due for a visit from the English in-laws-to-be. It was the first time they had met. They were driving down, would stay a couple of days, and then continue on south to complete their holiday.

He had noted with trepidation how the impending visit had fired up his wife, and provided her with another reason to increase her already frenetic activity. She seemed to view the event as an inspection by Les Anglais, of both themselves and their premises. While nobody nowadays ever exercised a veto on marriages—children had become far too independent for that—she wanted to impress and do justice to their situation. They were, after all, representatives of a long line of minor nobility in the area, and, though now in relatively reduced circumstances (what would the eighteenth century counts have thought of them renting out a barn in the grounds as a gite, for God's sake?), their family traditions were a matter of great pride.

Their magnificent stone-built farmhouse-cum-manor was in good repair; indeed, it was virtually indestructible by natural forces. If a lick of paint could preserve their heritage and image, then Madame would see that it was done. Unfortunately, it fell to him to carry out the work. There were now only three weeks before the wedding, and he was being constantly nagged that he was falling behind Madame's timetable for the garden and house decoration.

The garden was to be at its high summer best, with masses of blooms in every bed; all traces of minor decay in the house, of which there were plenty, were to be repaired, or at least covered up. He had been given a list of the windows that had to be painted, and had been reminded ad nauseam that the garage doors would have to be stripped and painted—they, apparently, were a disgrace.

Madame had emphasised that the lawns, especially, would need to look at their best; many of the guests would be English, and one knew how critical and knowledgeable they were about lawns. The present crop of molehills across the green expanse by the house was driving her into a fury, though he himself accepted it philosophically enough. To him, it was another welcome sign that Nature can always thwart Man's ambitions, which, by his reckoning, was how it should be. When he had put this view to Madame one day, in her exasperation she had suggested that perhaps he would like to stand out there on the big day, in his dress suit, and explain that to the guests.

After they had eaten their midday meal, Monsieur spent the afternoon bedding-out geraniums and levelling the molehills, not without feeling a sneaking envy of the moles. The idea of a life hidden out of sight, where you could go about your business undisturbed, appealed to him. But, no doubt, there were also domineering moles.

The day of the Russells' visit dawned, and he was busy for the whole morning sand-papering the wooden frames of the huge old windows, until his fingers were raw. He was not looking forward to the visit. He spoke only poor English, though he'd had a basic grounding in the language at school. Besides, he never liked putting himself out to be polite to strangers. The only consolation, as he saw it, was that, when they had visitors, his wife was distracted from her nagging, and burdened him with fewer jobs. With luck, he might be able to slip away from time to time to the farm.

The Russells duly arrived in the afternoon, after a journey of several hours from the port. Since it was sunny, they all sat outside and drank tea. Monsieur felt that he and his wife had fumbled the introductions. He could see that Mr and Mrs Russell were thrown out by a few phrases they didn't understand, and he and Madame were tense by trying to impress. Consequently, his mind seemed to go blank when it came to any words of English. The prospect of a couple of days of such uphill communication appalled him. If only they knew better English! Or, of course, if only their daughter had married a Frenchman!

"You 'ave 'ad a good crossing? Yes?" pitched in Madame.

"Yes, very smooth, thank you. Like a mill-pond, luckily. And we found you here easily, too," replied Mrs Russell effusively. "Thanks to your map. Apart from a slight hiccup at the last crossroads."

"A he-cup at the crossroads?" Monsieur was determined to take part in the conversation, come what may, particularly with the attractive Mrs Russell. "'Ow is he-cup?"

"Oh, I shouldn't have said that. It's just an expression we have. Makes it complicated. What I meant was, we took the wrong turn. But we got here in the end." She smiled cheerfully.

Monsieur sipped his tea and weighed up the new pair as the conversation got under way. They were an incongruous couple. Mr Russell was perhaps in his late fifties, staid, reserved, what he imagined to be the typical Englishman of years gone by; dressed, despite being on holiday, for the office, complete with tie. Mrs Russell, on the other hand, was a very different proposition; not only was she much younger, she was from a different mould. She seemed lively and chatty, and, though not strikingly glamorous, she was pretty, and was one of those women who generated a kind of magnetism; he could sense the waves already.

"My French isn't very good, I'm afraid," she explained, speaking slowly, "but I attend adult evening classes to improve it, so this will be excellent practice. I shall have to be careful of those *faux-amis*, false-friends we call them, words that look the same, but mean something different—I could get into trouble." She giggled.

Monsieur could not miss the opportunity. "'Ere, madame, you will find not *faux-amis*, only good friends."

As the initial tension dissolved, it transpired that the tea-pot had gone cold. Monsieur offered to bring out a bottle of his special cider. Although he made large quantities, he guarded his stocks jealously, and was not inclined to waste it on the ill-deserving. This, therefore, was a gesture of some significance.

"You are 'ighly 'onoured," added Madame while he was away, showing her relief that he had chosen to be civil to the guests.

Monsieur filled their glasses, then stood and proposed a toast. "To the wedding. *Bonne santé*. Good 'ealth. Cheers."

There were smiles all round, his lingering rather longer than the others.

"I will give you a tour of the 'ouse tomorrow, and tell you its 'istory," he beamed at Mrs Russell.

Over the evening meal, produced with almost defiant efficiency by Madame, it turned out that all had several common interests; Madame and Mr Russell were keen bridge players, while the other two were reluctant at cards, but shared an interest in history and architecture.

"I go with my wife each week to bridge, but am a very poor player," shrugged Monsieur, with a resigned grimace.

This was an understatement. He actually loathed card-playing and nursed a smouldering resentment about the evenings he was forced to spend on it. He did admit, though, that sometimes it led to his meeting ladies who later became conquests.

"'E will not concentrate on the cards, that is 'is problem," said Madame.

He smiled disarmingly at the guests and gave a mock-conspiratorial grimace.

After breakfast the next morning, they discussed the wedding arrangements with some difficulty, and many misunderstandings. He felt rather sorry for the Russells, for his wife was as determined as usual. Because she was so doggedly religious, she insisted that there was no room for negotiation on any aspect of the church ceremony, and even the civil part was to be according to the letter of French custom. He did succeed, however, in persuading her to tone down some details to help the Russells. After all, it was only polite to make some gestures, they were guests in his country.

The morning passed with Monsieur's guided tour of the house and a walk round the gardens. They were all getting on better, and even Mr Russell had left off his tie and ventured into the conversation. Much mirth was generated by one of his sallies, when, owing to his mispronunciation, the French side had thought he was telling them he had kidney trouble, instead of referring to a bad queen in French history.

Monsieur, too, had struggled with the nuances of intonation, and, in telling of his activities as a youth, was frustrated at the Russells' blankness when he repeated time and again that he had belonged to the organisation of "*bade-en-poule*".

"Bade-en-poule?" Mrs Russell had queried. "Sorry, I just don't know what you mean."

"It was started in England by this man, I am sure. We wore short trousers, and a kind of scarf, and we went to stay in tents in the summer. I 'ave forgot the name of the boys, but I am sure 'e was *bade-en-poule*."

Eventually, the penny dropped for Mrs Russell.

"Oh, yes. I know what you mean now," she said, almost helpless with laughter. "Baden-Powell. That's how we pronounce it. The boys were called scouts."

"That is it," replied Monsieur, waving his hand in triumph. "That was the man, and I was a scout, yes."

At lunch, the conversation turned once more to bridge.

"We 'ave a bridge party this evening, unfortunately," announced Madame, looking scornfully at her husband. "I wish 'e was a better player. 'E always lets me down."

"Tonight, chérie, why don't you take our friend 'ere, Mr Russell? I am sure 'e is a much better player than me. I can entertain Mrs Russell by telling 'er more of the local 'istory. And she can also practise 'er French on me."

He looked round for approval with a wide grin. It was readily agreed.

At seven o'clock Madame Chevalier and Mr Russell climbed into her little Renault. As she prepared to drive away she stuck her head out of the window.

"Hervé! Don't forget to water the flower-beds, and make sure you do all the tubs and hanging-baskets as well."

"Yes, chérie. I will start now." He gave a mock salute as the car lurched away.

Monsieur managed very successfully to run the hose-pipe round the flowers at the same time as chatting up Mrs Russell. He had also been able to point out to her some more features of the house, its different window styles, the unusual gables. He found some English phrases coming back to him, and was delighted that she was so readily amused. They got on like a house on fire. When he finished the watering, they sat on a seat in front of the house and drank one of his bottles of cider, becoming more and more confiding.

When they reached one of those language barriers which neither of them could translate, she just giggled and raised her glass. He fixed her with those twinkling, imploring eyes, shrugged comprehensively, and beamed his smile. He brought another bottle, and they stared, fascinated, as the foam brimmed and fizzed to the top of their glasses.

"I would like to make a proposition to you," he ventured. "Unfortunately, I do not 'ave enough of the words in English to be very polite, so I say in a mixture of French and English. I want to play a little joke on my wife, and I would like you to 'elp me."

"Go on, monsieur, I'm all ears, as we say."

"I want us to pretend that I 'ave seduced you this evening." He leaned towards her conspiratorially.

She stared at him, wide-eyed. "Good God! or, *mon Dieu*, I should say. Whatever put that idea into your head?"

"Just a joke for 'er, that's all. I think it might put a stop to the nagging. And, of course, we only pretend! *Naturellement.* Well, what do you say?"

"I suppose there's no harm, in principle. But how do we make her imagine that something's happened?"

"Simple. I explain as we go along. They will return at about eleven o'clock. She will leave your 'usband downstairs and come looking for me all over the 'ouse. We 'ear 'er coming up the stairs, so she will find us just emerging from my bedroom—we 'ave separate rooms nowadays, unfortunately. *Voila!* She draws the obvious conclusion, but out of shame she cannot tell anybody else—it is purely between the three of us. *Magnifique*, do you not think?"

She stroked her throat nervously.

"Well, it sounds all right in theory, but I don't want my husband to get even an inkling, though he's not a suspicious man."

Suddenly, she made up her mind.

"Yes! You're on! Why not? Anything for a laugh. A real *entente cordiale* between us."

They chinked glasses and toasted the scheme.

"And this," he added, tapping the cider, "is the cordial."

They could hardly stop laughing.

It began to grow dark and cool. Bats had now replaced the swifts flitting round the gables, as he brought yet another bottle from his store across the yard. He looked at his watch and checked his calculations.

"I think we now must go inside, to make sure we are in position in time, just in case they come back early."

They climbed the creaking staircase together, he with the bottle, she carrying the glasses.

It was about quarter past eleven when the bridge players returned. The headlights swept across the front of the house and disappeared into the garage. The two were chatting in very relaxed style as they entered the hall. They went straight into the kitchen, where Madame put the kettle on for some tea.

"I will go and find the others. I expect they are in the *salle à manger* watching the television."

She checked the rooms downstairs and then set off to the first floor. She paused on the landing. Her husband's door was half-open, and, unsuspecting, she looked in. He and Mrs Russell lay entwined in the bed, their bare shoulders showing above the sheets, both sound asleep.

For some moments she remained transfixed, then she padded to her room and stood sobbing. It was some time before she roused herself, then she briskly splashed cold water on her face at the washbasin, and dabbed her eyes with her handkerchief. She looked at herself in the mirror, then went downstairs to rejoin Mr Russell in the kitchen.

"They seem to 'ave gone to bed," she announced, her face gaunt and bleak.

They had their tea and biscuits and continued their earlier conversation. Madame, though, appeared pre-occupied and vague, and her English disintegrated.

"You must excuse my English. When I am tired I cannot translate. My brain is confused."

It was soon afterwards that the culprits awoke. Hearing the voices downstairs, it dawned on Monsieur that his plan had misfired, and would have to be abandoned. They both panicked and pattered about the room trying to locate clothing. Mrs Russell dressed in a frenzy.

"I must get back to our room before he comes to bed. Thank God nobody saw us," she whispered. She grabbed her shoes and tiptoed onto the landing in her bare feet.

Monsieur closed his door and sat on the bed. There was no point in getting dressed. He checked round the room for any of Mrs Russell's clothes and then climbed back in. He lay propped against the pillows, arms behind his head. He chuckled slyly. It had been a good ploy. He'd achieved one of his objectives. His satisfaction, though, was tempered by having failed in his attempt to frighten his wife into jealous submission. Well, he reasoned, at least life would be no worse than before.

He did not know, of course, that from now on her nagging would have a sharper, hostile edge.

Elements for Change

It was geometry, the first lesson on Monday morning, and the form-room was a hubbub of cheery voices, banging desk lids and the thudding of hurled school-bags. As usual, Simon Hodge was dreading the beginning of another week. He knew it would be a repeat of the last—of struggling to cope with theorems, those perplexing circles and triangles drawn on the blackboard by the beetle-browed and intimidating Mr Crossley. There would also be the worry of guessing at French grammar, and being ridiculed by fierce old Mr Hardaker, to the general amusement of his classmates. In each lesson he would pray for the bell to clang out in the corridor to end his misery, like a boxer clinging to the ropes.

A whole week stretched ahead, broken only by a morning of science, which he loved, and an afternoon of football, which he was good at, but would probably be rained off. Hard though he found much of the school-work, what Simon was dreading most was another week of Goldman. Ever since they had come together as thirteen year-olds the previous autumn, Goldman had gone out of his way to wield power over him, to intimidate and bully him.

There was nothing violent, no fighting or beating-up. That wasn't Goldman's style. He was far too sophisticated for that. The malice that glinted in the thick lenses of his spectacles seemed to penetrate to Simon's very core, probing his insecurity like a laser.

The two boys shared a double desk for most lessons, well within whispering, nudging and pinching distance. Now, as Simon put out his faded red geometry book, he felt a flash of hope, because Goldman still hadn't arrived. Perhaps he was ill and off school? He wasn't away often, unfortunately.

Simon's thoughts went back to the carefree weekend he'd spent at home with his parents and brother, marred only by leaving his homework until Sunday night, which had brought forward all his worries about the impending school week.

He surveyed the room of chattering boys, all chirpy and happy with their banter and rivalry, confident in their ability to cope with the coming lesson. Except him. Simon quailed with apprehension, his stomach churning. Any minute old Crossley's footsteps would echo in the shiny, green-tiled corridor. Instead, into his mesmerised gaze loomed the bulky figure of Goldman, big for his years, padding through the doorway. Simon's heart sank.

Goldman shuffled sideways between the rows, beaming smugly to left and right, his school-bag brushing against the desks. He threw open his desk-lid with a flourish and began to unpack.

"Hello, Goldie," ventured Simon, in an attempt to start the week on a good footing.

Goldman ignored him, but sat down and commenced polishing his glasses on an immaculately ironed, white, initialled handkerchief. Finally he turned to Simon. "I see your lot lost again on Saturday, Hodge. Why don't you support a decent football team?"

Simon winced inside. There was to be no truce, then. No easing into the week. This was the first pin-prick of provocation, and the screw would be turned on him cleverly, relentlessly, from now until the final bell on Friday afternoon.

"They only gave away the goals in the last five minutes," Simon countered. "The *Express* said they'd played quite well!"

It was so irritating. Goldman wasn't much good at football, and, because of his religion, couldn't play on Saturdays, but he conveniently affected to support the more successful of the city's two teams, while Simon's always teetered on the edge of relegation.

"That's the whole point, you pathetic creature. That's why they're such an abysmal bunch, giving away two goals in the last five minutes. And as for the *Express*, you shouldn't admit to reading such trash. But I must say, it all fits. It all fits."

Goldman shook his head in mock sadness, and sneered as he replaced his spectacles. At that moment Mr Crossley swept into the form-room amid a sudden aura of tweed jacket and pipe tobacco. He glowered expansively, seeming simultaneously to catch thirty pairs of eyes, quelling every sound. The geometry lesson got under way.

After half an hour, Simon began to think he might get away without being asked a question. Relief was beginning to diffuse through him. Mr Crossley had rambled on, covering the board with theorems, several times rubbing it all off in a cloud of chalk before Simon could finish copying it. He could never keep up. Then suddenly Goldman said something he didn't hear properly.

"You what, Goldie?" he whispered.

Mr Crossley turned from the board and spotted him in a flash.

"I wouldn't have thought you could afford time to talk, Hodge." His deceptively pleasant tone was one all the boys recognised and feared. "Perhaps you'd care to demonstrate your skill in solving the next problem?"

Simon blushed and fidgeted.

"Yes, sir."

He looked hard at the diagram on the board, frowning to show that he was concentrating, then peered at his book for clues. He couldn't fathom any of it. Goldman's knee jabbed against his, deliberately to interrupt his thinking. His mind went totally blank. He became aware of the lawn-mower whirring by in the playing field, of the beautiful diagonal patterns created by the shadows of the windows on the wall. But geometry couldn't reach him. He froze, until finally Mr Crossley's voice, still insidiously calm, broke in.

"Very well, Hodge. Write out a hundred times, for tomorrow, Geometry is more important than talking to Goldman. Got it?"

Simon writhed inwardly. In any case, he would have had homework enough to occupy him for two or three hours that evening; now he'd had this extra piled on, and it was all because of Goldman. He seethed until the end of the lesson.

"That was your fault, Goldman," he protested, as they packed up their books.

"It's not my fault if you get caught talking. And you're such a cretin at geometry, anyway. If you'd been smart, you'd have known the answer."

Goldman leaned his large, greasy head towards him, hissing, "You might as well face it, Hodge, you're thick. Too thick to be in this form. Come to that, I don't know how you passed the entrance exam. at all."

"I'm good at English," Simon flared. "And I'm good at science as well—I get better marks in science than you do, so there! And I'm going to be a scientist."

"Science! Ugh!" interrupted Goldman scornfully. "Science is inferior to the arts. Science is for nerds and boffins. It's all you're fit for."

Simon looked at Goldman with horror. How did he manage to be so powerful, so superior, so like a grown-up? He was, after all, only thirteen, like himself. But Goldman was an adult in miniature. From the top of his well-groomed, wavy black hair to his shiny black shoes, there wasn't a blemish. None of the usual boyish scruffiness, the daily wear-and-tear. He remained for the duration of each day exactly as he had been turned out at eight-fifteen from his lawyer home; sparkling white shirt, school tie knotted impeccably, blazer uncreased, cuffs stark and unsmudged. He could have sat behind the desk in his father's office and the clients would scarcely have noticed the difference.

Goldman didn't seem to hold the masters in the same awe as did Simon and the other boys. He almost regarded himself as their intellectual equal. He was always respectful, of course, never a hint of being cheeky; he was too clever to step over that unseen threshold where authority might feel challenged, and react accordingly. Goldman had such an easy confidence in his precocious ability that it was impossible to imagine him having butterflies in his stomach.

Now he glared at Simon through his tortoise-shell-framed glasses and announced with disdain: "You'll be going down to a lower form at the end of the year, Hodge. Just as certainly as Rovers will be relegated."

Simon boiled to the point of wanting to take a swing at the podgy, smirking face, but he held back, instead muttering an inadequate, "Aw, shurrup, Goldman."

Though Simon was quite happy to tumble and fight when necessary with most of his fellows, there was something about Goldman that put him off. Was it because he wore glasses? No, there was more to it than that. It was more to do with Goldman's grown-upness, his superiority, that stopped him. It would be like hitting a lady teacher. He could just imagine a dishevelled and bloodied Goldman picking himself up from the dusty form-room floor, broken glasses in hand, calmly and superciliously admonishing him in that prematurely deep and scholarly voice:

"You think that's the way to solve problems, do you, Hodge? Well, remember, the pen is mightier than the sword."

It was probably this feeling that Goldman would triumph in the end, and have the moral high ground, that made Simon and his classmates grudgingly wary of sorting him out physically. After nearly two terms of this school year, Goldman remained unchallenged.

At lunch-time Simon had an interlude when he was able to recover his self-esteem by playing well in an impromptu game of football on the playing field. He dribbled strongly and scored three goals, though there was a raucous dispute over whether or not his last goal had actually passed inside the pile of blazers serving as a goal-post.

His next humiliation came late in the afternoon, when the form was having the last lesson, French, he and Goldman again sitting together in a double desk. Simon had dreaded it, because he'd struggled with the homework, and knew that much of what he'd done was probably wrong. Goldman had goaded him that he was no good at French, racking up his already churning apprehension.

The French master, Mr Hardaker, was a severe, irascible man, with greying hair brushed straight back, but not quite flat, giving the impression of a bad-tempered porcupine. Nobody took liberties in his class, and he saw to it that each boy had to do some translation. Escape was impossible. And today was English into French, which meant that Simon's guesswork would be wilder and even wider of the mark than if he had a passage of French for translation into English.

Up and down the rows the boys took their turn to translate, most managing tolerably well. When it came to him, Simon received a sly dig in the ribs from Goldman's elbow, a reminder that the pressure was on, reinforced by a kick on the ankle. A few boys sniggered in anticipation of some sport. It was every bit as bad as Simon had feared. After staggering through the first few sentences, he stuck.

"Come on, Hodge," boomed Mr Hardaker, menacingly. "I would like a room with a view of the sea! How do you translate 'I would like'?"

Simon had gone blank with fear. He felt that it was probably something odd, irregular, but his mind was addled. He heard Goldman whisper behind his hand. He was wary of his tips, because he often deliberately told him the wrong answer to make a fool of him. There would only be a few seconds before Mr Hardaker lost his temper, so to guess at anything might be better than keeping silent. Again he heard Goldman muttering.

"J'aime, you fool, it's j'aime."

"J'aime," piped up Simon, tentatively.

"Screw his neck, somebody," bellowed Mr Hardaker, scowling.

The boys at neighbouring desks gleefully leapt on him, roughly grabbed his neck and tried to twist his head round, in the time-honoured tradition for grammatical offenders. There was general merriment.

Simon reddened and a sense of isolation welled up in him. Even his friends took a delight in manhandling him, and again it had been Goldman's fault, telling him the wrong words on purpose. He shouldn't have trusted him.

Since it was the last period of the day, after the bell he'd be able to catch the bus; at least there he'd have a few friends from other forms to lark about with, and could turn his back on Goldman and school for a few welcome hours. Except for the homework, and the hundred lines. The reminder sent a pang through him.

When the lesson finally ended, he was determined to ignore Goldman's taunts.

"Got you that time, Hodge. What do you mean, my fault? You're supposed to be able to think for yourself. You're part of an intellectual elite here. Though it strikes me you're not up to it."

"Yes I am, you'll see!"

Simon grabbed his books and school-bag and made for the door, unable to bear being near his persecutor a moment longer.

There was a straggle of boys to josh with as he walked down the long, tree-lined school drive and onto the road leading to the bus-stop. For some reason, none of those who normally travelled with him were in time for the first bus, so he went upstairs and sat alone on the front seat.

As on many days, he felt sad and angry, smarting at his treatment by Goldman, and worried by much of the school-work. How would he ever come through it all? He wanted to tell his parents, perhaps get them to complain to his form-master. But he'd often thought of that before, and dismissed the idea; he didn't want his mum and dad to think he was unhappy, and besides, where would he stand with the other boys if he was a moaner, someone who couldn't handle it? No, he had to keep his problems to himself, he'd find a way to deal with it somehow.

As the bus lumbered and rocked along through the suburbs, he consoled himself that at least the next morning was science, his favourite subject. In that he did excel, building on the knowledge he'd already acquired through his childhood enthusiasm for his hobbies, biology and chemistry. In the science lessons, especially the practicals, he really came into his own, and Goldman was inept and out of his depth.

Yes, he thought, that was the chink in Goldman's armour, and the place to teach him a lesson that would stop his bullying. Perhaps an opportunity would present itself in science the next day.

The morning found the boys meandering into the science block. Simon was thrilled straight away merely by the smell of chemicals pervading the corridors. Their practical laboratory had long wooden benches covered by decades of ingrained stains, though polished into an antique patina. The wall cupboards were laden with exciting bottles of coloured powders and solutions, He was in his element.

Their science master, Mr Jolly, was already there, writing instructions on the board. He was small and energetic, and, though he was in early middle-age, to the boys he appeared almost like one of themselves, such was his enthusiasm and constant activity. He joked, he positively effervesced, as he spent the lessons initiating them into the wonders of the scientific world. Simon adored him.

The boys drifted in pairs to their places and began putting on laboratory coats. Simon was reading the details of the experiments on the board as Goldman sauntered to join him.

"Well, Hodge, what madcap experiment are we undertaking today, in this despicable subject? I'm relying on you to help me, as usual."

"Why should I? You don't help me, in fact you get me into trouble on purpose."

"That's different, you nerd. You should be clever enough to see through it—I just keep you on your toes."

Mr Jolly surveyed the class from his raised podium.

"Come on, settle down, chaps. Today I want to show you more marvels of chemistry. There are two experiments; first, you're going to prepare nitrous oxide by heating a mixture of ammonium chloride and sodium nitrate. The chemicals you need are clearly labelled in front of you. You will weigh out five grams of each."

Simon could see that Goldman was showing his disdain by pointedly looking at a book and not listening. This could be his chance. He had recognised immediately that the magnesium powder put out for the second experiment could be switched to mix with the sodium nitrate for the first, and, when heated together, would produce a moderate explosion to frighten the life out of Goldman.

As they all started to busy themselves at the benches, Goldman languidly looked over his spectacles.

"What do we have to mix with what, Hodge? Some of these powders, is it? This really is the most tedious two hours of the whole week."

Simon pushed the sodium nitrate and magnesium powder towards him. Goldman shuffled off to weigh them, still grumbling.

Simon had nearly finished the first experiment and was jotting notes into his laboratory book, when he noticed Goldman light his bunsen burner and begin to heat the glass test tube containing the powders. He watched nervously as Goldman's mixture steamed and bubbled. Suddenly Goldman lost patience, and shook the tube vigorously.

There was a loud, splintering bang, and simultaneously a howl from Goldman. He was holding his hand, which was bleeding from several places. His lab coat and white shirt collar were spattered with stains. His glasses were cracked, but intact.

"This is your fault, Hodge," he whimpered. "You told me which chemicals to use."

"You must have mixed them up," replied Simon calmly. "Anyway, you're supposed to think for yourself, as you're so clever. But it does prove that science is more powerful than the arts, doesn't it?"

They stopped their argument abruptly, for Mr Jolly was bearing down on them to investigate.

Tom

The rain had started just as we were going into the church, and now, with the funeral service over and the little procession filing out behind the coffin, it had come on steadily. As we passed gaps between the yew trees, cold gusts of January wind caught us from the side, and we had to struggle to hold our umbrellas. The vicar and the family arrived at the end of the open grave, and the coffin, in that characteristic yellowish wood, was lowered for the burial.

I stood in the lee of a yew tree, while the vicar intoned, most of his words being carried away by the wind. The deceased's elderly sisters clutched each other's arms, while one of the undertaker's men sheltered them with an umbrella. The coffin was lowered into the grave and the vicar held out a terracotta bowl of dry soil for the ritual throwing of earth. It was a wise precaution on the undertaker's part to provide it, for the earth around the grave had been turned into mud. The family laid their wreaths, then huddled together in their grief, staring bleakly into the grave as the rain dripped down from the swaying branches.

It was hard to comprehend that we were here, that we were really burying Tom. He had gone so suddenly. I thought of the parson's little eulogy during the service. Yes, he had lived all his life in the parish, he had farmed the same land year in, year out; he had taken a great interest in his Shorthorn dairy herd, and, indeed, in all animals, and Nature herself. But no speech, certainly not a clergyman's second-hand platitudes, could convey even the essence of his life, nor the details of such a man's struggles, hopes and frustrations. If there was any consolation in his sudden death, it was that he had not suffered or lingered, but had worked right to the end, dying literally with his boots on, where he fell in the field.

For me, there was the consolation that I had visited him and his sister not long before, when they had been in grand form and we had talked of old times and about their plans for retiring. He had been chopping logs when I arrived, but he put down his axe, and in no time we were discussing his dogs and admiring the vegetable garden, always his pride and joy. The runner beans had just reached that jaded stage of early autumn when a few of the leaves were turning yellow, and the pods were knobbly and no longer worth picking. There were some fine rows of onions, and he was particularly proud of the tomato plants in a lean-to greenhouse.

"We had tomatoes as big as your fist," he had said. "Nay, bigger."

We leaned against a wooden water butt in the yard and chewed over the world's news as seen from the depths of his countryside. Tom kept a watching brief for all of it, through the media and his local sources; the postman, animal feed salesmen and shopkeepers. The politicians might think they could do what they liked, but they were being closely monitored and judged by old-fashioned standards. Flashiness was distrusted here; if something seemed to run counter to rural common-sense it was rejected out of hand, and no amount of weasel-words was going to convince him.

"It don't make sense to go importing cattle from them foreign countries after we've spent all these years getting rid of the diseases. No sense at all," Tom had argued. "We're throwing away the whole point of us being an island. But that's politicians, you see, Robert. Always slippery dealing."

I looked at his unshaven, weather-beaten face. He was so strikingly like his father had been in appearance and mannerisms, and even his voice, with the strong local accent, that I felt I was in the presence of that earlier generation in the days when we were much younger.

Their farm was remote and could only be reached by a rough, unmetalled track nearly a mile long. It was buried in its meadows, which sloped down on all sides. A sluggish, muddy brook at the bottom of the cobbled yard drained the croft by the shippon, where the Shorthorn cows would stand waiting to go in for milking. In wet weather the field churned to a quagmire and the brook would spill over on its way to the pond a hundred yards further down. Then the geese made their way up the floodwater, cruising arrogantly to investigate their additional territory. There were always pigeons on the roof, and hens and guinea-fowl squawking and scratching about the yard and fields.

In years gone by they had made cheese, and, as a small boy, I helped in the dairy as the milk was carried in churns from the cowshed. The stone floor and the huge shiny metal cheese vat echoed the clattering of buckets, creating an intimidating air of bustle, for the milk had to be processed by a certain time. The daughters were the cheese-makers, and they used to lean over the vat, endlessly stirring the curdling milk with their big red arms, bare to the shoulders. When the whey was drained they always gave me a cupful to drink, before the rest was carried to the pigs. Then the white curds in the vat would be sliced into squares and left to drain, to be gathered up later into coarse muslin wraps ready to go into the iron presses in the corner of the kitchen.

Though I was drawn, like all boys, to their pre-war Fordson tractor and other implements, my heart was with the livestock, and my favourite place was undoubtedly the cowshed. It was a long, ancient building of mellow brown brick, adjoining the house. The top half was a barn for hay and corn, a sanctuary for the cats, with round pitch-holes covered by wooden doors. For much of my youth the milking was done by hand, and before I was big enough to help, I used to stand by the various members of the family as they crouched on their wooden stools, their heads pressed against the cows' flanks. They would look up from time to time as they squirted the milk into the pail between their knees, and answer my endless questions.

There were so many strange words I heard about the farm, but could never quite understand; was that one a heifer? No? Well, that one, then? Not that one, either? I must have had a roan heifer pointed out at some time, and consequently thought that all roan cows must be heifers. I would tell them interminably about what I was doing at school, about worthy conkers I had, what my pals had got up to, and about our village school football team. They must have found me a nuisance, but their good nature prevailed. They took a genuine and kindly interest in children, and, with so few visitors, they were intrigued to meet any representative of the outside world.

Eventually, the time came when the farm was "put on the electricity", and the paraffin lanterns they carried about in the cowshed were replaced by electric lights, and a milking machine was installed. I still stood and talked to Tom and his father as they milked, but now it was about milk-yields and butter-fat content, and what I had been reading in the *Farmer's Weekly*. By now I knew what a heifer was, and probably its human equivalent also. From the barn in the background came the purr of the milking machine's engine, and our conversation was punctuated by the tick-tock of the suction in the clusters on the cows' udders.

The corn harvest was another activity I particularly enjoyed. There was the exhilaration of being outdoors in summer weather, and the fun of working on the tractor or harvester. Tom taught me to work this binder, since it required less skill than driving the tractor, but was still a vital job, and they were always short-handed. Tom would drive the old, faded orange Fordson, which pulled the binder along by the standing corn. As the corn was scooped onto the moving canvas trays to form a sheaf, it was my job to pull the lever which released the sheaf onto the ground. On a hot day this was a mesmerising process, and there were times when I nodded off to sleep, to be wakened by a shout from one of the men stooking, telling me in no uncertain terms that the binder had jammed.

The family did not socialise much, though the womenfolk did belong to the local Women's Institute. Tom and his father were only irregular attenders at the cattle market, held on Mondays. There they could meet a few acquaintances and chat about the state of farming, while leaning on the stock pens. They virtually never visited the local pub, though on a few rare occasions when they had visitors and a bit of free time, it had been known for Tom and his sisters to be allowed out to make the half-hour walk across the fields to the village. Even as a boy, I sensed Tom's plight, and I was elated for him when we were out on these little jaunts. I felt a keen sadness that he could not have more time off from his life of constant toil.

During the war, Tom had been in the Home Guard. This must have been a real treat, to have a regular reason to get away from the farm and meet other men of his own age, who had a broader view of life. For years afterwards, he talked about the characters he met there. He was in awe of their sharp worldliness, and not a little suspicious; some of that sort can come to a bad end, was his judgement.

After the war, and the disbanding of the Home Guard, the only hobby Tom had was pigeon-racing. This he took up enthusiastically, for it combined his love of creatures with a weekly escape route to meet Life at the Pigeon Club. Of course, it had to be kept in its place; work always had to come first, and only when all the jobs were completed could he allow himself to dally in the pigeon loft. He had built it by converting one of their old mobile hen-houses on iron wheels, had painted it with vertical black-and-white stripes, and fitted it out with nesting boxes. It was an exciting new venture, and was just becoming popular throughout the country.

Tom delighted in the birds, stroking them in his great, rough, cracked hands, while the others cooed and bobbed in the boxes. He had all types, some with chequered markings, some greys, others pied, or blue, or reddish-brown. He would explain it all patiently to me; how the races were organised, the exotic places they went to, the clocking-in, the possible prize money. The chance of a bit of extra money was an added attraction, for Tom was not paid a formal wage, and the family was never far above the bread-line.

We were intrigued and excited by the pigeon scene. Where were these places his pigeons had raced back from? Mangotsfield? Where on earth was that? Tom later found out, by careful questioning of a fellow fancier, from whom he no doubt tried to hide his ignorance, that it was somewhere near Bristol. Bristol! By 'ell, that was Down South with a vengeance.

"Aye, it must be a hundred and twenty mile off, Robert lad," Tom had proudly told me, as he fondled one of the birds that had made the journey.

We wished that they could tell us about it. As we stared into those sharp, glassy, orange-ringed eyes, we realised that here was a bird that had seen more geography than we had. It had been to Bristol and looked down on all the country between here and there. Not only that, it had come back in two hours. What did it take on the train? Best part of five hours. We stared at each other and at the bird in wonderment, as the magnitude of this communications miracle sank in.

I do not think Tom was ever as truly happy again as on those Saturday afternoons waiting for his pigeons to return. There was the excitement of watching the distant sky for that hurtling speck, of distinguishing it from a high wood-pigeon, then noting how it lost height as it approached. Was it ours? Then it would land on the loft roof and we would have the frustration of watching it strut about, chest puffed out, cooing, wasting precious time. In its own good time it would pop down into its nesting box, where we would catch it, remove the race-ring from its leg, put it into the recording clock, and punch in the time. Was it a winning time? Only that night at the club, when all the clocks were checked, would we discover.

The main thing was that the birds had returned safe and sound. That was Tom's first concern; he had sent his emissaries all those hundreds of miles and they had winged back at practically sixty miles an hour to return to this loft, to be with us. We marvelled at the homing instinct, we speculated on how it worked. And at the same time, we were frustrated that they still could not tell us about the journey.

As the years went by, his father could no longer help much on the farm, and Tom had even less spare time. His enthusiasm for the pigeons was squeezed out of him by work. Eventually, he sold all the birds. For a few years the loft remained in the field; nettles grew up round the rusty iron wheels and the paint flaked off, so that, from a distance, instead of its bold stripes, it took on the appearance of an old dog's greying muzzle. After that, some of the boarding started to spring and it was dismantled completely.

Then there was even less manpower on the farm than there had ever been and Tom's drudgery was never-ending. Old farmworkers who had been with them for half a lifetime had retired and not been replaced. Tom tried taking on young men, but could never keep them long, because he expected them to work the same hours that he did, to be dedicated to virtual slavery, and to have poor wages and not mind the remoteness into the bargain. Not surprisingly, the new generation would not have it.

Tom was mystified. "Trouble is, you see, Robert, young folk of today just don't want this sort of life. They want to dash about on fancy machinery, and, come five o'clock, want to be off out enjoying themselves," he had told me many times when we had discussed his labour problems. Enjoying themselves! Fancy having enjoyment as a high priority!

Tom and his youngest sister remained unmarried, the result, at different times, of misplaced loyalty, lack of opportunity, and emotional blackmail. They stayed on at home, running the farm, and spending an increasing amount of time caring for their parents. Farmers of that generation did not ever really retire, but continued to rule their kingdom from the house. There was no handing over of control, but rather a tacit admission that, though they could no longer do much in person, instructions would still be issued about what was to be done, and when. It was amazing how much parents could deduce about the progress of the farm work by watching shrewdly from the various strategic house windows.

Have those goslings got enough water? The turkey poults aren't growing like they should be. When are you going to worm those sheep? We always used to have done them by now. Don't you think that bottom field's ready for silage making?

The daily niggling and advice was endless, and would have driven many a one to distraction; it took patience and affection to absorb it without rowing. Tom, though, recognised that it was meant for the best, that quite often their parents were right, and that allowances had to be made for old age and its querulousness. But it took its toll.

For a few more years Tom's mother was able to make a useful contribution to the family's work by doing the cooking, sewing and darning. That freed his sister for the outdoor jobs, especially the poultry and the calves, though she could pop into the house from time to time to ensure everything was all right.

Eventually, their mother's ulcerated legs kept letting her down and she was confined to the house, moving from room to room only with difficulty, hanging on to the back of a chair or a window ledge to steady herself. Father, too, was frustrated by his reduced involvement in the farm. It was a penance to him to have to spend more time in the house, and he never acclimatised to it. He would sit in the kitchen and smoke his pipe, a geriatric terrier at his feet, but every few minutes he got up and went to the window to look yearningly across the fields. He saw not only the tractor crawling slowly up the hill on the horizon, but in his mind's eye saw harvests of long ago, when the corn was carried in, not by tractor, but by his Shire horses. He could see them as plainly as if they were in front of him now. By 'ell, what a grand pair they'd been.

Now he was confined in the womenfolk's domain. Bluebottles buzzed up the lace curtains. It was a world of geraniums and old cacti standing in the window ledges, of the canary singing and hopping about in his cage in the sun, of cheese presses and food preparation, of mending spread across the table. A man felt in the way here. If he sat by the fire, they would want to open the oven door to take out the bread, and he had to drag his chair over the flagstones. His dog, too, relocated herself with an effort, and as she settled down again managed, with a glance, to convey a sense of grievance to the culprit. Apart from his pipe and a pile of wooden spills for lighting it, the only masculine thing in the whole kitchen was his twelve-bore shotgun hanging on the wall, the firelight winking on its barrels. After an hour or so of the kitchen he could stand it no longer, and he would reach his hat from behind the door and set off to the yard to potter about in the buildings, to fiddle ineffectually at repairing a piece of machinery, or top-up a water trough, or simply lean over the sty-wall and watch the pigs.

As the next few years slid by, it was not only their visitors who observed how they were all ageing, they themselves noted it all too keenly. Each one would take me aside and confess their worries about the latest illness that one of the others had suffered.

"The doctor said he'd never seen anything like it in all his time. Didn't know how she pulled through," Tom had told me after one of his mother's illnesses. "Strong as a horse, he said she was, and might easy go on for another ten years."

She did not, though. Six months later she was dead, and his sister now had to divide her efforts between the kitchen and the farm-work, baking in the evenings, and rushing in during the morning and afternoon to put the meals on to cook. Father did his best, but he never seemed able to have things organised and ready on time, and after a few failures and rows, she found it simpler to do everything herself. He was eighty, and you can't expect much when they reach that age, she felt.

Little more than a year later, I received a message from Tom that his father had been taken to hospital, and that the outlook was not good. When I called at the farm Tom was accepting the inevitable with his customary realism. An exploratory operation had been carried out, but had revealed cancer.

"They found summat they didn't ought to. That's the trouble, Robert. And I'm afraid they can't do nowt about it. It's spread too far, and, what with his age, and everything…So, it looks as if it's just a question of time."

It turned out, though, that there was not very much time, and a couple of weeks later he was gone.

Tom and his sister had a grand clear-out, and decorated their parents' bedroom, which had not been done for decades. They kept the ancient brass bedstead, because it might come in for visitors, but piled it high with women's magazines, knitting patterns and hat boxes. They also changed things round in the sitting room, which had never been permitted in mother and father's day. For most of their lives, this room had never been used, but had been kept for best and for momentous family occasions. In their parents' declining years the new television had been installed there, so they could watch it from more comfortable chairs. Now they brightened the place up, replaced the dark, gloomy curtains with lighter fabric, and removed some of the funereal Victorian ornaments to the attic. The sepia photographs of family groups, and heavy-framed paintings of grandparents were, however, left in pride of place on the walls, and the glass domes containing a stuffed kingfisher and a snipe still occupied each end of the mantelpiece. Nor did they throw out the fox and badger heads on the back wall, or the gigantic, polished bull's horns over the door. They were all part of their family heritage, and each represented one of their father's escapades when he was in his prime.

Tom and his sister settled slowly into this new phase, and grew used to having only the two of them to cater for. The toil, however, went on, unrelenting as ever. They, too, were now reaching an age when physical work was harder to cope with, when limbs that were tired at bedtime were stiff and aching next day, when colds and coughs that they would have thrown off easily as younger folk now went onto their chests, and they wheezed and coughed for weeks on end.

Tom told me how, one night, as they sat by the fire after supper, he had suddenly announced to his sister; "I'm going to give up milking."

She had looked up from her knitting, astonished. "You mean, get somebody in to milk for you?"

"No, I don't. I mean get rid of the herd, the whole bloody caboodle. Give it up altogether."

"But, we've always milked, Tom," she protested.

"I told her, Aye, and don't I bloody know it! But that doesn't mean we've always got to! There's times I can hardly manage it. I'm getting jiggered. It'd give us a bit o' money from the sale o' the cows, we'd save on the feed bills, and we could run on some beef cattle, which would be a lot less work."

"Well, if you reckon you know what you're doing…"

"I do. I've been turning it over in my mind for a good while, and it's just got to be. There's still quite enough work."

So it was that they decided to give up the dairy herd, despite the sadness at ending an unbroken tradition of dairying on the farm going back probably a couple of centuries. Within a few months the sale was arranged, the cows sold, and the buildings stood empty and silent. The cats, of course, stayed on in the hay loft, and Tom continued to put down saucers of milk for them in the old cowshed, but now it was milk that they had the indignity of buying from the village shop, instead of producing themselves.

Tom and his sister gradually got used to staying in bed a bit later in the mornings, and not having the tiresome drag of the evening milking. They soon began to savour the extra freedom, little as it was, now they were no longer tied to cows' tails.

The routine of the rest of their days did not alter much, and they were still pretty well occupied. There was no getting away from the fact, as they both frequently acknowledged over meals, that now they were getting on in years every job took so much longer. They could not carry as many buckets as they used to do; nor as fast, nor as far. Most of all, they were reaching a frame of mind in which they did not really care. If things did not get done quite so well, or quite so often, let them be. They could only do so much.

Under these circumstances, it was not surprising that the farm began to show signs of neglect. Tom noticed it and it grieved him, because all their lives they had taken a pride in their surroundings and the way they farmed. Some of the window frames needed a coat of paint, and there always seemed to be dog hairs or mud from their boots on the kitchen floor; the crockery from previous meals lay about unwashed for longer and longer, and, outside, hedges grew straggly, clumps of thistles appeared in the fields, and a sheet of corrugated iron on a barn came loose and flapped in the wind. Though they had reduced the amount of work considerably, it was still a struggle, and more than they could cope with.

They were now turned seventy, and when the next winter came, rattling at the same time through the barns and their chests, they mooted the idea of selling up and buying a little cottage in the neighbourhood, where they would have no work, no ties, and would be able to get out and about. They both agreed that they needed to enjoy themselves and travel a bit, see places they had only heard about, while they still could. They were going to have a taste of the life they had missed, instead of being endlessly tied to work.

Throughout the next summer they weighed up the practicalities of giving up the farm, and sold off some of the beef cattle and poultry. The decision had been made in principle, and they were content in their own minds. Now the idea was firmly lodged, they were looking forward to retiring and to the new lifestyle.

As Tom and I talked in the farmyard, on what proved to be our last meeting, he was convinced that moving was the best thing for them, and he was excited at the prospect of leisure and no hard, physical work. They would sell the farm in the spring, and then have the whole summer before them to rest and make pleasure trips.

"We've got our eyes on a little place that'll be coming up for sale not far away, and that would just suit us rightly," he said.

As we shook hands, I wished him luck with the sale.

"Oh, we'll be all right, don't you worry. Next time you visit us we'll be living a life of comfort and luxury."

He laughed uproariously at the sheer, wild, self-indulgence of the idea.

Now, by a cruel blow, all that he had looked forward to had been denied him. He had never had comfort or luxury in his life, and he had left it too late. A lifetime of desperately hard toil and dedication had simply come to an end before he was ready.

I sheltered under the yew tree until the family mourners had gone and most people had left the churchyard. The gravediggers were waiting for a respectful interval in a hut in the far corner, before shovelling back the earth. As I approached the grave, the muddy grass squelched, and streams of rain coursed down the piles of red soil on either side. Raindrops splashed onto the coffin lid. But the rain and earth did not seem to be a desecration, more a welcome, for these were the elements in which he had spent his life. This was his true resting place.

Not Catching It

orry, love. I didn't catch what you said." Bother! David's gone out into the garden now. We've just got back from the hospital and he's going to tell me what the specialist thought about my eyes. The trouble is, my son will not speak up. Always mumbles. I am speaking up, Mother, he says. Mind you, it was just the same before I went deaf. He never was easy to hear. He's quietly spoken, I suppose you'd say. But it's so frustrating for me. You'd think he'd make a bit more effort, wouldn't you? I mean, he knows I can't hear him. I watch his lips, guess at what he's saying, but I often get the wrong end of the stick. Then he speaks up all right. Really raises his voice. I can see the irritation in his eyes. Fairly flashes it does. He's very patient mostly, but sometimes it annoys him to have to repeat things. Most folk are the same. They're tolerant at first, but that soon wears out. They resent making the effort to say things again. So they shorten it, simplify it, and practically shout as well, so that you feel a simpleton, an imbecile, instead of just deaf. Sometimes I could burst into tears, being shouted at like a child.

I must say, though, that he's a good lad to me. He's done everything he can to help me with gadgets. He installed one of those circuit things round my living room, with a movable microphone so I can hear the telly better, as well as people talking; it doesn't make a lot of difference, though. He does what he can to fiddle with my hearing aids—there's always something wrong with the damn things. If it isn't the battery that's on the blink, I haven't got the volume set right. I have endless trouble with the tiny controls now my fingers are so clumsy. If I turn it up too much, then all I hear's a terrible din because it picks up and distorts every bit of background noise, but I still can't hear what's being said. God! You talk about being frustrated! I could scream sometimes, I get so worked up.

And the audio-technicians and doctors don't help much, either. They change my hearing aid for a different type, perhaps with a softer sort of plastic or a longer tube, or some such thing, but it doesn't usually make much difference. I used to be quite optimistic that if only I could find the right sort of aid I'd be able to hear again. But I've given up hoping now. There's just nothing they can do, especially at my age. My hearing's gone completely in one ear, and there's only a bit left in the other, and that's failing every year. I've just got to put up with it. Coming to terms with your disability, they call it nowadays.

Some of the clinic people are very nice. They're doing the best they can, but they know it's hopeless. Others don't like old people and don't make any attempt to cover it up. You can see they're bored and resent the time they spend on you. Try this hearing aid, take it or leave it. The fact that the thing doesn't fit properly and I'll have a sore ear in a week doesn't bother them in the slightest. Little madams, some of them are. I do feel like saying my piece then, I can tell you. It's hard enough getting to the clinic, but if it's been a wasted effort it gets me boiling— I'm the one who's stuck here on my own with an infernal gadget that doesn't work. Locked away in my own world like an outsider looking in at life through a thick, soundproof pane of glass.

Folks don't understand what it's like, you see. How can they? I sometimes say to David: "I just wish that you could be deaf for a day, and see how you'd cope with it!" I don't really, of course. I wouldn't wish this on anybody, but I do think people would be a bit more considerate if they'd had some. If they only knew what it's like to be in a group of people chatting away, and to be right outside it all. You can see their lips moving, they laugh at some joke, they're sharing the experience, but you're left out, and the isolation of it stabs you. It hurts so much. Often, friends will take the trouble to explain what was said, and you can try to join in, but there's been a pause and the moment's gone. The trouble is, I feel I'm being talked down to if they stop the conversation and explain, yet I feel peeved and lonely if I'm ignored. There's no pleasing me, somehow. What I'd give to be normal!

My main consolation is that I've got my sight, that's what I always tell myself. I'm still taking part in the world if I can see. People can't steal up on me unawares so easily. But to be blind and deaf, that's something I dread. I just can't imagine what that must be like. I've had a bit of trouble with my eyes in recent weeks, which is why we've been to the hospital today. I can still read fairly well; you know, the paper, magazines, the odd book, and the telly a bit, though that does make my eyes very tired. But I daren't think of not being able to see. And yet I can't help imagining what it would be like. I have to put it out of my mind, though, before it gets too realistic. I'm frightened, I suppose. Just couldn't face it. I think I'd put an end to it all. I really would. Though you'd have a job to do that if you were blind, when you come to think about it. It wouldn't be that easy.

When you've got your sight you can enjoy trips out to places; you can still appreciate the countryside. Perhaps I can't hear the birds singing or the lambs bleating, but I love seeing the fields and trees, the nice houses, the shop windows in towns. In fact, my son came and took me out for a lovely ride in his car a few weeks ago. We visited a beautiful stately home. It was sunny and warm to walk round the gardens, and the house inside was fabulous. Magnificent furniture and paintings. I couldn't catch much of what the guide said, unfortunately, but we were able to linger in each room and read about it on little wooden boards. There again, it makes all the difference being able to see and read. Funnily enough, it was there I first had the trouble with my eyes.

We'd gone into one of those big, stately bedrooms and were looking at a painting hanging on the wall—a huge, ornate, gilt-framed thing—and I realised I couldn't focus on it. A cavalier on a white horse it was, apparently, but I could only just make out a shape. I thought at first it was because we'd gone from a very bright room to this rather dingy one, but I was exactly the same when we moved on. The light didn't seem to make any difference. We sat and had a pot of tea and scones in the cafe afterwards, and gradually I could see better again, but one eye wasn't right. I said to David, I've never had that happen before.

Do you think I should get it seen to? He thought I should wait a few days and only have it looked at if it happened again. Right enough, I suppose; there's no point in bothering them for nothing.

Anyway, the same thing happened a few days later. I'd been bending down to take some washing out of the machine and I couldn't see properly across the kitchen. A horrible experience. I sat down for a while, and it improved by the afternoon, but I still went to see the doctor. I managed to get a cancelled appointment—normally you have to wait days to see him now. He seemed a bit doubtful about both eyes and said he'd fix me up to see the hospital. Needed more tests, he said. Tests! Seems to be all they can think of these days.

David came and took me to the hospital this afternoon. He took half a day off work, which was nice of him. Going by car made it a lot easier. I find the bus journey an ordeal now. When they'd done these tests and examinations and what-not we waited a bit and then saw the consultant. Of course, I couldn't hear most of what he said, so I had to rely on David discussing it with him and he's going to tell me later. The specialist seemed a nice sort of man, kindly, but very serious. He certainly was telling David a lot; didn't rush us, like they do so often nowadays.

When we came out, we hunted about till we found the cafeteria, because by then we were both ready for a cup of tea. It's one of those modern places that's all bright green pipe-work, you'd think you were in the boiler-house, but the tables are clean enough. I think the women serving are volunteers from the Friends of the hospital—they looked that sort. Anyway, we had a pot of tea and a sticky bun each, and David said he'd discuss with me what the specialist told him when we got home, where it would be quieter and I'd have more chance of hearing. Apparently, they'd found a bit of trouble at the back of my eyes and they've given me some drops for it. I have to be sure to use the drops faithfully night and morning. I'm so thankful it isn't serious, my sight's everything I've got.

Take now, for instance. I can just look through the window to see where he is in the garden. Imagine not being able to do that! It doesn't bear thinking about. Oh, there he is, he's on the seat under the cherry tree. He looks quite thin on top from this angle. I wish he'd get a new sports jacket, he's had that one for years. I see he's taken his cup of tea out with him; to have a rest from me moaning, I expect. He looks a bit glum, I wonder what he's thinking about?

In fact, David was sinking into the gloom that so often pervaded him when he visited his mother and was reminded of her predicament. But this time he was locked in the mental turmoil of how to break the eye specialist's news. If he got it wrong, he could devastate her. On the other hand, might it not be better for her to be prepared now, rather than shocked later?

If only he could have a proper conversation with her it would make it so much easier. This was something that needed delicacy, but there was no chance of that. Just communicating with her at all had become so difficult. He had to stand right in front of her, speak slowly and practically shout. Then she seemed able to cotton on by a mixture of sounds, lip-reading and plain guesswork. It was so laborious and trying. It actually restricted what he said; he always went for getting the main message across, and omitted the little extras and asides of normal conversation because it was less trouble. The message today, though, was stark and painful.

He felt mean at his impatience; he loved her and was desperately sorry about her deafness, and sad that nothing could be done. So why did he have the sudden bursts of annoyance at her inability to hear him? Was it sheer frustration? Irritation at not getting through to her? Surely she was the one entitled to feel frustration and despair? He couldn't explain it. In restaurants and public places it was even worse; he had to speak so loudly that everyone around could hear. That inhibited chatting and annoyed him even more. Yet she looked so vulnerable and pathetic, gazing about her in her isolated world, with that bland, half-smile of the deaf. It presented to the world a contentment that couldn't possibly reflect her inner torment.

David sipped his tea and tried to imagine not hearing the birds all around him, or being without radio or music, tapes or television. It was inconceivable. Sound was inseparable from his life; the conversation of friends, voices, laughter, traffic. The whole bustle of living involved sounds. His mother, though, was cut off from it all. How desperately lonely and depressing it must be.

His thoughts came back sharply to the immediate problem. The specialist had said that the disease in her eyes was serious and progressive, and that the treatment could only delay the process, not cure it. Ultimately, she would go blind, though he couldn't predict how soon. The consultant had left it to him to break the news, because, as her son, he would know how best to deal with the situation, and how she would take it.

What was he to do for the best? His first instinct had been to tell her everything, because he had always believed that people want to know the truth and cope better when they do. But the more he considered it, and put himself in her position, the more he realised that the worry and despair would overwhelm her. She had enough to struggle with already. Surely, it was better for her to carry on as she was, unaware of the possible danger? After all, it might take two or three years to lose her sight, and in that time, well, who knew what might happen? She had a bad heart, and probably hadn't many more years left. He owed it to her to gamble for her peace of mind. Yes, he saw it clearly now; that was the best plan. He'd just have to be extra careful not to give anything away with careless comments.

David picked up his cup and saucer and walked back into the house, bracing himself for a long, awkward chat. His mother was sitting in the kitchen with several dark brown medicine bottles arranged on the table. She was peering at the labels, but looked up as he walked in.

"I'm just trying to get clear what all these are for, and when I have to take them. These new eye drops are night and morning, which is the same as my heart tablets. They'll be in competition with each other," she laughed.

"Not so much a competition as a race, Mum, I'm afraid," he said quietly to himself, as he pulled up a chair.

"Sorry, love, I didn't catch what you said."

The Hedgehog and
the Fortune-teller

martin and Felicity swung rucksacks onto their backs and followed the courier who had met them out of the airport. Emerging from the subdued light and relative coolness, they were suddenly confronted by dazzling sun, heat, cascades of red bougainvillea, and the pressing attentions of a jostling crowd of drivers and porters.

"'Allo! 'Allo, sir. You want taxi? Taxi?"

"No, thank you."

They caught up with the courier, side-stepping a couple of persistent young men, as their driver came forward, smiling, to take the luggage. The car was surrounded by bicycles and scooters wobbling and swerving, and by a throng of shouting people, milling about in no obvious direction. Dusty buses, a face or limb pushed through every window, hooted and tried to pull away, belching clouds of black exhaust fumes as the engines throbbed and spluttered. Martin stood by the boot while their cases were loaded, and was surprised by a tug at his arm.

"'Allo! 'Allo!"

Two small, brown-skinned boys, shoeless, stood by him, holding out their hands and pointing to their mouths. Quickly the driver interposed himself and opened the rear door for them to get in. The children were just tall enough on tiptoe to press their faces to the window, rolling their eyes reproachfully as they took in the interior, the visitors' clothes and bags. The taxi moved forward, its horn blaring to clear a path between the bicycles and pedestrians. This was their introduction to India.

Gradually, their taxi disentangled itself from the slower traffic and reached a main road, where the driver took to the overtaking lane, hooting impatiently at every small van or lorry he encountered. Martin and Felicity peered out eagerly for first glimpses of scenery; large buildings, parks, and rows of palm trees flashed by as they cruised along broad avenues, stopping only occasionally at traffic lights to allow a swarm of assorted vehicles to cross. They swerved round camel carts, hounded motor rickshaws, and loudly menaced a small, open lorry filled to overflowing with standing workers, who waved and cheered as they swept past. Martin and his wife exchanged wincing glances, wishing to absolve themselves from the driver's behaviour.

At last they pulled up in the driveway of their hotel. Immediately a uniformed doorman appeared, sporting a red turban and flamboyantly curled white moustache. Two minions opened the boot and staggered off with the luggage.

"Good afternoon, sir, and welcome," announced the oily commissionaire, with a calculating smile, obsequious and insincere.

Their room was on the third floor, and had a panoramic view of the street below. They explored the lavish facilities, admiring the coloured marble and furniture.

Martin took off his shoes, threw himself into a chair and looked through the restaurant menu. "There's some good Indian food on, by the look of it."

Felicity was still examining the drawers and wardrobes prior to unpacking.

Martin decided that a couple of beers were called for, and they savoured the ice-cold tang for some moments without speaking.

"By God, that's welcome." He contemplated the gaudy kingfisher on the bottle's label, and went over to the window. Every kind of transport known to man bobbed along, jostling and changing position as in a kaleidoscope.

"That's amazing. It reminds me of ants scurrying up to an anthill, carrying bits of vegetation. Look at those cows, too."

A group of grey, humped cows had decided to cross, and now wove languidly between the oncoming vehicles, looking as if they were falling asleep on their feet. Cars hooted, but the beasts took no notice, simply bringing them to a halt by sheer bulk.

"Well, it's certainly different," said Felicity. "I never thought I'd see cows wandering about in city traffic. I suppose we'd better unpack and change into something a bit less sweaty. Then, it'll be about time to go off for an evening meal. I'm getting a bit peckish."

In the early evening they ventured into the town. It was dusk, and the air was cold. Round the first corner they nearly stumbled over a family getting ready for the night in the open on the pavement. They had hung a tattered sack from the railings to the ground as a pathetic shelter, and the emaciated woman, wrapped in a dark shawl, was squatting by a fire of leaves and twigs, over which she held a small pan. Four children crawled over each other on a blanket, and against the wall they could just make out a huddled form swathed in rags, perhaps the father.

The next street was lined by small, open-fronted booths. Smoke billowed out of one and they paused to look at the pans of lentils and stews bubbling on the fires. A man stirring a pot in a cloud of steam beckoned to them, but they moved on.

"Smells good, doesn't it?" said Martin. "All the same, to judge by the general grottiness, it wouldn't be a wise place to eat. The likelihood of picking up some illness there is probably quite high."

"Yes, I'm sure we'll find somewhere a bit more appetising. Though you do wonder if we aren't all getting too twitchy about food and illness—it borders on hysteria, caused by the media's reporting."

Further down the street were some shops and restaurants with solid fronts and plate-glass windows, and other trappings of conventional premises. Encouraged by a printed menu on the door in English, they wandered in. It was drab and hot, the tables with chipped Formica smeared with grease, and the whole place reeking of boiled feathers and chicken skin. They ordered chicken tikka and vegetable biryani, and were pleasantly surprised by how good the food turned out to be. It was also very cheap.

On the way back to the hotel they took another route in even busier streets, and found themselves constantly hailed from the road by taxi drivers cruising by, or accosted by beggars and hawkers.

"Clean your ears, sir," offered one enterprising fellow, brandishing a cotton-bud. "Is very good—make you feel better."

The most persistent were the shoe-cleaners, young men carrying satchels full of brushes and polish, who sidled up as they walked and eyed up their footwear critically.

"Your sandals very dirty, sir, if I may say so. Let me clean. I do very good job, sir. Make very clean, very cheap."

"No, thank you," insisted Martin. "They're quite all right. They're often much worse."

"I make much better, sir, and only twenty rupees."

This dialogue continued as they walked, the youths often adding that the sandals were wearing at the heels and needed urgent repairs.

"I can mend, sir. With very best heels. Look."

Then they would whip out a selection of heels, and even soles, claiming to be able to effect a complete repair on the spot.

"No, thank you, all the same," Martin stalled, the initial politeness rapidly giving way to irritation as he discovered how difficult they were to shake off.

"My God, they're persistent. They never take no for an answer. How do you get rid of them without being downright rude?"

It was something they had not encountered before, and found awkward to deal with. It did not seem right to get angry with someone who was pleading to be allowed to earn his meagre subsistence, but, on the other hand, they found it an affront to their insular privacy as Westerners to be pestered for something they had not requested.

"Do you think they can be insulted, or are they so thick-skinned that it's a calculated sales technique?" asked Felicity.

"I imagine they're pretty tough. I don't think you'll hurt their feelings. They just try it on. Win some, lose some, that'll be their approach."

They negotiated the traffic and reached the hotel without incident. It had been a tiring day and they were glad to turn in early.

"It's a fairly sharp start again tomorrow, isn't it, darling?" shouted Martin from the bathroom.

"Yes, the car's supposed to pick us up at eight o'clock. They serve breakfast from seven, so we'll have plenty of time."

The next morning they were in the restaurant as the sun was coming up, and from their table they had a good view of the gardens. Birds and gophers were already busy in the palms. The moment Felicity had finished eating she got out the travel schedule and a map.

"We've quite a distance to do today. A hundred and fifty miles, I should say. Well across Rajasthan. And there are a few temples and palaces to see."

"Yes. It should be very interesting." A piece of the brittle bacon splintered under his knife. "Damn this stuff!"

They packed and assembled their luggage in the entrance hall. Precisely at eight o'clock a driver appeared and introduced himself. He was short, quietly-spoken, middle-aged, and wearing a blue shirt with a green, obviously home-knitted, sleeveless pullover. To him it was still winter.

Once again, they were on the road, this time heading out of the city into an ever more rural landscape. Villages became less frequent. The flat, farmed countryside of wheat and sugar cane gradually gave way to dry hills, dustier roads, and more camel carts. The trees were sparse, smaller, and not so luxuriant. They drove by tiny hamlets of shacks with thatched roofs, often with women washing clothes at a well, and camels tethered under the trees. The car bounced about on the road, the driver making no attempt to negotiate round the potholes, and at times they were thrown up so violently that their heads banged against the roof.

The sheer size of the country was beginning to dawn on them. Martin looked at the map and realised that, by the end of a hard day's driving, they would have covered about half the length of his finger in one corner of the country.

"I wish this guy didn't drive at such a crazy pace," he groaned. "It really is very wearing. My neck's murder. Perhaps he gets a bonus if he arrives early."

"More likely, he gets penalised if he's late," replied Felicity.

It was early afternoon when they arrived at a large, sandstone fort on a parched hillside. In the air-conditioned car they had not appreciated how hot it was, and now the heat and brightness reflected uncomfortably from the sandy ground. They were met by a well-dressed guide wearing a tie, who spoke good English, and took them straight away to a small garden restaurant in the trees.

"The intention, you see, madam and sir, is that you have a snack here and then I will take you round the palace and the temple—for us a very holy place. It is very interesting for you, also, I think."

"Ok. That sounds excellent. We're certainly ready for something to eat, it's been a long morning—a six-hour morning, in fact."

They sipped lime juice and had a meal at an outdoor table, while green parakeets squawked and fluttered in the trees, and mynah birds hopped and perched on nearby chairs. Then they set off to walk up the winding track to the fort.

The hill-top palace was on a colossal scale, with superb design and craftsmanship. Supporting pillars in red stone were beautifully carved with intricate patterns, many with elephant motifs. They were astonished by the detail of the inlaid precious stones, by the ceilings of thousands of tiny mirrors, and by the carved marble screens, like lacework, through which the ladies of the court would have peeped out. Some of the alcoves contained statues of various gods. The guide went down a staircase ahead of them, and Felicity turned to Martin quickly.

"Why does that god back there have an elephant's head and more than one pair of arms?" she whispered.

"That's one of the things I do happen to have read about. He's the son of Lord Shiva and he's called Ganesh. I believe he's the patron god of writers."

"And what about the extra arms?"

"Ah. There you have me. Presumably, if you're going to be super-effective, then it's symbolic of your special powers to have several pairs—many hands make light work, and all that."

The temple was in a corner of the quadrangle, and could only be reached by a flight of steps, where families of grey, lean monkeys scrambled and squabbled over morsels of food thrown by visitors. Brushing the animals aside, the guide indicated where to leave their shoes and they followed him inside. It was dark, and there was a strong smell of perfumed smoke. He rang a large bell hanging in the centre of the hall and they went across to stand at a rail with a group of others, while priests gave the worshippers the red paste to apply to their foreheads. In the gloom it was difficult to make out the detail of the statues beyond. They were moved by the fervour and complete absorption of the worshippers, who appeared to gain immediate serenity from the experience. They shuffled out in their turn, and picked up their shoes from the rows, relieved to find them still there.

After the tour, the guide accompanied them on to the town, and the hotel where they were booked in for the night. When they had showered and rested up for a while, they turned their attention to the evening meal.

"We could have a drink first in the bar," suggested Felicity. "I'm desperately thirsty again. We never seem to get enough to drink, and it's so hot. Going round palaces is all very well, but the concentration does tend to sag when you're thinking more and more about how thirsty you are."

"Yes, though that was a fabulous place. I wouldn't have missed it."

By the time a couple of beers had exerted their relaxing effect, the early start and the strenuous day's travelling combined to sap their enthusiasm to explore.

"What do you say if we just eat here in the restaurant, and have an early night?" Felicity said. "I don't know about you, darling, but I'm knackered."

Martin, stretched on his back on the bed, nodded. "Me too."

In the restaurant they found a table in a quiet corner, and from the mountains of food laid out, helped themselves to a selection of main courses, including various curries, though they carefully avoided the salad dishes.

"What did you think of that temple and all the rituals?" began Felicity.

"Well, the worshippers seemed to be taking it all pretty seriously," said Martin, shaking his head in wonder. "It's amazing that there are so many gods and goddesses, and different representations of the same ones. It's hard to see how educated people, at least, can really believe in gods which are in animal form. I suppose it's linked with re-incarnation as well. Hard for us to get our heads round. It's so alien to Western religion, isn't it? And, as you know, I don't subscribe to that any longer either. Actually," he went on, "it was seeing the religions in operation in the Far East that finally shaped my thinking—the fact that Hindus, Moslems, Buddhists and Christians are all pursuing different paths, all convinced they have the true way. They can't all be right!"

Felicity began peeling some fruit. "Yes, but the point is, when people believe in their particular brand of religion it can work for them. It doesn't matter whether it's true or not, it gives them something to hang on to. They're absolutely certain about the hereafter, and it provides inner peace, contentment."

"But that could be a fool's paradise," Martin objected. "I wouldn't like to be living a lie, to spend my life believing in something that, ultimately, turned out to be false. To me, it's crucial to get it sorted out, based on a rational appraisal of the evidence from all sources, religious, scientific, philosophical, the lot. It's a pretty important matter. Once you've got it straight, you can have genuine contentment."

"That would be a much more difficult type of contentment to achieve, though," Felicity countered, "because it may not hold out any hope for anything beyond. Your so-called contentment would actually only be a grim acceptance of man as he is."

"Precisely!" burst in Martin. "Precisely. Man's a biological species, just like any other animal. When he stops living he's just as finished as a dead hedgehog lying by the roadside, that's been hit by a lorry. You could call it my squashed hedgehog theory of human destiny." He laughed. "In the final analysis, we're all hedgehogs, no more than that. I admit, though—realism does take a bit of accepting. It's not so comforting."

Felicity looked at her watch. "We seem to have got into deep stuff tonight. It's too late to venture out now, even if we had the energy."

Martin called the waiter, signed the bill, and they went back to their room. He lay in bed for some time reading his book on India before switching off the bedside lamp.

"It's a funny business, when you weigh it all up, isn't it?" he said into the darkness. "You know, lots of people here believe in astrology and predestination—that everything that happens is pre-ordained by Fate. How can anyone really swallow that? It can't possibly be true that what we're going to do tomorrow has already been decided somewhere, now can it?"

There was no answer from his wife, and the steady breathing told him she was sound asleep.

Next morning he awoke to find Felicity drawing back the curtains, the sunlight streaming into the room. He lay staring at the opposite wall, sluggishly.

"Come on, then, rise and shine! Another day's beginning. I wonder what's in store for us? More sights to be seen. This seething sub-continent's waiting to be explored."

"It's just coming back to me," Martin murmured. "I had an absolutely dreadful nightmare. I woke up in the early hours, and it was a mighty relief to find it wasn't true. You know how it is when nightmares are so vivid you're convinced it's actually happened?"

"What was it about?"

"I dreamed we had an accident in the car. The driver was overtaking in his usual reckless fashion, and we hit something head-on. The driver was killed and we were trapped in the back. Somehow a doctor appeared and decided to amputate my legs on the spot, with a huge meat saw."

"No wonder you were glad to wake up! You must have had too much to eat before we went to bed. You were pigging-in. They say that makes you dream."

"Like all dreams, though, it wasn't quite like reality. In this one, as I watched him sawing across my leg, the blade went all wobbly and wouldn't cut properly. It was frustrating in a peculiar sort of way. I was willing him to get on with it. Then I woke up."

After breakfast they had an hour to spare before setting out on the next part of their journey, which was only a hundred miles. It was a good opportunity for a look round the town. People stared at them as they wandered by the booths and stalls, and there were the usual attentions of hawkers. Outside one booth was a board advertising fortune-telling, and an elderly man in a long white gown was sitting nearby in the shade. As they approached he called to them.

"Tell your fortune, madam, sir, very useful."

In view of their conversation, it seemed an ideal chance to experience the astrology at first-hand.

"I'll give it a whirl, damn it," said Martin. "You come in as well."

The fortune-teller needed five-hundred rupees before he would start. He sat opposite Martin and looked hard into his face for some moments without speaking. He had a mop of white hair, his face was deeply wrinkled, but it was his eyes that held the attention. Brown and sad, they were large in proportion to his face, and Martin felt himself mesmerised by them.

At last the old man came out of his reverie and asked him his date and day of birth, and a few other personal details. He consulted sheets of yellowing paper and flicked through dog-eared ledgers with gnarled and deformed fingers. Next, he took his hand and studied the palm. At last he looked up.

"Some of the future is not good, sir, I am afraid. I see an accident, sir. No, I can't say when, but could be bad accident. Rest is good, though. You have happy children."

"The children are already grown-up, so that isn't telling me much!" Martin laughed.

When the session ended, they thanked him politely and walked back along the street.

"That was just as I thought it would be," exclaimed Martin. "Total rubbish! Hogwash! Apparently, many people do take it very seriously, and won't do important things on days when it's not right with the stars—even the politicians! They also use it to analyse people for jobs, or as husbands and wives. It's astonishing that intelligent people can be so superstitious."

The driver was already waiting. It was cool in the car, and soon they had threaded their way through the straggling outskirts and were on the open road, resuming the pattern of staccato hooting, pulling out, racing for a gap, and then swinging in just in time.

"Business as usual on the roads," observed Martin wryly. "I was reading that part of the problem with lack of driving discipline is that, because many of them believe that everything's pre-ordained, that whatever is going to happen, will happen, they feel they don't need to take much care. It's sort of…out of their hands. Now, me, I like to think I have some influence over events—braking, for a start. On the other hand, this driver's been good, in a hair-raising sort of way. I'm beginning to trust his judgement. I just assume he's going to make it each time."

They were now on one of those long, straight stretches of dusty narrow road, the heat shimmering in the distance. The surface was rough and bouncy, and they came up behind a decrepit small truck lurching along. The driver gave it his customary fanfare, and, despite the fact that a large lorry loomed from the opposite direction, pulled out to overtake. The truck still erratically held the middle, and was doing a fair speed. More pipping and blaring, and their driver edged forward until he was racing alongside. The gap between them and the oncoming lorry was getting a bit tight. Surely he should drop back? He did not seem to have enough acceleration.

Still he raced doggedly for the space, now down to what seemed to them only two or three car lengths. He was just pulling clear of the truck when the car struck a particularly rough patch of road, which threw them up in the air. Instead of cutting in, the car kept straight on. For a few seconds they saw the inevitable, had a clear view of the huge, orange-painted lorry high above them, then saw only its massive radiator, like a wall, blocking out the windscreen.

Reflexly, they pressed their feet onto the floor, rigid, panic-stricken. Terror rushed up through their stomachs and chests, stifling the breath in their throats. Then it was all in slow-motion. The impact was deafening. It seemed to take an age for the crumpling of the front of the car, the shattering of the windscreen, metal buckling and being pushed in, and further in. Would it ever stop? It was pushing nearer and nearer to them. They were twisted sideways, the front seats were being heaped on top of them. There was an unreal moment when all was quiet, and then falling glass tinkled and liquid dripped from the metal tangle in front of them. They tried to struggle free.

"Get out quick, in case it catches fire," Martin shouted.

Felicity was pushing frantically at the door, with no success. There was blood on her face and arms. Faces appeared at the buckled window frames, shouting. The rear door was tugged open and they dragged her out, sobbing.

Until then, Martin had not noticed the pain, but when he tried to move he realised his legs were pinned under the driver's seat, and the throbbing, searing heat rushed up into his thighs and seemed to radiate on into his abdomen and back. He flopped back, sweating and clammy, panting with terror and pain. Now he saw, in a distant, detached way, that in the tangled mass of metal and upholstery a couple of feet in front of his face, was the crushed body of the driver. He could make out one grotesquely distorted shoulder, and see that the shirt and green pullover were soaked with blood. He could not see his head anywhere.

People were now reaching into the back of the car and pushing at the wreckage in an attempt to free him, but it was no use. Mechanical equipment was needed. Martin had always been rather claustrophobic, hated being trapped, and now he had a sudden panic to get free. He heaved his back upwards, his arms shaking with the exertion, but all he did was provoke a spasm of pain, which flooded up from his legs and actually seemed to be three-dimensional; it was like a great block of solid pain encasing him. He sobbed brokenly to himself, and slid into unconsciousness.

They were not far from a good-sized town, and eventually an ambulance and rescue service vehicle arrived. After much difficulty, they managed to cut him free. Felicity sat by him in the ambulance, totally numbed, and only vaguely aware of the cuts and bruises all over. It struck her as eerie that, only that morning, Martin had told her of his nightmare of a car crash, and then the fortune-teller had mentioned an accident.

They arrived at the hospital, a run-down building with plaster flaking off the outside walls, the signboards amateurish and tatty. They left him in an emergency room while they took his wife to another department to have her injuries treated.

Martin's first impression when he came round was of light at the far side of a cavern of darkness. He could make out frosted glass and metal window frames. He rolled his eyes, and was aware of movement on the ceiling. It was a large fan, like an aeroplane propeller, going round and round noiselessly. He felt dizzy again watching it. Where on earth was he? He moved his head and recognised a very surgical sort of room; over there was an instrument cabinet, and he could see some gas cylinders. The smell was very much of a hospital; disinfectant and polish and medicines. Slowly, recollection of what had happened seeped through him. That was it, he'd been trapped in the back of the car by his legs, and had had all that excruciating pain. His heart pounded with fear as he recalled its intensity, dreading another wave. He moved his arms and felt his thighs; they were bound up in thick sheets. He tried to move them; the muscles tweaked, but he had no feeling further down, and had no sensation of his feet, either.

He panicked and tried to sit up, but by the time he had raised himself onto one elbow he felt dizzy again, and he lay groggily peering towards his legs, panting and sobbing. Was he paralysed? No, he had some movement in his thighs, so the injury wasn't spinal. Thank God for that. It must be severe crushing to his legs, probably at about knee level, where they'd been pinned by the driver's seat. That bloody idiot, he thought. Why, oh why didn't the maniac drop back? There had been no hurry. No need to take any risks.

Suddenly, he thought of his dream. What an amazing coincidence! Of course, it was just a coincidence. One in a million. Curious, too, that the fortune-teller had talked about an accident. But then they can throw out any old suggestions and cover anything; even a cut finger would count as an accident for their purposes. Could the old chap really have foreseen this? Of course not. Just an incredible coincidence.

Martin's thoughts were interrupted by two doctors in white coats coming into the room and standing, hands in pockets, either side of the trolley on which he was lying.

"How are you feeling now? You have very severe injuries to your legs, you know. We have given you a pain-killing injection, so it won't be too uncomfortable at the moment. I'm afraid it might not be possible to save the legs, though. We will do our best, but if the damage is too bad, we will have no alternative. It would be too life-threatening."

Again, Martin panicked. It was outrageous. Was this really happening, or was it another vivid nightmare?

"Look, please do everything you can to save them. I've always been very active, a keen walker…"

It seemed ridiculous, but he was about to say that he'd always used his legs a lot, and he still needed them. His thoughts jumbled up incoherently. It was bad enough for this to happen anywhere, but to be taking place in a one-horse town in the middle of India was horrifying. Did they know what they were doing? Was he getting treatment and skill as good as if he was at home? He doubted it, and went cold. He suddenly realised that he might need a blood transfusion, and instantly thought of Aids. Christ, it was a fair bet that they didn't screen blood for HIV here.

"Please will you sign this consent form, sir? A nurse will come for you in a few minutes. I assure you we will do our very best. Do not worry."

They went out, their footsteps echoing down the corridor.

"I'd like to see my wife and talk to her. Where is she?" he shouted.

His cries went unheard, and he lay back, drowsy and confused, but his mind soon started up again. Perhaps he ought to try praying, just in case there was something in it? Please, please, please God, may they save my legs! I'll do anything, if only they can be saved. He tried to summon up a clear image of Christ in his mind. He usually did that by thinking of pictures in stained-glass windows in English country churches, or by visualising a large painting of Jesus they'd had at his Sunday School as a child. Please, please, may it be all right. The irony was not lost on him, even now, and he felt ashamed that, after all he'd said about religion over the years, all the rationalising he'd done, here he was, praying for divine help. Still, it couldn't do any harm, and this was a desperate situation.

A nurse and porter came in and wheeled his stretcher-bed out of the room. As they rumbled along the corridor, he could see the palm trees through the windows, and noticed that it was a hot, sunny day. Of course, he'd forgotten, it was always hot and sunny in India. He should have been on holiday today, sightseeing. He felt a pang of sadness and wished it was just an ordinary, uneventful day.

They wheeled him into the operating theatre. Another glossy, cream ceiling with large bright lights. A doctor took his arm, and he felt the cuff being wrapped round above his elbow and pumped tight.

"Just a small injection, and then you'll go to sleep. Please take deep breaths."

Martin thought of Felicity, of the children, his parents. He made an effort to steady his breathing and keep control, to resist the panic as his head suddenly swirled and everything became more and more distant.

They lifted him onto the operating table, unconscious. The surgeon came towards the table from scrubbing up.

"Right, then, are we all ready? This one's a double amputation."

The Wind-Up

He braked hard and squeezed tight against the hedgebank as the oncoming car suddenly appeared round the blind corner. His car was almost stationary as the other flashed by without slowing, their wing mirrors missing by a hair's breadth.

"Bloody maniac," he exclaimed, and looked in the rear-view mirror to watch the big red BMW receding into the distance down the lane.

Alan Baxter drove hundreds of miles a week in his Rover, his job required it, but nowadays he felt that he spent too much time on the road, and there was little pleasure in driving. It wasn't just that there was more traffic than twenty years ago, but that drivers were more ill-mannered and aggressive, the mood uglier. The urban traffic was bad enough, with its endless queues and pushiness at roundabouts and traffic lights. The really sinister aggressiveness, though, was on the open road, or here on the lonely country lanes, where the competitiveness became personalised, a kind of duel.

He was frequently followed for miles out of his village by idiots in white vans (it always seemed to be white vans or Ford Escorts), who drove so close that he couldn't see their number plates in his mirror. The other common offenders were young women in high off-roaders returning from the school run. Did these buffoons actually realise what they were doing, the risks they were taking? What did they think would happen when he had to brake sharply, a regular occurrence?

He considered the lane ahead; it was barely two cars wide in many places, blind bends with jutting hedges every hundred yards or so, and no verge to swing on to in an emergency. To do even forty miles-an-hour here was dodgy, anything more plain reckless; there were tractors, horses, and, at least morning and evening, a fair number of cars cutting through from one main road to another to avoid the towns. It was the same everywhere— "rat-runs" the local papers were calling country roads now. This morning, it seemed to him an apt description.

Alan Baxter was a courteous, thoughtful chap, and he worried about traffic in the future; the lack of any apparent solution to all the transport problems disturbed him. It wasn't as if he was against cars. Far from it; his livelihood depended on driving to places he couldn't reach by any other means. Nor was he a sedate old fogey; indeed, he'd been quite a tearaway with cars and motorbikes in his twenties, and was still proud of his times to various parts of the country. He could dash about with the best of them.

And yet, he could detect a very clear change in attitudes on the road now, and it wasn't simply a middle-aged perception. It was quantifiable. He'd only to count the number of near-scrapes, the regular smashing of his wing-mirror by passing cars, the frequent minor spats with kids who lost patience and overtook in crazy places where he was observing the speed-limit. Perhaps that was it; perhaps people had become more impatient, more intolerant, more violent. The curious thing was that they seemed to behave so much worse in cars than mingling personally in everyday life, as though the little tin box provided anonymity and a protective shell.

He sighed and glanced in the rear mirror. A black car was approaching rapidly. Although there was little traffic in mid-morning, he knew that the road ahead was narrow and winding for many miles, with few opportunities for overtaking. There were several crossroads, however, so perhaps it would turn off. He looked again, and saw the Volkswagen badge on the radiator, a Golf of some sort, with a crop-headed young fellow at the wheel.

Baxter kept plodding along at a sensible speed for the conditions; he certainly wasn't going to race this guy on the straighter stretches, or take the bends too fast. It wasn't a racing circuit, he told himself. The black Volkswagen pursued him for miles, filling his mirror, from time to time pulling out as if to overtake, then dropping back. It didn't turn off. At each junction Baxter looked into his mirror, hoping it would take another road, but each time it swung in his direction, gathered speed, and locked onto his tail as inexorably as a missile.

Was it a kind of sport for these kids, he wondered? Was this oaf just so bored sitting there that latching onto the car in front was a bit of exhilarating fun, like the dodgems at the fair, or a roller-coaster ride with added driving skill? Baxter couldn't begin to understand the mentality. But, of course, he recalled, youngsters do like taking risks for the hell of it—he could still remember feeling that thrill himself. Just about.

To throw off the VW, he decided to drive slower, so that on any straight stretches the fellow could pass. Unfortunately, the road continued to wind and there were no opportunities. His pursuer was now so close on his tail that virtually all he could see in the mirror was the Golf's windscreen and the menacing figure in the white T-shirt.

The road next ran through an area of woodland and widened slightly. Here's where I lose him at last, thought Baxter, and braked gently. The Golf flashed its headlights and indicator and overtook, but, to his horror, its brake-lights glowed red immediately, and it cut in and scrunched to a halt in front of him, forcing him to pull up, with no room to manoeuvre.

The man in the white T-shirt leapt out of the Golf, and in a few strides was bending and gesticulating at Baxter's window. He was in his early twenties, mean-looking, hair so closely shaved that he appeared almost bald, arms tattooed, his jeans with a tear at each knee. He rapped on the window until Baxter pressed the electric button and it rapidly slid down.

"Are you trying to wind me up, Granddad?" he snarled.

"Certainly not. I was wondering why on earth you had to drive so close. You'd get there just as quickly if you were twenty yards behind."

"Don't tell me how to drive, dickhead. People of your age shouldn't be on the road, dawdling along at that speed. You were slowing down just to nark me, weren't you?"

Baxter could see how agitated the youth was becoming, as he pushed his head halfway into the car, the bristle-covered veins bulging on his scalp.

"As a matter of fact, I was slowing down so that you could overtake easier; and anyway, nobody can sensibly drive any faster on lanes like this. It'd be lunacy."

Baxter's heart was pounding, he was afraid and vulnerable in such a lonely spot, at the mercy of such a character. It was years since he'd had a confrontation like this.

The youth leaned in closer, his face now only inches away.

"You calling me a lunatic? I think we're gonna have to re-arrange your features, Granddad."

He made a move to head-butt Baxter in the face, but the older man reflexly recoiled, and, at the same instant, grabbed the neck of the T-shirt and held it fast. With his right hand he pressed the window button, and, with a whine, the pane slid up.

He held the bunched shirt until the edge of the window pushed against the youth's throat and would go no further. Then he pulled the head down with both hands, so that it was wedged at the larynx, the neck tightly compressed between the glass and the frame. Raucous squawks came from the head, the arms flailed on the roof of the Rover with echoing thumps, and he could see the torso and jeans thrashing from side to side against his door.

With some difficulty Baxter edged himself over the gear-lever, and slid sideways into the passenger seat to give himself more room. The distorted face trapped in the window had turned purple; the swollen tongue protruded from a mouth blowing bubbles, the eyeballs were turned upwards grotesquely. As Baxter waited, though, it was the noise that sickened him most; moist, choking gurgles, which gradually died away. One arm slipped limply down the windscreen, the chest pressed against the window. A rope of saliva drooled and swung from side to side with the car's rocking, as Baxter scrambled out of the passenger's door.

He trembled all over with the enormity of what he'd done, but his mind cleared enough to realise what was necessary to make it look like a bizarre accident. Taking a handkerchief from his pocket to avoid leaving finger-prints, he opened the Golf's door, pressed the button to lower the window, and then returned to his car.

The road was clear. It was the sort of place where perhaps only one car came by every twenty minutes; he might be lucky. He opened his door carefully, supporting the body until he could reach the window button and release the head. At all costs he must prevent the body touching the ground. He grappled closely with the limp corpse and managed to carry it upright for the few yards to the Golf. Once he'd dumped it into the driver's seat, and wasn't struggling with the weight, things became easier. He closed the door and got in at the passenger's side. With the handkerchief he pressed the button, and, as the window ascended, pushed the head with all his strength, keeping the neck on the edge of the glass as it was dragged upwards. The corpse was twisted up from the seat, but the head remained satisfactorily jammed out of the window.

Now he had to move quickly. Leaving the engine running, he went round to the driver's side to confirm that the pane had trapped the neck along the original injury. When suddenly confronted by the disfigured face he was appalled and panicked. Glancing swiftly up and down the empty road, he threw himself into his car, reversed to give himself room, and drove off at high speed.

A mile or so further on he came up behind an elderly couple in an old Ford, tootling sedately along at thirty miles-an-hour. He was shaking with reaction and impatience, but the road was too narrow and winding for overtaking. Baxter saw the irony of the situation. He made himself take a deep breath, and dropped back twenty yards. This was one aspect he hadn't learned about when he was a paratrooper.

Shifting Relations

"It's no use, Dad. If we can't find some money from somewhere soon, you'll have to leave here." Philip shuffled his armchair closer to his father's and spoke slowly and deliberately. "Do you understand that? The money from the sale of your house has nearly all gone."

He had not yet dared to tell him that he was to be allowed only two weeks more. He waved his arm in a broad sweep, taking in Manningford Court's tastefully-furnished resident's lounge.

"This place is costing you £450 a week. It's very elegant and comfortable, and I know you like being here, but when your money runs out you'll be in the hands of the Council's Social Services department, and they'll move you to one of their homes, which will be a lot more basic and cramped."

"Oh. I see. I wouldn't like to leave here, they're such nice people," was all his father could muster.

The two of them stared gloomily at a patch of multi-coloured Axminster lit by a beam of sunshine from the window. Manningford Court, a converted country mansion in several acres of grounds, had style and elegance, and had suited his father very well.

Old Mr Swindlehurst slowly scratched the top of his balding, liver-spotted head in a gesture which had always reminded Philip of Stan Laurel in awkward situations.

"I suppose," drawled the old man hesitantly, "I could sell some letters. It's the only thing left of any value. But I don't know how much they'd fetch nowadays. And I haven't got many. It's a devil when you don't know how long you're going to live." He chuckled wheezily.

Philip was surprised.

"What letters do you mean, Dad? I know you used to collect the odd manuscript years ago, but I didn't know you'd any left. Where are they?"

Mr Swindlehurst sat upright and looked hard at his son. Despite being in his eighties, frail, and intermittently vague, he was often quite sharp; he still dressed smartly in sports jacket and Paisley tie, and spent a few minutes each morning polishing his brown brogues until they shone like conkers.

"I collected a few literary manuscripts and letters at one time, mostly by nineteenth century novelists. But I sold most of them off to pay for holidays and odd things we needed. They should be in that old black metal trunk that went to you when the house was sold—I hope you've still got it. Not been chucked out in a clear-out or anything?" This was a wry reference to Philip's wife, who was ruthlessly tidy and unsentimental.

Philip was uncertain. He remembered it at the time of the removal, with piles of other junk. So far as he knew, a cursory glance inside had not registered anything of interest, and the trunk had been consigned to his loft, to be out of sight and out of mind.

"Well, if you look in that trunk you should find a couple of box-files. Any letters there are will be in one of those. The files will be labelled something else on the outside—to put off burglars, you know. Just in case."

"I'll go up into the loft tonight," said Philip, glancing at his watch and getting to his feet. "Don't get up, Dad," he cautioned, forestalling his father's futile attempt to rise.

Driving home, Philip worried again about his father's predicament. He had hoped for months that some funding would appear to keep him at Manningford Court for the time he had left. His father was in a pretty terminal state, what with his heart and his lungs, and the doctor was now talking of months or weeks only. This business about some letters that might be saleable was right out of the blue.

To Philip's relief, that evening he located the trunk in a dark corner of the roof-space. There had been a few re-arrangements of the loft's contents in the two years since his father had moved, and the black trunk now supported a box of Subbuteo, a doll's house, and some dusty lampshades. There was a generous sprinkling of dead bluebottles on everything.

Rummaging into the trunk's contents, Philip found catalogues, guide-books, family photographs, a schoolboy's stamp album three-quarters empty, and, finally, a marbled green box-file. He dragged it out. The spine was not helpful: Made in England, patent with Lock Spring. Under this was scrawled in felt-pen, "Instruction Manuals".

Philip felt his excitement mounting as he peered inside. On top was a brochure about a sewing machine his mother had had years ago, under that several on other appliances, but at the bottom lay four unsealed, buff envelopes, held together by a rubber band. This looked promising. In the silence the cold-water tank dripped beside him like a heart-beat.

Sitting on the splintery joists, Philip impatiently opened the first envelope. There was a typed sheet of headed paper from Dalrymples, a London firm of antiquarian booksellers and dealers in manuscripts, detailing the provenance of the accompanying letter. It was apparently written by the novelist Trollope to an acquaintance in Essex, thanking him for keeping his horses, and sending him money to cover the cost of their keep. Not exactly a spicy revelation of English literature, but it looked very genuine. The letter itself was an off-white sheet of folded octavo, with faded, spidery writing on all four sides, and dated 1873.

He studied the signature. Anthony Trollope. It was amazing to think that this piece of paper had actually been held in Trollope's hands all those years ago; that for a brief moment it had been a part of his life. Philip, in the solitude of the loft, could almost feel a bond reaching back to the previous century. He could see the attraction such letters would have held for his father, always more concerned with the past than the present, always a bit of a historian and a dreamer.

What would that be worth now, he wondered? There was no sign of a price or a purchase date. His father would probably have been keen to keep secret how much he had paid. He put the documents back in the envelope.

Squatting up in the roof was uncomfortable, so, gathering up the file and the envelopes, he scrambled down the ladder. Downstairs, he sat at the kitchen table and opened another packet. Again, there was a sheet of headed paper, this one from a different dealer, bearing a typed description of the manuscript; Zola, Emile (1840-1902), to an unnamed correspondent, 1 page 8vo in French with integral blank leaf, Paris 1887. The letter concerned the forthcoming publication of the novel, *La Terre*.

Philip peered at the faded, angular writing. He could not make out all the French words, but the large, bold signature was obvious enough. He recalled that his father had always been a devoted admirer of Zola; indeed, in his retirement he had immersed himself in nineteenth century literature almost to the exclusion of reality.

There was something eerie about this piece of Time he held in his hands; Paris, 1st March 1887. This really was a tangible fragment of 1887, a captured moment, a man's thoughts embodied, to be passed on potentially for ever from generation to generation. What had Zola done after writing the letter that day? Had he walked in the Paris streets, gone, perhaps, to meet other writers now famous? It was an awesome feeling.

The third letter was by P G Wodehouse, another of his father's favourite authors, written in 1950 with a New York dateline, to someone who had evidently praised one of his books and requested an autograph. It was a kind and cheery letter from Wodehouse, which ended by thanking the woman for her interest. Yet again, there was no clue about the date his father had acquired the letter, or how much it had cost.

What would these documents fetch now? He really had no idea, but, clearly, the quicker they contacted a firm of antiquarian book dealers, the better. They might provide enough to keep his father at Manningford Court for another few weeks—which might well be his last.

Pre-occupied, Philip opened the final envelope. This was lumpier than the others and he drew out a handful of papers. There were three pale blue envelopes, raggedly opened, addressed in bold writing to his father at his old office, and three other folded blue letters in the same hand.

"Darling," one began. There was no address, and the dateline was simply Thursday. "Thank you so, so much for another blissfully happy time. If only such nights were possible more often and we could be together more. I'm missing you dreadfully this week…"

Philip stared in disbelief. He turned to the end and read, "Dying to see you again in two weeks' time. Lots and lots of passionate love, your hungry, impatient and devoted,—Dorothy."

The other letters were similar, none dated or with an address, all passionate and longing, and indicating a love affair conducted secretly, irregularly, and with considerable strain to both parties. He looked at the pale blue envelopes. They all bore a London postmark, were dated 1959 and 1960, and had stamps that were now almost collectors' items in themselves. The last envelope he opened also contained a leaflet advertising a weekend literary gathering for March 1960, with speakers' names and times of their lectures. His father's lover, for this was clearly what she was, closed the accompanying letter "You'll see that I'm speaking just before tea and, with a bit of luck, we should be able to get away then, if I'm not too pestered with questions. Desperately looking forward to seeing you again Darling, and being in your arms once more. Your frenzied, ecstatic, wildly passionate—Dorothy."

She was speaking just before tea. Philip turned to the leaflet. The slot before tea was described as; "The flawed heroine in the historical novel" by Dorothy Minshull.

The letters to his father were signed Dorothy! That was it. His father's lover must have been Dorothy Minshull, the novelist. Surely not! But here was all the proof. Absolutely undeniable. Philip could hardly take it in. He was aware that his father had always been interested in literature and the world of books, though being a solicitor, he was not professionally involved. But to have had a romance with Dorothy Minshull was just, well, so utterly improbable. And none of the family had been aware of it. Or had his mother known? How long had it gone on? From the postmarks, these few letters covered just over a year, but that did not necessarily represent the lifetime of the affair, the whole opus of the correspondence. These were just the ones that had survived. How and when had it ended, he wondered? He knew that Dorothy Minshull had been dead many years. She was probably a few years younger than his father.

Philip took the bundle of papers to his wife Maureen in the lounge.

"Did you find any letters?" She looked up from her magazine.

"I certainly did! There are three literary ones, by Trollope, Zola and Wodehouse, which are really interesting. They might be worth a bit, too, probably will help to keep him at Manningford Court for a few weeks longer. But these—" he waved a sheaf of the blue writing paper, "—these are something else. You are just not going to believe this."

"Why, what are they? Rare, valuable?" asked Maureen.

"Possibly," said Philip, sitting down on the sofa beside her. "But more than that, these—" again he pointed to the pile in front of him, "—are letters from Dad's girl-friend, one we never knew he had. Dorothy Minshull, the novelist, believe it or not."

He paused, and then burst out; "They are a complete betrayal. Of Mum, of us children." His face hardened. "I just feel completely let down. The old swine."

"Wow! A girl-friend. That doesn't seem quite like him, does it? Though I suppose if it was nearly forty years ago it hardly matters now." Maureen was ever the realist.

"Yes, it does," Philip snapped. "We looked up to him as kids, loved him, trusted him. If we'd known at the time, we'd have been shattered. Totally disillusioned."

He stood up and prowled about the lounge shaking his head. He had very much his father's physique, was tall and slim, despite being in his early fifties.

"And what about Mum, for God's sake? What would she have felt? Did she know, come to that?" The question hung in the air, as their thoughts ran off along a myriad tracks.

Philip finally stopped pacing, plonked himself down heavily, and sat gazing unseeingly at a dried flower arrangement in the fireplace.

"So, what are you going to do?" ventured Maureen. "Confront him with the letters and accuse him of betraying you all? Are they actually worth anything is more to the point in his present financial crisis? Dorothy Minshull is well-known. She had quite a little niche in the historical romance world at one time. And she might have been dead long enough to be of interest to aficionados who collect such stuff. Hardly in the same league as those others you mentioned. It's worth a try, though."

"I don't know what to do. I'll sleep on it."

Philip brooded for the rest of the evening. It was part of his nature to worry away at problems, completely self-absorbed. They seemed to gestate in his mind, until all of a sudden a decision would present itself and he would bring it forth, accept it, act upon it, and then, as often as not, lose all interest.

At breakfast he had made up his mind, and was able to answer Maureen's enquiry by stating his intention to visit his father that evening, tell him of his discovery of the letters, and give him the opportunity to explain.

"I shall be very understanding, very low-key; you know the sort of thing, more in sorrow than in anger. We'll see what he says, and take it from there. You're probably right; it was a long time ago, and there's no point in starting a row."

Maureen poured him another cup of tea. "It's possible your mother never suspected anything, if it was always a long way from home."

"That's right. I hope she didn't. After all, infidelity doesn't actually hurt the injured party if he or she doesn't know about it. It's only a metaphysical sort of harm. I suppose that it's just the risk they might find out that makes it wrong. The greater the risk, the greater the wrong-doing—marriage vows apart, of course," he added, "but that's a special social case."

Maureen chewed her toast and surveyed him thoughtfully. "So, if you can get away with it, adultery isn't wrong? That's your philosophy, is it?"

"Well, not exactly. That's not what I meant. But then you're into the whole question of wrong, and what's that, anyway? You must admit you can postulate situations where detection would be impossible and the harm nil. And these days, you might not be married. You wouldn't even be breaking a social convention then. What would have been damaged?"

"Trust?" suggested Maureen, with heavy irony. "Plus some of those feelings you expressed last night—betrayal seemed to feature prominently in your outrage. And you were only taking a child's perspective. What do you think a wife would feel?"

"Mm. A good point. Life's a complicated business."

Philip was losing interest in the argument and drifting into woolly mode, realising, as so often, that he had failed to pin down the most intriguing aspects of the problem. What the hell, he thought. There aren't any real answers, anyway.

"I must be off to work. I haven't even got the car out yet. I'll take all the letters to Dad tonight and see about selling them, so I'll be late back."

When Philip arrived at Manningford Court that evening, he found his father in a semi-circle of residents watching the news in the television room. They went back to his rooms. His father's smartness masked his frailty, and he made slow progress, leaning on his stick and pausing every few yards to take great labouring breaths.

Having got him installed in his armchair, Philip showed him the three literary letters. "These are fascinating, Dad. Each one's a little piece of history. When did you get them?"

"Oh, goodness knows. Thirty-odd years ago, probably more. It seems a shame to sell them, but I suppose I'll have to. I couldn't bear to leave here. We'd better get in touch with one of the dealers and see what they'll offer. I'm sure they're still in business."

Philip hesitated before continuing. "There were some other letters, too, Dad. From the novelist Dorothy Minshull. Do you remember them?"

His father glared at him and took in a huge gasp of sustaining air. "Letters from Dorothy Minshull? What? In that box-file?" He paused, looking at Philip shiftily. "Did you read them?"

"Couldn't help it. I thought they were the same sort of thing as the others. But they weren't, were they?"

"They were private—my letters, and you'd no business reading them," said his father, almost shouting in his agitation. "We were friends for a long time; she meant a lot to me."

"More than friends, I should say, judging from the contents."

His father ignored the remark. The dangerous curiosity nagging at Philip got the better of him. "Did Mum know about it?"

For a few moments Mr Swindlehurst peered with bent head at the letters in his hands, then looked sharply at Philip, bristling with haughty aggression, his jutting jaw trembling visibly.

"It's really nothing to do with you, Philip. As a matter of fact, she did find out eventually. Unfortunately. But luckily, she took it very well; she was a brave woman…"

"Brave," cried Philip, flaring. "Brave! She wasn't taking a lifeboat out. She'd been deceived and betrayed by you. Why didn't she leave you? You deserved it."

"Because people didn't in those days. Not often, anyway. Largely on account of you children, when it finally came down to it."

He put the letters down on the coffee table, leaned back in his chair, and pressed his fingertips together pompously. "And she still loved me, so what would have been the point?" he added smugly.

His attitude ignited Philip's smouldering anger. "The point, Dad, would have been that you were killing her love stone dead. And using her like a doormat. I'm disgusted," he spat out. "You deceived us all and you don't even seem to be sorry or regret anything."

His strategy of calm understanding had evaporated at the thought of his mother's heartache. He had always been close to her, and the discovery of her suffering, even at this late and irrelevant stage, struck him to the core. He looked at his father with mounting distaste; his total lack of remorse, his pomposity, his imagined superiority, were all undiminished by his physical frailty. Philip sensed his sympathy for him and his present predicament ebbing away. His father liked it here at Manningford Court because it was genteel, and he was a snob. Well, Philip vowed, from now on, he could just struggle, for filial assistance was going to be reduced to the bare minimum.

Mr Swindlehurst had now recovered himself sufficiently to assume the superior demeanour of a solicitor with a client.

"I don't think we can usefully say any more about this, Philip. So far as I'm concerned, the matter's closed," he said coldly.

"In that case," retorted Philip sharply, "we'd better discuss more urgent matters. I've never actually spelled it out before, because I was hoping some funds would turn up, but you can only stay here for two more weeks. There's £900 left, that's all. After that it's the Social Services."

He found himself relishing the astonishment on his father's face.

"These letters are the only source of extra money, so you'd better get selling them. And quick. Phone or write to one of those dealers, tell them what you have—then keep your fingers crossed." He could not resist a hint of mischief. "Perhaps for sentimental reasons you don't want to sell the Dorothy Minshull ones?"

"Oh, there's no point in keeping them. Money's more important than sentiment now."

"I thought it might be," replied Philip, with a bitter smile. "I'll come again at the weekend; by then you might have had a response, and we can plan better."

"Before you go, Philip, what are these other residential homes like? Bigger than this, more people?" Mr Swindlehurst was obviously disturbed.

"Oh, not bad, I believe. A lot more old folk, of course, and a broader social mix," he slipped in pointedly. "But that makes it livelier. Plenty of organised activities going on, communal singing, jolly games, you know the sort of thing."

Predictably, his father's face fell.

"I don't think that sounds like me at all." His chest was heaving.

Philip was gleeful. "Oh, it'll shake you up a bit. Give you more interest. See you at the weekend, anyway."

By his next visit his father had received a reply from Dalrymples, the booksellers, and he tossed it across the table. Yes, they were very interested in purchasing the letters by Trollope, Zola and Wodehouse, particularly if they had good provenance. Their value would obviously depend on condition, so they would have to see them before committing themselves. An estimate might be in the region of £200-£400 each.

"That's not bad, is it?" said Philip, looking up. "Probably about a thousand for the three. Better than a poke in the eye."

"Wait till you've read the rest," grumbled his father.

The letters from Dorothy Minshull, it appeared, posed a few problems. The booksellers pointed out that they would need to verify the authenticity, check the handwriting, do some biographical research, in short, there were no end of obstacles. And, to cap it all, they added that Dorothy Minshull was not very sought after by collectors, and the letters would not be worth much, even when proven.

Philip frowned. "It's a pity you didn't have a letter by the Beatles, Dad, a signed record sleeve or something. Now that would have been worth a bit!"

Mr Swindlehurst snorted. "Riffraff."

"Rich and famous, though, and collectable," continued Philip breezily. "However, that's by the way. We obviously can't take the letters up to London, so I'll send them by registered post."

His father was very much on edge. "How much longer did you say I can stay here?"

"There's just over a week now. I should think that's a bit tight for Dalrymples to mull it over and get a cheque to us, knowing the post. I think we can forget getting anything for the Dorothy Minshull letters, but we'll bank on a thousand for the others. That'll give you an extra two weeks—three from now. I'll arrange with the office here that I'll pay in advance for you, and we'll square it up between us when your money arrives. But after that you'll have to move. I'll get in touch with the Social Services people."

As Philip had suspected, the payment from Dalrymples did not arrive until the beginning of his father's final week as a resident of Manningford Court. He took the cheque to show him as proof that the deal had gone through, but the old man was too agitated to pay it any attention.

They sat on their own among the exotic plants in the lavish conservatory adjacent to the lounge and looked out across the lawns and flower beds, which were a mass of colour. His father talked with wistful excitement.

"Isn't that a magnificent view, Philip? Peaceful. In fact, it's just like living in one's own country house, being here. The thought of moving's getting me down. I was awake half the night worrying. It's not just the surroundings. The staff are nice, and the residents are so interesting. One of the ladies used to be a concert pianist, and she gives little recitals sometimes. The chap down the corridor from me was a colonel in India, and he tells us amazing tales. Fascinating people, a really good crowd. Do I have to leave?" he pleaded.

"'Fraid so, Dad. No reprieve. It may be luxury here, but it's also very hard-headed commercial luxury. No money, no stay. Anyway, I've been to see the place the council have arranged for you, and that's also very pleasant, so there's no need to get despondent." He turned the screw again. "It's in the town, of course, but I'm sure you'll be very happy there."

"How big are the rooms?" butted in Mr Swindlehurst anxiously. "Will I have two, like here, because I've got such a lot of stuff, you know?"

"I'm afraid that is a bit of a problem." Philip noticed that he didn't care, as he previously would have done, about his father's feelings, and had no compunction about putting the facts brutally. "You'll have only one room, and it's not very big, but it does have a washbowl and a fitted wardrobe, a chest of drawers, all you'll need. You'll have to share a loo and bathroom down the corridor."

"Oh, my God. Sounds dreadful. And how many people are there? More than here, I suppose? What are they like, did you see any?" he added, as though it was a tribal reserve.

"Yes, like old people are; you know, doddering about, sleeping, coughing. There seemed a lot of lively chatter, though, and shouting to one another, laughing."

"Hm. Common, by the sound of it," said his father haughtily.

They returned to his rooms to survey his possessions and weigh up how many of his belongings he could take with him. Quite a lot would have to be jettisoned, including books and some favourite pieces of furniture. Mr Swindlehurst sat on the edge of his bed. He had become more and more despondent as Philip had ruthlessly reeled off the items to be got rid of. He looked up at him, and, with bitterness in his voice, said "This move will kill me, you know that?"

"Nonsense. You'll soon make yourself at home. You'll enjoy it, if you let yourself."

The removal went very smoothly; there were so few effects left that Philip hired a small van and then made a second trip in the car to pick up his father.

Mandela House had been built about ten years, was of bright, starkly pointed brick, and had large, aluminium-framed windows. It was situated near the centre of the town, and the nearby roads were noisy with traffic. The foyer was large, of shiny linoleum, but rather dingy. The echoing corridors, too, though admirably wide for cleaners' trolleys, were always redolent of cooking, and though the lack of carpet did make it easier for the residents to shuffle their feet along, the floors were unforgivingly hard if one did happen to fall.

Mr Swindlehurst's little cell was less than half the size of one of his rooms at Manningford Court, but it was nicely wallpapered and had all the basic amenities, including a red emergency cord by the bed. After they had got their breath back, Philip helped him unpack and arrange the drop-leaf table, his bookcase, and two chairs in the best positions. The geometry of the room dictated that there was really only one place that each piece could usefully be in, and when the puzzle had been solved it was just a matter of stowing away suitcases on top of the wardrobe, and shoes and other clutter under the bed.

The old man surveyed his surroundings gloomily, his face desolate. "This just isn't me, Philip. How has it come to this?" He shook his head in resignation. "Well, anyway, it won't be for long."

"Oh, come on, Dad. Cheer up. There's lots of new people to meet, plenty going on. It'll take you out of yourself. I'll pop in tomorrow and see how you're doing."

The following evening Philip made his way from the foyer towards the residents' lounge. He was greeted by the sound of a noisy, tinkling piano and many raucous voices raised in communal singing, punctuated by rhythmic clapping. He stood in the doorway at the back of the room. A large, jolly lady in a shiny dress was energetically conducting the ceremonies. "If you're happy and you know it, clap your hands…" they sang. How they sang, how they clapped.

Philip at last spotted his father, sitting alone at the edge of the group. His face was set in a morose trance. He looked a picture of isolation.

Diagnosis and Treatment

J t was the first time they had met. Dr Forsyth noticed his new registrar appear while he was stuck on the telephone before starting a ward-round. He was staring vaguely towards the doorway, twiddling the cable into knots, when Dr Jennings peered in. Seeing he was occupied, she stood at the other desk and shuffled through a pile of patients' notes.

He was immediately struck by her looks; short, dark-haired, her figure amply hinted at beneath the white coat, her manner self-contained, shy. He studied her face as she read; though not classically beautiful, there was something about the round, full cheeks and dark eyes, her slightly wistful look, which affected him straight away. His responses to the colleague on the line became mechanical.

"Get some more blood tests done and I'll see him again tomorrow. OK? Right. 'Bye."

Paul Forsyth got up, introduced himself to Dr Jennings, and welcomed her to the department. During the ward-round he paid as little attention to her as he could, dealing mainly with the other doctors, but he found himself trying to impress her with his knowledge and experience, hoping she liked his jokes. He was aware of where she was standing in the group around the bed, but didn't trust himself to look at her directly.

When they had seen all the patients he returned to the office to jot down remarks, and she brought him a bundle of files and X-rays. As she put them on his desk he noticed her wedding ring. Well, there we are then, he thought, as she went out. He felt disappointed.

Driving to the hospital next morning Paul Forsyth was

thinking about Dr Jennings and looking forward to their contacts in the coming day. Sitting at the traffic lights, he recalled her delightful smile, how wisps of black hair fell over her forehead. He repeated her name to himself; Susan. Charming.

They met on the way to the wards. He was all a-twitch, his stomach churning with excitement, and had to make a determined effort to avoid burbling inanities.

"Do you have far to travel?" he asked, curious to know where she lived.

"We live out at Fordham, so it's not too far, takes about half an hour in the car."

He wondered about her husband. What did he do? Did he travel with her? Fordham was an ordinary, drab suburb, though it had suddenly acquired a rosy, exciting glamour.

The ward-round got under way. Again, he was conscious of putting on a performance for her benefit. He became a model consultant; he sparkled with knowledge, his experience was profound, his concern for his patients obvious and genuine. He impressed as if his life depended on it. And yet he was also nervous. Why did it matter what she thought of him? After all, she was just another junior doctor working on his firm for a spell. Then she would be gone.

When the round ended he had to stay behind at a bedside with a colleague. He felt a pang as he watched her drift off with the other juniors, and found that he was taking no notice of what was being said, in fact, felt resentful that he was detained.

At lunch-time Paul was in the canteen with a group of colleagues, when Susan Jennings joined the queue at the food counter with a chattering gaggle of friends. He watched her surreptitiously as she went to a nearby table. Though he dared not look in her direction, his contribution to the conversation flagged. My God, he told himself, this is just like being an adolescent again, hoping for a glimpse of some distant girl way beyond your reach, waiting at bus-stops, hanging around the students' union for the remote chance of a meeting. He squirmed inwardly; surely it hadn't come to that? He had been happily married for fifteen years, and in that time had been immune to pretty faces and alluring figures. So what was happening? He certainly wouldn't deny the existence of love-at-first-sight; he'd been mighty susceptible to it throughout his 'teens, but why her, and why now?

At home that evening, Paul Forsyth was moody and pre-occupied. His three children regaled him, as usual, with their school activities; this had been absolutely great, that hadn't been fair, there was too much homework—the usual jumble of lively intensity that filled their days. His wife, Elizabeth, produced the evening meal and told him about her day. Afterwards, he glanced at the newspaper without concentrating and contemplated the scene around him; his home, his wife, whom he'd loved faithfully all these years, his children, who were a constant pleasure and for whom he'd do anything.

He peered cautiously at Elizabeth over the paper; she looked more or less as she did when they were married, still pretty and attractive. Surely he still loved her? Yes, of course he did. On his mental screen appeared an image of Susan Jennings and he compared the two. Was she more beautiful than his wife? Well, to be honest, different; and, of course, younger. One was familiar, the other unknown and exciting. What was he going to do? He could keep it to himself and hope it would wear off, or he could ask her out, in which case he was risking either a dreadful rebuff, which would make him look foolish and provoke gossip, or getting into an affair, which might rock or wreck the boat.

"You look thoughtful, darling. Something worrying you?" asked Elizabeth.

"Mm? Oh, no. Just planning tomorrow, that's all. Nothing special."

The kind, caring soul; he was ever so fond of her, and glad she couldn't read his thoughts. He felt guilty for even contemplating deceiving her.

During the night he awoke frequently, and each time rationalised a little more his proposed self-indulgence. Perhaps if he were to see her a few times they could become friends, and that would put the mystery and glamour into perspective, she would lose her distant, unattainable attraction, becoming mundane. Did he really believe that? Well, it might work. Deep down, he suspected there was a tiny part of him hell-bent on romantic excitement. Go for it, it urged. He made up his mind to ask her out at the first opportunity.

It was a fortnight before he had a chance to approach her, a time in which he had become further ensnared, every glimpse of her feeding his infatuation, when she filled his thoughts and dominated his imagination. Externally, of course, he seemed the same, but inside he was in turmoil, constantly thinking of her, taking little interest in anything else. The similarity with his teenage loves was embarrassing; it was painful, miserable, exciting, delicious. His judgement was definitely affected, and he only hoped that nobody noticed.

He contrived a meeting with her in private, ostensibly to discuss a patient, and, as the conversation ended, his heart raced and throbbed in the silence before he took the plunge.

"Er, Susan. I was wondering if I could meet you one evening for a meal to discuss that pneumonia project you're going to do?"

Susan was clearly surprised by his approach, and held his gaze warily for some moments. Paul felt himself wilting.

"Yes, I suppose so," she agreed hesitantly. "At least there wouldn't be the interruptions there are during the day. I'll get all the patients' data jotted down." Her eyes flashed a warning.

They met the following Thursday in a pub-cum-restaurant close to the hospital. The evening was going well, though he was a jangling wreck and Susan seemed to him to be patently on edge. Having discussed the project in business-like fashion for an hour or so, their conversation moved on from nervous chatter to revelations about their background and careers. Paul was desperate to prolong their meeting and tried hard to amuse her with anecdotes of his working life, and of characters he'd worked for in various hospitals. But in each pause he could sense an underlying uneasy tension, as if she was thinking, what next?

Paul had not been intending to make any reference to his romantic feelings, but a combination of the wine and her lovely little face destroyed him.

"Susan," he found himself starting. "I've got a confession to make." He saw her expression harden just perceptibly, but pressed on. "There was another reason behind meeting you tonight. I wanted to tell you I'm in love with you."

"Oh!" The word hung in the air, sharp, final. Then there is a problem to solve, it said.

"I just fell for you the minute I saw you," he went on hastily, to fill the silence. "And it's grown over the past few weeks. I thought it might help if I told you."

He felt pathetic and vulnerable. He was metaphorically prostrating himself abjectly at this girl's feet. Here he was, her boss, laying himself open to ridicule before a junior. If this were to get round the hospital, he'd be a laughing-stock. How would she take it? What kind of woman was she? For half-a-minute his fate hung in the balance. Was she already planning how to amuse her friends with this scene next day? Why, in God's name, had he taken this risk? He looked imploringly into her dark eyes. She is stunningly beautiful, he thought.

Still she surveyed him, and he bumbled on again, afraid of the silence.

"I thought you could help me somehow…perhaps, to er, get it out of my system," he finished lamely.

She gave a tense laugh.

"As though it's a disease, you mean? And you're looking for treatment."

"Well, it's getting to be like an illness. I do have the diagnosis. I can't think of anything but you nowadays. I'm mad about you. Perhaps we could meet from time to time—simply as friends, you understand, and then I'll get you in proper perspective; realise that you're not actually a goddess, though that's hard to imagine."

Susan gave an acknowledging, rather than a mirthful, smile.

"I don't know. I've got a husband, and we're perfectly happy; you've got a wife and family. What about them?"

"Oh, they mustn't know—that wouldn't be fair to any of them. But anyway, I'm only proposing we meet as friends, there can't be any harm in that, can there? And you would make quicker progress with your pneumonia project."

As her decision hung in the balance, Paul couldn't help slipping in a little hint that their liaison might help her career, though he felt slimy for doing it.

"I suppose it would be all right," she announced at last. "But it's strictly as friends." She gave him a meaningful look to emphasise her words.

"Strictly. Thanks, Susan. I appreciate it."

They met once a fortnight for a couple of months, having little difficulty in providing excuses to their partners for an evening out, since late hospital meetings were commonplace. At first, Paul's conscience troubled him when he lied to Elizabeth, but the guilt was always readily displaced by the excitement of being with Susan. Gradually, he desensitised himself.

His greatest problem was in coping with the time when he didn't see her. The empty evenings seemed interminable, as he wondered what she was doing. Worst of all were the weekends. Would they never drag by? Each Monday morning he was in a ferment at the prospect of seeing her again, and he inwardly jumped at every vaguely similar white-coated shape he saw in the hospital corridors. Ward-rounds had become a delicious pleasure, and occasionally the working day would provide him with a special smile or a meaning glance from her that was proof of their growing closeness.

Paul's breakthrough came as they sat in one of their rendezvous pubs. By now, all pretence of discussing her project had been abandoned and both acknowledged that they met for the pleasure of each other's company. Over the previous weeks he had steadfastly refrained from mentioning his feelings, but tonight she looked inspirationally stunning.

"You look ever so beautiful, and I do love you," he said, almost apologetically. "It hasn't gone away, I'm afraid."

Susan was flustered. She scrutinised the bracelet on her wrist and twisted it round uneasily before speaking.

"No, it hasn't, has it? I think it must be infectious. I'm feeling the same about you." She looked up at him, eyes bright and brave.

"But, Susan, that's marvellous. Oh, I love you, I love you, I love you," he cried, clasping her hand. "I'm ever so happy—I can't believe you feel the same."

Inevitably, as their affection deepened, they were not satisfied by meeting every week or two, and Paul was always keen to snatch a lunch-time drink or an extra evening at a pub in the country, where they were unlikely to be recognised. They found it harder to give plausible excuses to their spouses, and occasionally one of them would fail to turn up for a tryst because an alibi had gone awry. Then panic would set in. Paul, detained at home with the family, would be in an agony of frustration and fear at what Susan would think of him, though unable to let it show; while Susan waited at the rendezvous with increasing desolation enveloping her, and filled with greater irritation at the restricted life they were forced to lead.

They spent more and more time planning assignations, dreaming up elaborate excuses, and struggling in the web of deceit they were so avidly constructing. They lived in constant dread of being seen together away from the hospital, and planned the arrival and departure of their cars in side-streets and car parks with the precision of bank-robbers.

"God, I just bumped into Dr Jackson as I crossed the road," she panted breathlessly one evening, as she threw herself into his car. "I hope he didn't see you waiting here."

Furtiveness became a way of life. If anything, Paul was more jumpy than Susan, perhaps because he was older, or because he had so much more to lose. His family responsibilities weighed heavily. He was frequently withdrawn and tetchy at home. He was still fond of Elizabeth and the children, of course, devoted to them, in fact, as always, and wouldn't hurt them for the world. But now he'd got this extra dimension added to his life, and struggling to maintain the geometry of it all was tearing him apart.

Since Elizabeth didn't know of his affair, he excused himself with his new logic: she wasn't actually being hurt, was she? There was always the risk, though, he had to admit, that she'd find out sooner or later, and then what? He dreaded, and daren't contemplate, the consequences. Was he still in love with her, he asked himself every day? Well, yes, he was; not as passionately as fifteen years ago, naturally, that was understandable, but certainly in love with her in a modified, familiar-friendly sort of way. She hadn't changed much, was still pretty well the perfect wife. But here he was, madly in love with a girl ten years younger. Could he be in love with two women at the same time, he wondered? Of course, it all depended on how you defined love; he could certainly see that there are different degrees and stages of love. He pounced on the concept instantly; that was it, stages of love. He was at a different stage of love with two women.

So that meant, he mused, that his present passionate love for Susan would also eventually burn down to a lower flame, as had his earlier passion for Elizabeth. Was that the inevitable effect of Time on all love? In acknowledging that it probably was so, a seed implanted itself deep in his subconscious.

For a month after Susan's declaration they lived on an emotional roller-coaster; when they were together they came alive and were blissfully happy, apart, they descended into aching misery and loneliness. They had made a definite decision that they would not go to bed together for the present, and, as a result, their passion had been restricted to pounding preliminaries in one of their cars parked by lonely hedgerows. It was clear to both of them that the situation was untenable, and frayed their already neurotic existence to breaking point.

One night, after a particularly quarrelsome meal in a distant pub, they acknowledged that their relationship had reached a turning point. They sat in the dark in the car park, mesmerised by the rain pattering on the windscreen.

"Susan, we can't go on like this, you know. We've either got to progress further, whatever the consequences, or we stop seeing each other. This is playing havoc with both of us."

"I know, darling. I've come to the same conclusion. It seems so ridiculously ironical; all or nothing. Your idea of wearing out your infatuation was completely wrong, wasn't it? All we've done is get ourselves hopelessly entangled. I'm desperately in love with you—I just couldn't contemplate life without you now."

"I feel the same, obviously. Do you think we should leave home and live together?" Paul froze as he uttered the words; he'd always sworn that he wouldn't hurt his family, but now he was being pulled in two directions, events drifting out of his control.

"How about us having a weekend away first? Perhaps a session of sexual head-clearing would do us good, and we'd also have time for some serious talking about our future," Susan suggested.

He was surprised at her boldness in making the commitment, but overjoyed that she loved him so much that she wanted to. They would finally be really happy, and possess each other as they'd longed for. He put his arm round her and she snuggled her head against him.

"OK, if you're sure. But we're going to have to come up with some pretty watertight excuses."

A few weeks later they had invented a bogus weekend conference for the benefit of their spouses, and arranged to meet at a hotel in a town two hours' drive away. They travelled separately on the Saturday morning, Paul waving goodbye to his children with a heavy heart, weighed down by guilt. As he drove, the problems built up in his mind. It was irritating enough that he had any doubts, because for months they'd been desperate for sex together. He was beside himself with excitement at the prospect, but, at the same time, was nervous at the huge step he was taking. His lies to Elizabeth, too, had pricked him more sharply than usual.

"A weekend conference?" she'd said, frowning. "That's odd at this time of year, isn't it?"

"Oh, they do have them," he'd countered breezily. "It's being sponsored by one of the pharmaceutical companies. I suppose weekends are the only time people are available." He'd hoped he sounded convincing. But shame at deceiving her in this ultimate way really hurt him and still festered. Would he actually decide after this weekend to leave the family and live with Susan? He'd no idea.

When he arrived at the hotel he found Susan in a bar at the rear. It was lunch-time. They drank lager, had a snack of sandwiches, and made uneasy conversation about the journey, the weather, the furnishings; anything to distract from what was in their minds. She looked appealingly beautiful and desirable and all his qualms vanished. On a wave of anticipation he marched up to the reception desk and registered them under false names, nearly forgetting the name he'd selected. I'd never make a criminal, he thought happily, as he drew their room key.

"If you've finished eating, darling, we might as well go up to our room."

They looked at each other with tense smiles, and picked up their small bags.

"This reminds me of that Groucho Marx receptionist quip— Mr and Mrs Smith and no luggage!" he said.

"Yes, that's us exactly," she giggled. "What room number are we? Not 13 by any chance?"

"No, 25 apparently. It must be up those stairs."

According to the Automobile Association handbook, from which he'd picked it, the hotel boasted three stars, but their room was dingy, the carpet threadbare in places, the ceiling cracked, and the curtains and bedspread cheap and gaudy. Paul opened the wardrobe to a jangling of wire coat-hangers and was assailed by a musty, sweaty odour, which rapidly pervaded the room. The view from the only window was blocked by the brick wall of a neighbouring building, adding to their sense of imprisonment.

Susan threw her arms round his neck and they kissed passionately, her body sinuously seeking his. They tried to shut out the alien surroundings and re-assure themselves. It was Susan who made the first move.

"I'm going to be ever so traditional, darling, as it's our first time. You get undressed in the bathroom and I'll jump into bed."

"Fine. Don't be long!" He forced a brave grin.

Paul kissed her again and ambled round the corner to the bathroom. Sitting on the side of the bath, he heard the rustling of her clothes as she slipped them off, and imagined how gorgeous she must look. He made no attempt to undress, as his worries made a final assault on his conscience. He was being torn apart.

He was madly in love with this woman, they were about to make love. Why was he holding back? He felt as if he was on the edge of an abyss; once he took this step there would be no turning back. This relationship, which had hitherto been fairly innocent, had unbalanced him, but not yet destroyed him. But it would do so, and with him would go his marriage and the happiness of the family so dear to him. Did they deserve to suffer for his indulgence? He was appalled and saddened by the madness of his situation. How, in heaven's name, had he got himself into this mess?

It was, after all, a Saturday afternoon, when normally he would be with Elizabeth and the children. What were they doing now? They would be missing him and trusting him. Trust. The word echoed through his brain; and he was about to betray them all, betray the trust and affection they'd built up over the years. He thought of his children, of the six-year-old, with her long blond hair, freckles and winning smile.

"Come on, darling. What are you waiting for? You're not shy, surely?" shouted Susan playfully from the bed.

He sighed deeply and went back into the room, sat on the bed by her and took her hand.

"Paul! You've still got your clothes on!" she laughed. "Are you teasing me? Trying to drive me into a frenzy?"

She stopped abruptly when she noticed his expression, more drawn and tense than she'd ever seen him.

"I'm sorry, darling." He paused, biting fretfully at his lip. "I just can't go on with it. It's a step I can't take. It's nothing about you, or me, or us. Much as I love you and want you, I just can't hurt my family. Now I realise that being faithful to Elizabeth is crucial. I won't betray her. I should have seen it before. I'm sorry."

He noticed how beautiful her bare shoulders and breasts were, how tantalising and inviting she was; now every part of her seemed to mock him.

Susan drew up her knees under the bedclothes and clasped her hands round them. She stared blankly across the room, as if searching for something, totally deflated. He hoped that some time she'd be grateful for his honesty, but now he could see she was shattered.

"Well, in that case, it's a good job we didn't go any further," she muttered bleakly, blinking tears onto her cheeks. "There's not much point in staying any longer, is there? I might as well get dressed."

Feeling that the quicker he got away from this scene the better, Paul picked up his bag.

"All right. See you downstairs."

He returned to the bar, where he ordered afternoon tea with scones and jam. When Susan joined him she had obviously been crying. They sat for a long time, had a second pot of tea, held hands intermittently, and, privately and aloud, wondered about their future.

"Let's not be too hasty," he suggested. "Give ourselves a week or so to crystallise our thoughts, then meet up and talk things over." She started to sob again, and once more he tried to console her. "I'm ever so sorry, Susan—it's all my fault from start to finish. I invaded your life, encouraged you into all this, and now it's me who's getting cold feet."

She pressed her lips together tightly and blinked back tears.

"Oh, I was a willing accomplice. And we've had a marvellous time so far. It's just that…well, I've grown to love you and now I just live for you, seeing you, being with you. I suppose if I'd stopped to think, I'd have known that it wasn't going anywhere—at least, not without a great upheaval, and innocent people getting hurt. And I wouldn't have wanted that either."

In the car park they kissed again and held hands, searching each other's faces for understanding, their memories coupling in a subconscious farewell. Paul broke the silence.

"You set off first, darling. Drive carefully. See you on Monday."

As she prepared to drive away, he leaned through the window and kissed her again. "Remember, I do love you," he said, clinging desperately to the moment.

She nodded, tears streaming down her face, then slowly drove away.

Paul travelled home in a turmoil, sadness and distress mixed with relief that at least he hadn't gone beyond the point of no return. He still had time to think the situation through calmly.

When he arrived home the children were playing in the front garden with friends. As he walked up the path, six-year-old Jane ran to his arms excitedly.

"Daddy, you're home early! Look, Mummy's done my hair in plaits." Proudly she showed him the blond lengths of twisted hair. "And she's made us some strawberry ice-cream for tea."

"Has she? Well, aren't you all lucky, love?"

Paul squeezed her to him for a long moment, his eyes closed. He knew he'd done the right thing.

Seeing him from the house, Elizabeth ran out.

"Darling, what's happened? I thought you weren't coming back till tomorrow. Is everything all right?"

He gave her a kiss and looked at her appreciatively. Dishevelled, and in her gardening clothes, she was still attractive.

"Yes, fine. Nothing happened. It didn't seem a very interesting meeting, so I came home. We'll be able to do something all together tomorrow."

Everybody's Happy

He'd always loved his pigs, so standing here in their midst seemed the perfect place to take his leave of the world, and of his worries. He took two cartridges out of his coat pocket and stared at them long and hard.

Why had he brought two? Surely one would be all he'd need? If the first one didn't finish him off he'd be in no state to fire a second. They were such beautiful things, too, despite their instant, terrifying, destructive power. Beautifully crafted in shiny red plastic and sparkling brass, they were almost ornamental. They rolled about nicely in his palm, tempting and fascinating. He couldn't really comprehend that in a split second one of these could bring everything to an end, an end to his torments. Peace.

He slipped them into the breech of the twelve-bore shotgun crooked in his arm. The brass ends and central pips twinkled back at him like a pair of seductive eyes, teasing. Go on, they seemed to say. We're ready. Are you?

The sows now began to stir as first light appeared at the eaves of the covered straw yard, and they became aware of him. A couple lumbered towards him, grunting in a soft, conversational way, looming white and massive in the gloom.

William Burden, even now, in this extreme, was proud of what he had achieved in building up the pig herd over a lifetime. In acreage, it was only a small farm, on marginal land, and he and his wife Ruth had worked like terriers in the early days. Originally, they had had a small beef herd and sheep, and had

175

fattened pigs, but the message at the time had been that you had to specialise to be successful. The old philosophy of mixed farming that he had been reared with had had its day. As the profit per animal had become so small, large numbers kept intensively was the way forward. To do that, you had to put all your effort and resources into one thing.

Like many others, he'd listened to the arguments, read avidly, attended meetings, and assimilated the new creed. Specialisation was the name of the game. From now on, pigs were to be his life. The sheep had gone, the beef herd had been sold, and with zeal he had converted the old stone buildings to house more pigs. In time, more and more of the land was swallowed up by long, low concrete piggeries, with tall, dusty food hoppers rising up alongside them. More tractors appeared and roared about the yards and fields, churning it all into a sea of mud. Great pits were dug to contain the animals' dung, ponds of foul grey liquid coyly known as slurry lagoons.

The air round the farm reeked of pigs, winter and summer; his overalls, his skin, even after a bath, as his wife complained, smelled of pigs. The pigs themselves, in their concrete palaces ("pig palaces" was a term of the time designed to delude farmers that they were providing luxury accommodation), were often wet and filthy, muck pasted on their sides and legs and cramped together too tightly for comfort. There had been constant problems with tail-biting, when, out of boredom, the pigs had crunched their fellows' tails off, and then, encouraged by the taste of blood, had chewed and chewed until there remained only a hideous bloody stump, which often became infected and festered.

William Burden, the go-ahead farmer, had accepted all this as an inevitable part of progress. He was fond of his pigs, of course, always had been, but these things were problems of intensification and had to be lived with—that was modern farming and that was the only way to make money. There was no question of having a different system, and, in fact, he hadn't lost any sleep over it.

For a time, make money he certainly did. Though pigs are always an up-and-down, cyclical market, his huge expansion had thrived and the family had been able to improve their lifestyle.

They had spent a bit of money on modernising the kitchen for his wife, on a couple of ski-ing holidays for the children, a newer second-hand Land Rover, and, finally, when things were going really well, he had lashed out on a new Volvo estate.

Life at that time, and it was not really many years ago, had seemed good. The bank was falling over itself to lend him more money. He had drastically increased the number of sows he kept, now up to six hundred, and, since he took the progeny right through to bacon weight, at any one time he had many thousands of pigs on the farm. At feeding time you could believe it. The noise, the intensity of the squealing in the various buildings, was out of this world. Hellish. He sometimes felt it was the souls of all the pigs he'd ever sent to the bacon factory screaming to get at him, to tear him to pieces in retribution.

Where had it all gone wrong? Burden, in his late fifties, tall, thickset and ruddy-faced, glanced down again at the cartridges snugly nestled in the breech of his twelve-bore and slid one up and down nervously with his finger and thumb.

It was difficult to say how the decline had started, or just when. A couple of years ago the price of pigs had plummeted, though he had not been unduly worried at first, regarding it as another of the temporary dips. But they had never recovered. Then Ruth had been off-colour for a long time and the doctors couldn't find out what was wrong. That had been another worry. The intermittent problems with the children had also added to the strain; again, nothing really drastic, just the regular minor crises that accompany adolescence—nevertheless, part of the drip-drip of tension and worry. Yes, he could see that it had all been sliding downhill for several years, gradually getting on top of him, everything contributing to his feeling of being hunted and pressurised, badgered by events beyond his control.

The reminder of his desperation jolted him back to the details of what he was about to do. It was still very early, the sun barely up, and only the first rays lighting the far end of the shed. Once more he ran through the procedure; he would kneel down, with the butt of the shotgun on the ground, and place the barrels in his mouth. He had experimented already, and had checked that his arm was long enough to reach the triggers. However, he had found that, with his hand extended, his fingers were at the wrong angle, so that he would have to pull the trigger with his thumb.

In fact, he realised now, if he yanked down hard with his thumb, it would probably slide on beyond the first trigger and almost simultaneously pull the second. He needn't have speculated on the merits of having two cartridges, after all, both would be used anyway.

Another idea now struck him. Instead of kneeling, perhaps he could balance the gun on the wall of the pig pen, and, by crouching slightly, be at about the right height. He tried to visualise the anatomy of his head. The barrels ideally needed to be pointing up inside his mouth towards his skull and brain, an angle guaranteed by kneeling. Having the barrels parallel to the ground would direct the discharge to the back of his neck. Did it matter? Wouldn't the massive, obliterating force of two columns of lead blow away most of his head and neck anyway, how ever the gun was positioned? It was bound to. No problem. So long as he didn't try holding it to his temple and have it wavering about. That was where it could all go horribly wrong and end up in hideous injury. No, he would stick to his carefully rehearsed plan; kneeling, barrels in mouth, right thumb on trigger.

One of the sows ambled up to him, chomping happily on a mouthful of straw, eyes glinting in that mischievous way pigs have. He scratched her neck affectionately, the thick, bristly skin familiar to his finger-tips. Pigs had been his life, his success, and now his ruin. But it wasn't their fault. Though he cursed them often enough, he bore no grudge. A combination of things had driven him to this state. He looked round at the clean, spacious strawed pen, warm and dry. A paradise for pigs. It was ironical that now, at the very time when he had greatly improved the conditions and welfare of his pigs, that he faced his greatest financial crisis.

Burden mused bitterly on how, over the past couple of years, he had radically changed his systems of husbandry, costing him a fortune as he borrowed to the hilt to finance it all, gambling on the future. He had got rid of the stalls for tethering his dry sows, which, to be fair, he'd never really liked, or thought remotely natural. In his darker moments he acknowledged that he'd never had the guts to face up to the cruelty involved in the sows' confinement, or go against the prevailing fashion. He had also replaced the farrowing crates, though he was sure it would lead to a lot more trouble with the sows as they gave birth, and would certainly result in more squashed piglets.

It depressed him to feel that farmers couldn't win these days; they'd become public enemy number one, and he was utterly perplexed. When the country had wanted mass-produced, cheap food and efficient farming, he, like the others, had thrown himself into it. But suddenly, the rules had been changed. Now, it appeared, the public no longer wanted that. The sentimentality of the times had caught them up. The urban consumer had a romantic view of the countryside; farm animals had to be happy (happy, for God's sake!), with few constraints, living an idyllic existence in perfect surroundings, eating a natural diet (whatever that was), and breeding haphazardly as the mood took them. Did they want to pay for all that would cost? Did they hell. He seethed once more at the very thought of interfering, urban do-gooders.

For some months now, he'd been losing about twenty pounds on every pig he sold, and the gap between his costs and earnings had widened catastrophically. He had pleaded with his bank manager to be flexible, and to extend yet again the period for his loans. He had now gone beyond the last deadline and the bank was threatening to foreclose.

In the early stages of the crisis he had discussed the accounts with Ruth. Together they had considered savings that could be made; they would do without this and that, cut back on luxuries, even sell things. All the family had felt the pinch, but it had not had the slightest effect on the huge deficit; money was bleeding away week after week. Recently, he had deliberately kept his wife out of the picture to spare her the worry, and told her only in vague terms that they were barely making out, hoping against hope that there would be a sudden improvement to save them.

Burden had been frustrated to realise that everything he understood about farming had been turned on its head. Agricultural strategists were even talking again of diversification being the key to survival. Diversification and mixed farming, for heaven's sake! When he'd been in mixed farming it had been ridiculed as old-fashioned. It had all come full-circle, but it was too late for him now. He'd made all the changes; had changed to intensive systems when that was the vogue, had changed again to the present extensive, welfare-friendly schemes, and where had it got him? Bankrupt with happy pigs.

The sows snuffled around him as they waited for feeding time, chewing playfully at his boots and sleeves, jostling at the gun barrels. Well, he thought, I hope you are all happy, for God knows what will happen to you after today. The sun had just appeared and there was all the promise of a summer's day ahead. Burden felt a twinge of regret as he realised that he would not see it. It was time to gather his last thoughts and make ready for his final action.

He snapped shut the breech of the gun, admiring, as he always did, the ornate scroll-work in the grey metal. When he had planned this, he had not thought of saying a prayer, because religion had been out of his life for so many years, but now, actually faced with eternity, he suddenly needed to clutch at the extra consolation. The first prayer that came into his head was from childhood, and didn't seem appropriate, dealing as it did with the future and being good. His mind ran feverishly through several others, and he muttered a mixture of fragments, ending with a specific wish for the safekeeping of his family.

His heart was pounding now, his guts churning, as his last moment neared. His hands trembled. What he was aware of most was an overwhelming sense of relief that his troubles were over; no more mental torture, no more self-persecution for having failed. He had already crossed over, got beyond the turmoil that had buzzed in his head for these past months, that had put his life on the edge of a black chasm from which there had seemed no escape.

He kneeled in the straw in his thick brown corduroys, and held the gun out in front of him, the butt resting on the ground. He had to lean forward slightly to be able to put the tip of the barrels into his mouth. They were cold and tasted tangily metallic. One of the sows persisted in trying to rub against him, and he fended her off briskly with his arm.

Now, at last, was the end of it all. Release. He reached forward until his thumb was on the front trigger, bit firmly onto the barrels, and closed his eyes.

He wanted his final images and thoughts to be of Ruth and the children. He summoned them up; they were all there vividly in his mind's eye, smiling, seeming to understand, to approve. He pushed hard with his thumb, his whole body tensed, his face screwed up, eyes tightly shut, teeth clenched on the cold metal. His heart stifled him with its racing. Nothing happened. His thumb did not budge.

Oh! the bloody safety-catch! How had he managed to forget the safety-catch? Couldn't he do anything right? He trembled from head to foot, cold sweat bathing his forehead and hands. He pulled the gun from his mouth and crouched in the straw, shaking, appalled by the anti-climax.

Now he was at their level, the pigs regarded him with curiosity, an object to be explored and played with. Their snouts nuzzled and jostled his sleeves, chewing splashily at his coat and displaying long rows of gleaming white teeth. He batted them away impatiently with his arm, as some desperate force pulled him back to his senses.

Was that escape an omen? A message to change his mind and try to go on living, to start again? Nothing of the bloody kind, he thought grimly. Just damn carelessness that he hadn't released the safety-catch. Time was getting on now and he needed to get it over quickly before someone came.

He dispensed with the previous rigmarole, and, almost in a panic lest he should lose his nerve, slid off the safety-catch and knelt down. A few feet away, the sows contemplated the scene placidly, their pink eyes twinkling in the subdued light. He took a last glance about him; certainly his pigs were happy, and in a moment he would be happy too.

Once more William Burden bent forwards, felt the stark chill of the barrels in his mouth, frantically conjured into his black mind images of Ruth and the children, and stretched his thumb down onto the triggers.

The sows, frightened by the explosion, leapt back a few yards with loud, barking squeals. After his body had rolled sideways into the straw they came to investigate. At first they tugged at his trouser-legs and sleeves playfully, but quickly became bolder, gnawing deeper and more ambitiously, with happy, high-pitched grunts.

Last Farewell

he body was in a black plastic bag in the boot of the car, where he had laid it carefully next to the tool kit. As they pulled up at the traffic lights they did indeed resemble a funeral; their car was old, stately and black, and old, stately Harold and his wife Mildred wore solemn mourners' expressions. They had been prepared for the end for some time. The vet. had told them that Henry's kidneys had packed up, and when a cat gets to fifteen there's really nothing to be done. They had decided that, when he had his next bad turn, they would take him in and have him put to sleep.

They had had a few sharp rows, of course, about how bad a turn had to be to qualify. Harold, who doted on their cats, always insisted on giving him another twenty-four hours, and Henry had repeatedly rallied, though skinny as a rake. This time, though, even Harold had to admit that Henry was moribund, and had no recognisable quality of life.

Mildred had been much more cavalier about the whole thing, pointing out that he did have seven other cats, it was not as if Henry was the only one. No, Harold had thought, but he was the oldest, and, though he did not say so to her, he knew that Henry was rooted in nostalgia, and associated with a period in his life when he had been a lot happier. Henry was a link with better times. Aloud, Harold told her that he damn well hoped he was never on a life-support machine with his continuing existence depending on her say-so, because she would have him switched off to save the electricity.

They drove on out of the town, wending their way into the lanes, gradually climbing up to their cottage on the hillside.

"What are you going to do with him, then?" said Mildred, to break the gloom that enveloped them.

"Bury him! What the hell do you think?"

He took out his annoyance on the gear lever as he changed down for the final corner before their home.

"I've got a nice, peaceful plot lined up for him, and I'll put him there this afternoon."

The car rumbled over the flagstones of their yard and stopped abruptly, tipping them forwards. Mildred did not risk asking him where he had selected for the grave, because she could tell by his mood that she would only be snapped at.

They had a cold lunch, Harold, in a withdrawn silence, battling resolutely through a pork pie, Mildred flitting, as ever, from kettle to pantry, pantry to table, then to the sink. A selection of their seven cats sat by the hearth, either washing acrobatically with a back leg stretched in the air, or gazing thoughtfully into the fire. Most of them were related; three generations of tabbies, and a similar family of black cats. They did exactly as they pleased; came and went as the mood took them via a cat-flap in the back door. They distributed themselves around the warmest spots in the kitchen according to a subtle hierarchy, which was constantly being challenged by the young and enterprising. Rows broke out among them much as they did between Harold and Mildred, a sudden flare-up ending a period of sullen brooding.

Harold got up from the table, taking his mug of tea to the window. He was grey-haired, stocky, and still strong, even in his seventies. He always wore both belt and braces, the belt stretched out of his sight under the paunch. The dual support reflected his view of life, distrust and canniness. Now he tucked his thumb into his braces and sipped tea while checking the landscape.

The cottage had a panoramic view of the valley and beyond to the encircling hills. He could see anyone driving or walking up their lane long before they arrived; he could note when each farmer started making hay or cutting corn; when the cattle or sheep were moved from one field to another; if the train pulling away from the distant town was on time. It gave him a proprietorial feeling, as if he were lord of all he surveyed. Indeed, his nickname down in the village was The Laird.

Satisfied that his landscape was in order, Harold turned his thoughts to burying Henry. Sad as it made him, in a way he always relished burying pets. There was a grim satisfaction in the ritual of putting them in the soil, their last resting place after they had shared their lives, about bidding them a last farewell. They were characters, after all. They understood him, they depended on him, and he understood them, and depended on them too. He was under no illusions about that. As he got older, he realised only too keenly that he was more and more at odds with his fellow human beings, who let him down left, right, and centre. He had been regarded as odd when he was still at work, and only middle-aged, but, since retirement, he had gradually withdrawn and become more eccentric.

Harold sighed as he looked back to life when Henry had been a kitten. He was still working and there seemed to be purpose in his existence. There was lively chat and joking with his work-mates. Mildred was still at the shop each day, and did not seem to get on his nerves as she did now. The silly, empty-headed woman. He could not understand how ever he had come to marry her. It had hardly been a wild, passionate romance. Their listless courting had simply become a habit, and he had actually fallen in love with the countryside where her people farmed, and could not tear himself away.

Originally, he had thought that, as a farmer's daughter, Mildred must be capable and good at organising, but even when he realised how hopeless she was, he still went ahead and married her, incapable of making the break. There had been no children, of course, and, as the years went by, they desiccated together. Now they were emotionally shrivelled, he channelling all his affection into his cats, Mildred, not apparently having any to channel, had become a robotic husk, who knitted and watched television, peering with gormless awe at a world she barely comprehended.

Harold's reverie was interrupted by Bella, the oldest tabby cat, jumping into the window seat and rubbing herself against him.

"What does the old lady want, then? Hm?" He stroked her head and Bella purred loudly, fixing him with adoring yellow eyes.

"Shall we go and bury Henry? We can't leave him in the car, can we? Are you coming to supervise? Yes, Dad, she says, I think I'll have to officiate—I am the senior cat now, you know."

Harold had many a conversation with the cats, using them like a ventriloquist as characters for whom he invented the parts in his fantasy world. He picked up Bella in his arms and went into the kitchen, where he encountered the scrawny Mildred, who was gazing out of the window.

"You know, Harold, I've just been thinking," she said, in her slow, hesitant way. "You could have Henry stuffed."

"Stuffed?" shouted Harold incredulously.

"Yes, you know, by one of them men that puts birds and things in glass cases. Taxi something-or-other they call them."

"I know what a taxidermist does," snapped Harold, "and we're not keeping Henry like that. It'd be obscene having him looking at us; with us, but not with us. It'd be degrading for him. Dust to dust's what I believe in. Anyway, it'd be morbid."

"But you are morbid, Harold. All them pets' gravestones and jam-jars of flowers in the orchard. If he was stuffed you'd still be able to talk to him—even you can't go talking to gravestones."

"I'm not morbid, woman. Just sentimental, that's all. I get very attached to the animals, which is more than you do. You haven't an ounce of feeling in you, for the cats, or me, either, for that matter!"

"Well, what a thing to say! You're going peculiar, Harold. That's what folk round here say about you. Do you know that? Peculiar, they call you—and they're right."

Harold could listen to no more, and, with his blood boiling, tore out of the back door to the shed where he kept his garden tools. Still fuming and muttering under his breath, he changed his boots, grabbed a spade, and collected the bag containing Henry from the car. He had always been prone to flying into tempers, but at least this time the fiendish energy produced could be harnessed to good use in digging a deep hole.

Reaching the orchard, he took off his jacket and carefully unwrapped Henry, who rolled out onto the grass, his legs stuck out stiffly, his hair wet and flattened on one side, his teeth bared. Even the pang of seeing him did nothing to mollify Harold's anger, and he slammed the spade into the turf with energetic thuds, in no time piling up a mound of soil. It became harder as the hole deepened, and he found himself struggling for breath. Suddenly his chest was full and tight, and the soil and the spade swam violently before his eyes. He felt the impact as he crumpled heavily on the ground, and then drifted into black unconsciousness.

Mildred was washing up, in her own kind of cold, vague, annoyance, from time to time glancing through the window to watch Harold digging. She saw him fall, and set off into the garden still wearing her flowery apron and yellow rubber gloves. As she bent over his purple face, she could distinctly hear his rasping breaths, but her repeated cries of "Harold, what have you done?" brought no response.

She tottered back to the house, negotiating the cats on the doorstep, and, as she began to telephone for the doctor, thought what a good job it was they'd changed their phone to one of the new sort with buttons, because she'd never have got the fingers of her gloves into the holes in the old dial.

They got Harold to the hospital pretty quickly, considering they were so far away, but, even plugged into all the machinery, he only fitfully regained consciousness. Two days after the heart attack, on the day he died, Mildred visited him for the last time. She was sitting by his unresponsive head, telling him something inconsequential for the sake of it, when suddenly he stirred. He put out his hand feebly, and it brushed against her head. His hand stroked her hair for a few moments, caressing her affectionately.

Mildred was deeply touched by his tenderness, and tears welled up. He began to mutter and she bent near to catch his words.

"Henry. Henry, old puss-cat. I'll be all right now you're here."

Blenkinsopp's Conversion

B lenkinsopp entered the committee room and wandered along the table in search of the plastic label bearing his name. He nodded to a couple of characters who had already found their berths, and were holding forth while polishing their spectacles on handkerchiefs.

As usual, he had been placed down at the far end, so that he would be viewing the proceedings from a position out on the wing, where catching the chairman's eye would be almost impossible. At least he would be able to analyse events undistracted. You mean doze, said his inner self. Well, yes; freewheel was perhaps a kinder term; contemplate the implications of everything; no, doze, insisted his inner self.

Blenkinsopp unpacked a file from his briefcase and hunted for the papers for the meeting. More committee members were arriving. Coats were hung on the stand, cheery greetings exchanged.

"Do we get coffee before we start?" asked one.

"No, it's supposed to arrive about half an hour into the first session," replied the lady secretary, a cheerful, resilient soul.

"Oh, hell. I could just do with a cup now. It's taken ages to get here."

The committee was made up of twenty people, mostly men, and they nearly all had appeared. Blenkinsopp sat down, took out his pen, and surveyed the table. God, what a bunch. A selection of eager apparatchiks, leavened by a few odd-ball specialists and peppered with the self-important great and supposedly good. He glanced at the agenda. A formidable list of items lay before them, some with daunting potential for discussion.

They were going to be kept there until late in the afternoon. His heart sank. How would he get through it? The secretary closed the door and immediately he felt trapped, almost claustrophobic, at the prospect of the boredom. He could probably permit himself one trip out to the lavatory, perhaps in the late morning or mid-afternoon, but that was all. Lunch would be sandwiches in the room, strolling about dropping egg and mayonnaise onto the carpet, while people cornered other members and wittered at them. No escape there.

The chairman opened the meeting by introducing a new member, a lady from some government department who was an adviser, and, he hoped, would be making her own input. Blenkinsopp winced. The jargon had started in the first sentence. Usually at this sort of meeting he kept a list of odious phrases, manglings of the language, and he had his sheet at the ready. Today, he wondered whether to do a comprehensive list of every atrocity, or simply record the new ones. It was hot, despite the open windows, and he felt rather lethargic, so opted for the latter. After all, many of the phrases, while still offending or amusing, had become so commonplace in committee-speak, that they had lost their novelty. The level playing-field and window of opportunity were now so notorious that they were eschewed by politicians.

He looked round the table again. With regard to hackneyed phrases, there were huge talents present, who, in the past, had come out with some gems. They were clearly gigantic sponges, who mindlessly soaked up trendy words at every meeting they attended, in every report they read, and exuded them without a thought. Blenkinsopp was still amazed that such people, so capable in many ways, could repeat clichés without apparently noticing. Like parrots, really. A sponge crossed with a parrot. A sporrot or a parronge?

The chairman was now outlining for the new member the committee's function, and Blenkinsopp felt a flutter of indignation at the smug, self-congratulatory tones. The committee barely carried out its intended duties, invariably refused to face difficult problems, fudged wherever possible, and was often over-ruled from above when important decisions were actually taken. It was nothing more than a cosmetic talking shop, as many of them would recognise, if they could be honest. He looked at the heading. How did a Committee differ from a Working Party, or a Panel, for that matter, and a Board, or a Council? He had served on all types and there was no detectable difference. They were all pretty hopeless.

He had just got half-way through a really lung-filling yawn, when the chairman swept round the table like a lighthouse with his smile and caught him in the beam. He managed to poke a hand towards his face and half-stifle it. Damn it. He couldn't even get physiological satisfaction, never mind mental.

The chairman launched into the Minutes of the Last Meeting. Did anyone have any factual corrections to the Minutes? Blenkinsopp sincerely hoped not. If feet started dragging at this stage it would be a long morning. But, of course, they had among them nit-pickers and eager-beavers, so points there were.

"Chairman, if I could draw your attention to page 3, line 12? I think that should read : 'if funds were to be made available'."

God! Wasn't that guy smarmy, thought Blenkinsopp, eyeing him morosely. A proper little Sunday School monitor; he even had an array of different-coloured pens in front of him. Everybody knew what was meant; why did this little jerk have to draw attention to himself? I'm here, I'm here. Please teacher, I've got my hand up.

Outside the window, a lawnmower had started up, and the gardener set off to guide it along the strip of grass parallel to the building. Wouldn't it be nice to be that gardener just now? Up and down without a care in the world. Institutional gardeners never seemed to have any cares, and were able to feel free while passing the windows of the office-prisoners. It reminded him of exams, both at school and university, when it was always summer, and you had to battle away indoors while the groundsman walked about with his lawnmower looking contented and wise. It was a gorgeous day, too, ideal for a day's walking in the country. He thought of some of his favourite walks. The tracks would be hard and dusty now, overgrown in places by nettles and brambles. The skylarks would be hovering high above the meadows, giving a sense of endless space and freedom.

He was interrupted by raised voices and a minor argument between two seasoned antagonists, who were contesting whether or not the Minutes were a true record of what had actually been said. It proved to be only a slight hitch, and, as the chairman put it, antlers could be unlocked. Very droll.

After an hour or so the coffee was brought in. An elderly woman pulled in the trolley, banging it noisily against a briefcase propped by the table, and her young assistant clattered the cups and saucers onto a side-table. There were plates of biscuits covered by plastic film. The waitresses in their green and red uniforms tiptoed about for a moment, as though trying to become invisible, and then departed. Blenkinsopp just caught a glimpse into the corridor, where he could see a few non-captives walking along. How he envied them! Lucky blighters, actually getting on with some real work. And yet, they probably envied "The Committee", having seen the real coffee and biscuits going in. They little knew how hard-earned it was.

The coffee produced an immediate loosening of attitudes. All except the most inflatedly pompous visibly unwound and allowed themselves a few limb movements; some leaned back, a couple put their arms above their heads; one adventurous soul, obviously strong on initiative, actually yawned and stretched at the same time. Men nodded and smiled to their neighbours. The half-time lemon, without the whistle. Not that it was half-time. Previously, the catering ladies used to bring the cups of coffee to each member round the table, starting, of course, with the chairman. That had been an orderly affair. The business had proceeded, with the more polite whispering a sepulchral thank-you as their cups arrived, the self-important merely reaching out in mid-sentence as if the cup had descended from Heaven.

Now, however, in the interests of efficiency, that had been superseded. The new system produced a much greater diversion, a better opportunity to study human nature, as Blenkinsopp gratefully acknowledged. It had been decided, nobody knew how, that the members would help themselves. It fell to the secretary to start the ball rolling. She leapt up from her scribing and addressed the shiny silver pots, peering into each to establish which was coffee, which milk. She then bore a cup ceremoniously back to the chairman.

Meanwhile, other little scenes were being enacted. The bold strode off to the side-table, ostentatiously poured their coffee, grabbed a handful of biscuits, and returned efficiently, oh, so effectively, to their seats. Ready to carry on, chairman, said their manner. I've got mine, bugger the rest. They probably didn't even notice how many people they pushed past. Blenkinsopp thought, as he watched it all from the left wing, that it would make a good pointer to character and effectiveness in the workplace ('strewth, he was beginning to use the words himself now), rather like those games on management courses. Put some pots of coffee at one end of a room and let twenty-odd people sort it out. It would reveal the leaders all right.

Now, by a process of natural selection, the field was left to a group of ditherers who had assembled by the coffee. Polite, diffident, but nonetheless desperate for a cuppa, they bumbled and hesitated. These characters could dither for England, thought Blenkinsopp.

"No, after you, I'm sure there's plenty for all of us," conceded one.

"No, go ahead, please do," implored another with negative assertion.

They filled cups and then offered them to other people, some of whom were fawningly grateful, while others had to decline because they took it black. More dithering, milling about and confusion. Blenkinsopp wondered what it was really like on a sinking ship or a crashed aeroplane. Did the British still persist in this absurd politeness? At last, as the group dispersed, he and his neighbour sidled up. There was just about enough left, if they pooled the dregs of several pots. And it was nicely cold, of course.

The chairman was still droning on. They were now into the main agenda.

"I think we can take the specialist reports next. Terry, how have your projects been going? Let's hear from you first."

Terry, who stood at the top of the pecking order for no obvious reason, simpered and smirked his introductory remarks, which washed over Blenkinsopp in a wave of "sharpening", "focussed", "targets", and other management-speak. He groaned inwardly at the prospect of many hours more of this and began to feel not only irritated at being shut up in this room, but actually felt physically trapped and threatened. Could he find an excuse to leave? Not a plausible one, anyway.

Terry was now justifying his expenditure and making rash claims for his department's capabilities. Of course, he would need more resources and the committee would have to vote him a bigger slice of the cake. Blenkinsopp became more irritated. His oppressed boredom, punctuated by indignation, was an explosive mixture, and, more than once at meetings, he had felt himself on the verge of making the most almighty scene. How would they all react, he wondered, if the normally urbane Blenkers, who only spoke when he had something worthwhile to say, suddenly flipped and waded into them?

Now he focussed on Terry's moustache, as it negotiated the bumpy ride over the stream of words; "buoyant", "dynamic", "pro-active", all burbled by. Then suddenly "to source from elsewhere". Blenkinsopp literally flinched with mental discomfort. Source? A verb? He wearily added it to his list for the day, below "Chinese walls", "envision", "the big picture", "post-implementation support", and the rest.

If he'd really applied himself today, he could probably have broken his record, which stood at fifty-four new phrases for a single meeting, an occasion in London a few months ago, when the civil servants and commercial whizz-kids had vied with each other in verbal stupidity. But, somehow, he didn't feel like it. He was particularly resentful at being stuck indoors on such a beautiful day, was tetchy and bored by not being required to make much of a contribution, and anxious that the small report he did have to present would have been anticipated by the earlier speakers, or would be torn to shreds.

Terry had now finally stopped talking, and there were sycophantic warblings from around the table. He lapped up the approval. He might be thick-skinned, thought Blenkinsopp, but it doesn't stop him absorbing the old oil. He tried to think of an animal that represented Terry's salient features, but failed. There was a haughtiness that put him in mind of a camel; it was curious how he achieved that, because he appeared to be looking down at you, even though he wasn't any taller. A snake? Certainly pretty reptilian, and yet too bulky. A weasel? The pointed features and moustache emphasised that all right, and he did look as if he was at one moment peeping over the grass, and the next ready to dive down a hole. No single animal carried the day, and he concluded that the perfect committee animal would have to be a fantastical, composite creature.

The next speaker was already in full spate. Big, boisterous, bumptious, and that was only the 'b's, Charles was ninety per cent objectionable, but, oddly enough, the remainder could be interesting, even charming. And, for the purposes of this committee, he wasn't too boring. He was so arrogant, and his opinions so outrageous, that he really livened things up. He was a turn. Even the emollient chairman was sometimes moved to query some of his claims.

"Really, Charles? Are you quite sure? It doesn't seem terribly likely."

At the same time, some of the committee members were muttering to one another "absolute crap", "poppycock", and worse. Charles was an acknowledged expert in his field, and the adulation he had received over the years from a small circle of acolytes had beguiled him into thinking that he also understood everything else. He had become a know-all. A great brain can function equally well in all spheres, was his reasoning. From being a loud-mouthed young hothead who criticised the Establishment, he had now, in later years, become a loud-mouthed greybeard who pontificated. In fact, more than one colleague had seen parallels between Charles and some football managers of a similar personality.

"It's perfectly simple," he was now saying. "Do what I say, and you haven't got a problem. I will guarantee you..."

Blenkinsopp observed him from his side-on position. His great shapeless bulk wobbled about as his arms flapped to make points. His voice came over as blah, blah, with words interspersed here and there. There seemed to be more noise than could be accounted for by actual diction, and Blenkinsopp wondered what the sound profile would look like on a frequency screen. Charles's voice seemed to send out a loud warning first, like an ambulance's siren, which told everybody else to stop talking, and to listen to him.

"The point is this…" He went on and on. Unfortunately, today he was in boring mode, not in his provocative and outrageous style. He was beginning to take himself seriously; then he lost the tiny streak of fun and his entertainment value evaporated.

Blenkinsopp began to glaze over. He had looked to Charles to liven things up. The committee members were an unprepossessing lot. Not a decent-looking woman among them; a couple of weary civil servants with cardigans and sensible shoes; one of them always seemed to have a cold, and perpetually dabbed at her red nose with paper tissues. He had long ago nicknamed her Kleenex. The men were little better, a mixture of the pushy-on-the-make, fawning sycophants and administrative coolies, with a group including Blenkinsopp himself co-opted as special advisers.

Do you really have to be here, Blenkers? His inner self was objecting, and putting the more fundamental questions that were below the surface, which he rarely addressed. Well, it would be very difficult to get out of attending these meetings. The bosses wouldn't like it, and you know what that means. Unsatisfactory reports. No promotion. But why be a slave to this nonsense, went on the inner self, when you could be free, independent, able to come and go as you please? A job outdoors perhaps? Nice idea, but it's not possible, as you're well aware, not before retirement.

The thought of that depressed him still further. He looked round the room at the committee and felt trapped again. The clock on the wall said ten years left to retirement. Could he take ten more years of this? A breeze outside rustled the curtains, at once mocking him and inviting him out to play. Come out onto the hills, it seemed to say; we don't have agendas and verbose reports here, we don't have people boring you with their eternal claptrap and second-hand opinions about things that don't matter; but we do have the larks shimmering, and the wind sweeping across the hayfields, and the cries of the peewits. We certainly don't have hassle, or pressure, or aggro, or whatever you care to call it.

He looked across to the horizon, to the edge of the city. He must somehow get out of this room. He panicked. Should he excuse himself and just wander about in the corridors until he felt better? There was no time to decide. It was his turn to speak. "And now, Mr Blenkinsopp, can we have your report please?" he heard the chairman saying.

Every face round the table was looking at him, waiting. The only sound was that playful little breeze, inviting him out. He seemed to rev up inside, like a racing car on the starting grid. However, to his surprise, he didn't charge into his opening words in a flurry of nervous energy, but was possessed by an icy calm. He disregarded his notes.

"Thank you, chairman. I've been looking forward to this opportunity of addressing you all and giving you my views. You don't very often get them, do you? You may even think I don't have any. And they don't really matter anyway, do they? So long as you can put forward those of your little clique, the ones who work your strings. Please don't interrupt, chairman, the only tolerable thing about you is your good manners. As you know, I've sat on this and many other of your idiotic committees for years, and I've hated every tedious minute of it, just as I've loathed and despised the devious, manipulating rats sitting round you."

For some reason, sheer astonishment, presumably, neither the chairman nor the others moved or made any attempt to interrupt him. Facial reactions were mixed; some literally had their mouths open like fish on a slab, others stared in embarrassment at their notepads. A couple of his principal adversaries smirked uncomfortably, but with glee behind the mask, because they could visualise telling their colleagues later how they had witnessed these goings-on; they had actually been present when Blenkinsopp snapped.

"It's high time you knew what I really think—I'm sure I'm not the only one who's sick and tired of items going through on the nod, sick of having to pretend we can see the emperor's new clothes. Well, in future, I shall be shouting loud and clear, the emperor's stark, bollock naked! Got it?"

Nobody moved. They just sat and stared at him in amazement. He was conscious of wondering why they didn't interrupt. It was like a stoat with a group of rabbits. Perhaps they thought it was all planned, and that he was dangerous and armed. Whatever the reason, he had got their attention, and was going to exploit his advantage to the full.

Verbally, he went round the table, dealing with his chief rivals one by one, lambasting their mistakes, exposing their sharp practices. One began to object; "I say, look here…"

Blenkinsopp cut him off.

"You're not going to say anything. You've always had too much say. Now you're going to listen."

He ridiculed each one in an appropriate way, words and images rushing into his head on a tide of fertile inspiration. He noticed out of the corner of his eye some members giggling as their colleagues were dissected, their well-known foibles paraded and lampooned. Blenkinsopp was a good mimic, and, shorn of his usual inhibitions, not a bad actor, and now he brought all his hidden talent to bear in a sparkling one-man show. He saw them all with animals' heads above their suits; a braying donkey, an offended camel, a wart-hog, even a goose, the characters he'd given them over the years. One of his ways of whiling away the time in meetings had been to write limericks about them all, and now seemed the perfect occasion to let them hear some. He had been particularly pleased with a couple of his efforts, because the names had required considerable ingenuity to find a rhyme. He greatly enjoyed the recitation.

He was now coming to the end of his tirade. He'd dealt with everyone and everything he could think of, and wound up with a few scathing remarks for the chairman to relay to their lords and masters about the running of their affairs. It just remained for him to extricate himself from the room before the spell which had gripped him wore off. He glared at the chairman with infinite disdain.

"I shall not be attending any more meetings. Good day."

With that, he picked up his briefcase, flashed a look of scorn round the table, and walked out, closing the door softly behind him. He sauntered down the corridor in a pre-occupied daze. Well, Blenkers, old son, you've really done it this time, whispered his inner self. Burned the boats pretty comprehensively, I'd say. No way back from this one.

He was still stoked up and didn't care. In fact, it was very exhilarating. He found he'd enjoyed dishing out a bit of hostility.

It made such a change after years of patient urbanity and reasonableness. He paused on the stairs. Perhaps this was the way forward to a new lifestyle? Become prickly and belligerent. Of course! There was enough evidence that it paid off, you'd only to look at some of the successful bastards he knew. You got nowhere by being reasonable. The formula seemed to be, behave as bolshily as possible and they shower resources on you. Throw a few timely wobblers, and you get everything you want.

Blenkinsopp meandered on through the institute and out across the square, feeling as elated as if he'd experienced a religious conversion. He felt as if he could take on anybody and win. Indeed, he was positively spoiling for an argument. Perhaps there'd be some trouble with a ticket collector, or a yob with a loud personal stereo on the train. Endless possibilities for confrontation. Nobody was going to push him about in future. He recalled how he'd been nick-named Soppy at school. Well, from now on, he was going to take the Sopp out of Blenkinsopp.

Great sentiments, put in the inner self, but you don't seem to be taking into account the fact that you've just done some serious damage to your career. There will be repercussions for yonder outburst. No, somehow he doubted that. He had a hunch that he would be treated much more circumspectly for a while, but that was all. Anyway, he hadn't done anything wrong; only ruffled a few feathers, pricked some egos.

Blenkinsopp arrived at the station, found his train, and settled into his seat. There wasn't a single thing to which he could take exception. Nobody was smoking in his non-smoking carriage, no stereos or mobile phones. Nothing on which he could practise. He felt like a man with a new weapon and nothing to shoot at.

Watching the countryside rattle by, he was filled with a great sense of relief, as well as the euphoria of beginning a new venture. Though he'd been taken completely by surprise by his outburst, he now recognised that he must have been on the verge of it for a very long time. It wasn't simply meetings that drove him so wild, they were just one aspect of being trapped in a high-pressure job he didn't like, in which frustrations mounted almost tangibly. It had all been bottled up for so long, until at last his safety valve had blown. There were lessons to be learned, and he would develop a new strategy for the future, which should see him through to retirement.

In the following weeks, Blenkinsopp noted a change in his personality and behaviour. Where previously he'd been conscientious, now he became slapdash and lackadaisical. He gaily ignored deadlines, laughed at criticism, threw correspondence into the bin, and took a delight in being rude and stroppy—in fact, he began to be dubbed Blinkingstropp in some quarters, which would have delighted him, had he known. Instead of keeping his thoughts to himself, he now told people straight out if he considered their ties appalling, their reports pathetic, their talent minuscule.

And he loved it. As each vanquished and perplexed colleague crawled from his room and tottered away down the corridor, Blenkers rested his elbows on his desk and shook with laughter. This was the life! If only he'd discovered it thirty years earlier, how easy it would all have been. There would have been no need to listen for hours to the whinging self-justification of his middle-managers, or to be bored senseless by cases for allocation of resources. He would have interrupted them brusquely in mid-sentence and shown them the door, as he did now. He had been too polite and considerate for forty years and there was a lot of ground to make up.

Eventually, Blenkinsopp began to notice signs of a waning of his aggressiveness. At first, it seemed to be simply more selective; someone might push in front of him in a queue and not receive their due verbal lashing; or a feeble report from a colleague would be accepted with something akin to the old sympathetic resignation, instead of being dissected. He was less prickly, not so easily crossed. Was the spell wearing off? Certainly he felt less jumpy, and his sense of not-caring-a-damn had mellowed into a less militant form, though he still didn't care-a-damn about most things. He had evaluated life afresh, changed his priorities, and come to the inevitable conclusion that most of what had hitherto concerned him was utterly trivial, and not worthy of his involvement. He exuded an Olympian detachment, which his family found irritating, engaged as they were in daily life on a lower plane.

The big crash for him came, however, at the annual budgeting meeting of his company. This was always a tense, set-piece confrontation between the most senior managers, at which they presented the cases for their budgets and staffing to the Board. It was highly competitive and often acrimonious. In Blenkinsopp's former existence it had been an occasion he dreaded, and in which he performed badly, though since his conversion similar minor meetings had seen him wipe the floor with the opposition. In fact, he had acquired a formidable reputation.

Today, however, for some reason, he felt diffident and unsure, in exactly his old way. He listened with increasing despondency to the chief executive's speech, and to the cases made by his rivals. He was withdrawn and gloomy during the discussions, and raised only an odd, perfunctory question.

When it came to his turn to speak he was nervous and unconvincing, and he knew that he had finally reverted to his old self. As he finished, he mustered a defiant glare for his audience before returning to his seat. He remained for the rest of the morning's business in a cocoon of pre-occupation, feeling isolated, hopeless and vulnerable.

He went for lunch with the others in a despondent dream, convinced that when the results of the bids were announced in the afternoon session he would be at the bottom of the pile, as of old. However, when the chief executive delivered the judgements, he was staggered to hear that he'd been given everything he wanted, and had come out very definitely on top. There was even special commendation for the strength of his case.

Hell's bells, he thought. How did that come about? I think I know, intruded his inner self. They haven't yet twigged that you've reverted. They think you're still the rogue elephant who might trample all over them at any minute.

Blenkinsopp settled back in his chair, lost in thought. He smiled contentedly as his future tactics dawned on him.

Pastures New

Jealous? He couldn't be. Not of a horse. Resentful, certainly. In recent months Robert Hartley had found it increasingly irksome that he and his wife had to spend so much time on their two horses; the early morning mucking out and feeding, the same again in the evening. He paused while the bucket filled under the tap, and watched sullenly as Wellington, the big bay gelding, chomped at his mash.

I'm your slave, you great brute, he fumed, but couldn't help admiring him, glossy brown and bulging with trained muscle. But that wasn't the point. Since buying them, the horses had taken over their lives, there was no time to do anything else. On summer weekends now Jennifer went off for long rides, or to events, leaving him, not being a rider, on his own. In winter, the necessary exercising and messing-about took up most of the daylight hours. Now they rarely had a day out together as they used to. Wellington and Hercules had driven a wedge between them.

Hartley strained to lift the water bucket onto the hook in the wall, and began to fork out the squelchy bedding. To be doing this in the cold and darkness of a winter's morning before work, he said to himself, was sheer bloody madness. Utter lunacy. His back twinged sharply as he braced himself to lever the fork in the packed wet paper. In fact, such was his anger, why go on doing it?

He straightened up creakily and looked out to the yard, his breath steaming in the dim light of the stable lamps. Well, when they'd bought the damned horses he had agreed to help, so he was duty-bound. A promise was a promise. And Jennifer would certainly be pushed to do it all before she went to work. It wouldn't be fair for her to have to do everything. As they'd said for the past thirty years, there had to be give and take in a marriage. Nowadays, though, he seemed to do all the giving. Jennifer was the one who rode the horses and derived the pleasure; he got absolutely none. Sweet sod all. Unless you called this pleasure.

He pondered bitterly. So that was the reason he was locked into this chore, was it? A cycle of obligation he couldn't break out of without fraying some more strands of their marriage. There was no doubt that, since the children had left home, things between them had changed. Was it all the horses' fault, or was it just because they were older? Wearier, more disillusioned with life? Bored? Or because Jennifer now worked full-time, had a career? Probably a mixture of the lot.

The barrow was piled high with soggy bedding, and he trundled it wearily through the yard towards the dung-heap behind the stables. The soft tyre made the going harder, straining his shoulders, building up his frustration. Their paths crossed as his wife carried out the nets of hay.

"Is that everything done?"

"It'll have to be, I'm late already," he growled.

Jennifer, however, insisted on a final sweeping-up, so he strode off towards the house alone, to indicate that he was turning his back on the whole damned business.

They went their separate ways to work and began another day in their increasingly separate lives. Robert Hartley mused as he drove into town. Today, for some reason, his irritation lingered more than usual. He was getting sick of this way of life, and the horses were the focus of it, an open sore, picked at daily.

It was at coffee time that an idea struck him. They were all sitting round in the office sipping from their multi-coloured mugs, and the conversation had turned to horses. After the usual banter about his, which were known to be a thorn in his flesh, one of the girls said she was looking for a replacement horse.

"Well, if it was up to me, you could have both ours as a gift!" Hartley said, with some feeling.

He had always got on well with Sally, perhaps because she laughed at his jokes, and was a vivacious, cuddly-looking girl ("girl", he thought wryly, she must be over thirty). There was a sort of sparky chemistry between them, though he couldn't put his finger on it.

Later, sitting alone at his desk, the thought came back to him. One of their nags would suit her down to the ground. Perhaps he could persuade his wife to part with the horses and they could re-organise their lives and make an effort to be together more. Start to rebuild some bridges before it was too late. He sighed; some of the bridges seemed already beyond repair. The likelihood of convincing Jennifer to sell the horses was nil. In the household's current priorities he trailed behind Wellington and Hercules by a few lengths.

Hartley was first home that evening, as usual, and had the preparations for the meal well underway when Jennifer turned up. Unusually, he plied her with a gin-and-tonic.

"You sip this, dear, I've got the food on the go already," he breezed.

"Good heavens! What's this in aid of? Have you got the sack, or something?"

"No such luck. I just think it's time we had a serious chat. About where we're going. Our daily life, and all that."

He busied himself with the pans on the stove, and vigorously whisked eggs for the omelettes, taking frequent gulps from his glass by the cooker.

"Do we need a chat? And what do you mean—where we're going? Life seems all right to me—I'm perfectly happy with it." She sipped, thoughtfully.

"Well, you may be, but I'm not." He poured the egg mixture into the pan as a distraction, but the sizzling only heightened his tension. "I don't think we spend enough time together. Not like we used to. Frankly, I feel we're drifting apart. We were much happier years ago. And the horses are the main reason. I just never see you. You dash in after work, change into your jodhpurs, and you're gone again."

He turned back to the stove and shuffled the omelette, pleased that, so far at least, he'd kept the conversation calm and on an even keel.

Jennifer's response, too, was measured.

"I didn't realise you weren't happy with things." Her face set in that haughty, slightly nettled look he knew so well. "Wellington and Hercules take a lot more of my time than yours."

"Yes, but you enjoy it. You like the feeding, the brushing, the hoof-picking, the whole tedious, bloody caboodle. It's your horsey hobby. To me it's just an infernal pest. And I'm beginning to resent every hour I spend. I could be doing other things."

She went over to the table, and he ran across, holding the omelette plates in an oven-glove. Next he opened a bottle of white wine, feeling that aid was needed to mellow her resistance. He pressed on while he still had courage and momentum.

"I can see some danger signals. We need to be together more, and the best way is to sell the horses."

"Sell them? Sell them?" she shrieked. "No way!"

He kicked himself for not waiting for the wine to work.

"Yes. You could still go riding—hire one by the hour at stables; but we wouldn't have all the work, the damned drudgery. It's even worse than having a boat. At least a boat doesn't have to be fed twice a day."

He decided to risk all. The situation had been getting him down for ages, and he'd nothing to lose.

"The choice is between me and the horses. I'm not putting up with it any longer." He softened. "I'm sorry, love, but it really is that serious."

"Oh, don't be so dramatic, Robert. We can improve things easily. I'd no idea you were getting into such a state about it."

He glared at her. "I'm not in a state, as you call it. I just recognise the state our marriage is in—you don't seem to. We can sell the horses and go back to our old way of life—as a matter of fact, I even know of a likely buyer for one of them."

"Forget it!" she snapped, flouncing to the sink with the plates.

They passed the evening more distantly than usual, Jennifer buried in a book on dressage tests, the silence broken only by the rustle of Robert's daily paper.

At supper the following day, she surprised him by bringing up the subject of the horses again.

"I've been thinking about what you said yesterday. I suppose we could sell one of them, perhaps Wellington. I'm obviously not going to give up horses, but I could manage with just Hercules. It would cut down the work, and the cost."

Robert glanced at her, intrigued. Had she scared herself by finally recognising that perhaps their marriage really was on a slippery slope? The trouble was, getting rid of one horse wouldn't make that much difference. But, at least, it was a start.

"Well, there's a girl in the office who's looking for one just like Wellington."

He tried to contain his elation, to stop his face registering any trace of triumph; it could be critical.

"What sort of money would we want for him?"

"As much as possible, obviously. Three thousand, I suppose." She looked gloomy at the prospect of parting with him.

"Right. I'll mention it to her tomorrow."

When he found Sally she was standing by the photocopier, hands on hips, waiting for it to disgorge. Robert had seen her like that a hundred times before, but today the tight pink shirt, her full shoulders, her large, smiling blue eyes, had a special effect on him. She was a very attractive girl. He became strangely nervous.

"Sally, er…you know we were talking about horses yesterday? Well, one of ours could be for sale, after all. You interested?"

She stroked her long blond hair back self-consciously.

"Oh, yes…I suppose I am. How big is he again? Sixteen hands or so, didn't you say?"

"Spot on, and muscular with it. He's a strapping brute, but I'm sure you could control him. He's got a heart of gold. No malice in him. And he's well into all the eventing tricks, dressage, fancy footwork and what-not," replied Robert enthusiastically.

The copier rattled out a sheaf and Sally turned to collect it.

"The problem is, though, you probably want a lot for him—what've you got in mind?"

Robert took a deep breath. "Well, my better half is thinking about three grand—but he's the finished article. Ready to jump on and go."

"Oh, yeah, I can see that. But it's still a lot. Though I have got the insurance money from Tinkerbell being put down. Tell you what. I'll have a look at him and see if he appeals."

In his office, Robert rolled a pencil back and forth across his desk. If they could get rid of Wellington, it would be a start for their rehabilitation. Though he couldn't see Jennifer giving up Hercules as well. Still, he could work on it. He thought of Sally standing by the photocopier, and found himself hoping for another glimpse of her during the day.

At home that night he waited for Jennifer to return, wondering how she would take his news of a possible buyer. At six o'clock sharp the front door slammed and she bounded through to the kitchen, dumping her briefcase in a corner with a snort.

"Hello, love. Had a good day?" he tried.

"Oh, so-so. The usual. Endless hassle and trivia. It'll be nice to get outdoors. Get some fresh air and work off the frustration on Hercules. No, I won't stop for a cup of tea. Must get cracking."

She disappeared upstairs to change. By the time he was half-way through his next cup, Jennifer appeared again in jodhpurs, and was hauling her riding boots out of the cupboard.

"I mentioned Wellie to that girl at work—she's quite interested. When can she see him? Saturday? You've not got an event or anything on, have you?"

Jennifer was already heading for the back door.

"You did hear me, did you, love? Would Saturday be all right?"

She paused in the doorway. "Yes, I should think so. Cook the potatoes and the other veg for about half-eight. Get those pieces of cod out of the freezer, they need using up."

She was gone, and Robert heard the Land Rover roar off up the lane. He sipped his tea desolately, and consulted his watch. She had been in for exactly five minutes. Long enough to cast one skin and take on another. Long enough to give him his instructions. The veg. The pieces of cod. Cod-pieces. The piece of cod which passeth all understanding. He sighed and his spirits sank. It couldn't go on.

On the Saturday morning Sally came to the stable, and they paraded Wellington up and down the yard.

"He's got absolutely no vices," extolled Jennifer." Quiet as a lamb, but plenty of energy."

"Sounds like the spec for a man," Sally burst out.

They all laughed, each with different thoughts. Sally rode

Wellington round the field and convinced herself he was suitable.

"Yep. He's just the job. I'd like him," she announced, as she slid down from the saddle. "Now what about the price?"

"We were thinking of three thousand," said Jennifer quickly. She knew what Robert was like when it came to selling things.

Robert shuffled round to Wellie's rear, thoughtfully eyeing up his hocks as the negotiations proceeded. It also gave him a good, dreamy view of Sally's jodhpured backside and thighs.

Sally was offering two thousand eight hundred, and an awkward silence enveloped the two women.

"We'd be happy with two-nine, I think, wouldn't we?" put in Robert. "How does that grab you?"

At that, Sally agreed to have Wellington, subject to a satisfactory veterinary examination. "See you on Monday", she shouted cheerily through the car window. Robert watched her drive away, and noticed a sense of emptiness. Monday was a day-and-a-half away.

He started mucking out Wellington's box, while Jennifer saddled up Hercules for her ride.

It took Sally nearly a fortnight to arrange the money and the examination, but eventually a date was fixed for the hand-over, and the Hartleys delivered Wellington in their trailer to his new livery stable in a neighbouring village.

Robert patted Wellington's long nose and offered him a mint as soon as he was installed. "There you are, Wellie, old son," he told him aloud." You're in good hands. I can't say I'll miss you, and it's not au revoir—it's definitely goodbye."

As they drove home, Jennifer put a brave face on it.

"I'm really going to miss him, after all these years. But still, we'll have more time together, won't we? That's what you wanted, wasn't it?"

"Too true. How about us having a day out tomorrow, for a start? A day walking in the hills, or a day at the sea, come to that?"

"I can't, I'm afraid. There's a jumping competition at Okeford Park, that I entered for ages ago. I'm taking Hercules."

Robert's hopes withered. "How about next week?"

"No. There's dressage at Melbury."

Of course, this was how it would be. Always something to come between them. Another event, another show. Hercules needed practice, Hercules needed schooling. Hercules needed some damned thing. He should have realised. Selling Wellie had made no difference at all.

He changed gear angrily and turned on her.

"Do you know, if we compare hobbies, the amount of time you spend on yours and I spend on mine? Has it ever crossed your selfish mind?" He paused. "No, of course it hasn't. Well, I'll tell you. I happened to look back through my fishing diary for last year. Do you know, I went fishing twenty-two times in twelve months, and that's often only for the odd hour or two. And how often do you ride? Let's say five times a week, at a conservative estimate. So that's over two hundred and fifty times a year." Months, years, of irritation spilled out of him. "Not to mention, of course, the infernal daily mucking-out, feeding, and generally waiting on the brutes. And you wonder why we never have time to be together! I often wonder if you want us to be."

Jennifer was taken aback. "You're being very unfair. It's not really that bad. And anyway, riding's my hobby, and it happens to be a time-consuming one. Animals can't be dumped in a corner when they're not in use, like a fishing rod. I work hard all week, and I'm going to enjoy my hobby."

She looked across at him defiantly. "We've got rid of Wellington, and that should give us a bit more time. But I've no intention of giving up riding, or of selling Hercules. And that's final." She turned away and stared fixedly through her side-window to prove that it was.

Back at work on the Monday, Robert had a good excuse to seek out Sally.

"How's Wellie settling in?" he asked, excited to be near her again. "He's eating all right? Not pining for me, or anything?"

"No. He's adapting well." She giggled and shrugged awkwardly.

"There's a spare head-collar and some other bits of his tack we forgot to give you," he went on. "Perhaps I could come down to see him one evening after work and bring them?"

He was almost pleading with her.

She seemed to have trouble getting words out. "Yes, er…I suppose you could. I'm sure he'd be pleased to see you."

She giggled nervously again. Robert noticed that she had twisted her paper-clip into a knot.

"OK. How about tonight?" he suggested. "I could meet you at the stable straight from here on my way home, say half-five-ish?"

"Yep. Suits me. See you then." She gave him a friendly grimace, and was gone.

Robert was twitchy with anticipation as he arrived at her livery stable. He had been thinking about Sally throughout the day. Why did it matter if he impressed her now? After all, she was simply a woman he worked with, who'd bought his horse.

Her car turned in and scrunched through the yard. She leapt out and hurried across to him. "Sorry I'm late. I had to call at the post-office."

They leaned on the loose-box door together and studied Wellington as he tugged huge mouthfuls of hay from his net.

"I must say, the old swine impresses me more now I don't have to look after him," smiled Robert. "He's a splendid specimen; just look at the power in those muscles." Wellie rolled his eyes and ambled over to nuzzle him, still chewing. "Mind you, we've still got nearly as much work with Hercules, so it hasn't made much difference. One of these days, I'm going to take a tin of cat-meat to Hercules, and I'll say, if you get ill, or go lame, Hercs, you'll be in one of these tins in twenty-four hours, and no messing. That'll petrify him."

Sally laughed, and he noticed those attractive little creases appear round her eyes. They chatted for half an hour, maintaining a verbal ping-pong. She was so fresh and amusing, and such good company.

When he got home, he found a note from Jennifer on the kitchen table. "Schooling Hercules. Do the veg for about eight o'clock. We'll have omelettes."

Instead of a pot of tea, he poured a gin-and-tonic. Veg for eight, eh? That was an hour-and-a-half away. The house was dark and silent. Damn it all. He was lonely. It had only just dawned on him in so many words. What he needed was company.

Robert persuaded Sally to let him meet her at the stable again the following week. At work now they seemed to find endless reasons for a quick word; they met by incredible coincidence all over the building. Surely, she must have realised it wasn't his concern about Wellie that drove him? But still, she seemed happy enough for them to meet.

This time, he helped a bit with the mucking-out, and when Wellie was tucked up and they'd stood about awkwardly talking, he was so powerless to leave her, so desperately clinging to her company, that he invited her for a drink. They drove separately to another village, and found an alcove in the pub's empty lounge. Mid-week in winter was ideal.

In their quiet corner they discovered and entertained each other. Robert, greying, over fifty and overweight, told endless anecdotes about his life. Sally, pretty and in her thirties, sparkled with life and laughter.

He returned with another round, however, to find her lost in thought, running her finger round a beer-mat.

"Robert," she said nervously, her voice changed now. "What are we actually doing here together? There's more to this than just Wellie, isn't there? Be honest, now. Have you thought it through?"

Her change of mood took him by surprise.

"No. I haven't thought anything through. Er…well, I'm here because you're good company, and you cheer me up, and amuse me. And…well, I was just desperate not to leave you at the stable. I dunno if that's an explanation—it's how it is, anyway."

"I think I get the picture, but do you know what you're doing? How it can affect us both? After all, you are married—what on earth would your wife think?"

It was his turn to stare, as he fiddled with a beer-mat. He spoke slowly and painfully, as he tore out each sentiment from his inner self and groped for the right words.

"We simply seem to have drifted apart in recent years. I suppose it's a common problem; marital boredom, even though we are ostensibly very compatible, pre-occupation with work. In our case, of course, the final straw's been the damned horses.

212

That's what's driven the real wedge. And somehow, Jennifer's not like she used to be. She thinks more of the horses than of me, probably."

He looked up suddenly, and made an effort to pull himself together. "Anyway, I'm not going to complain about her. That's private, and it wouldn't be fair—she's been a good wife for thirty years. But it looks as though it's a chapter that's coming to an end. Simply that."

He fixed her eyes with his, searching for the response he yearned, his face furrowed in a quizzical smile.

"Perhaps, like Wellie, I'm a mature horse who's ready for new pastures."

He leaned across and took her hand. "I've fallen in love with you." He smiled feebly, shaking his head, baffled. "There's no other way of putting it."

Sally kept his hand and squeezed it. Pure elation shone in her face. "I feel the same—it's been driving me crazy."

Robert lunged at her clumsily round the table, succeeded in hooking an arm round her shoulders, and they kissed.

For the next hour they held hands and discussed what they should do, how they should play it. The lounge bar was still empty, and the landlord had given up looking in.

"I'll tell Jennifer tonight, and see what her response is," Robert said. "A lot depends on that. It'd probably be best all round if we kept the status quo for a few weeks, took it slowly, but at least we'll be able to meet frequently in the evenings— that was what was getting to me."

He looked at her and beamed; he just couldn't believe that she felt the same about him. He kissed her again, for the hell of it. Perhaps love releases something in us like an amorous adrenalin; if so, Robert was awash with it.

They parted in the car park. Robert was so euphoric that he sang aloud all the way home. Snatches from his favourite operas bore him along. He was madly in love, and carried away by it. The notes died, however, as he turned into the drive. He had concocted no excuse for being late, hadn't the faintest idea of how he was going to break the news to Jennifer, or what would happen. Somehow, he just didn't care. At the front door, the memory of Sally came back and inspired him for the fray.

Jennifer was sitting on the sofa, reading. Before she could finish "Where on earth have you been?", he launched into his impromptu speech. He didn't sit down, because that would have surrendered the initiative—he was going to spell out how things were, not negotiate and end up asking permission. He paced about in front of her.

"Sorry I'm late, I should have phoned. The fact is, I've been down to see Wellie again, with Sally." He raised his hand imperiously. "Please don't interrupt. I've been seeing quite a lot of Sally recently, and er…as a matter of fact, we're going out together…" He tailed off lamely.

Jennifer was thunderstruck and cut in. "You're what? You're going out together? You sound like a teenager! Have you gone stark raving mad? Falling prey to some hussy who's stringing you along for a lark?"

Robert stopped pacing and confronted her angrily.

"To set the record straight, I made the first moves. I'm the one to blame, not Sally. I fell for her, and I'm in love with her. Luckily, she feels the same. I warned you that we'd drifted apart; well, this is the result. And you can figure out why."

Jennifer tried to hold back tears, but failed, and wiped her eyes with the back of her hands.

"So," she sniffed, "you're intending to carry on seeing her and living here—or what?"

"We can arrange that between ourselves, like civilised people," said Robert, calmed, but not weakened by the tears—he'd had too many mornings mucking-out, too many lonely weekends for that. "I'll probably move out in a few weeks, but you and I will have to discuss a lot of details first. I want you to have a fair deal."

Jennifer stared at him in disbelief, her red-eyed, tear-stained face registering the dawning despair.

"But Robert," she began, "what'll I do without you?"

"No problem, dear. You've got Hercules, and all your competitions and events, not to mention work—the busy executive and her career. You'll never miss me. I'm just an obstacle you take in your stride on the way round."

This was too much, and Jennifer ran off upstairs, sobbing. The bedroom door slammed.

Robert poured himself a whisky and walked jauntily round the lounge, thinking ecstatically of Sally, whistling tunes from *The Magic Flute*. He took a long drink and started making an inventory of the items he would take with him.

Three weeks later, he moved in with Sally. It seemed the best for all of them, the way things were. Her cottage had plenty of room, and for Robert it was heaven to be fussed over again, to feel affection. As Sally helped him unpack his cases, and looked for drawer space for his socks, he felt a surge of love and excitement. He grabbed her in the middle of the room in a great bear hug of emotion. This, he thought, nuzzling her hair, is bliss.

In the darkness at seven o'clock next morning, as the cold rain streamed from the stable roof, Robert energetically forked the soggy bedding in Wellington's stable. Then he wheeled the laden barrow briskly across the yard, performing flamboyant half-circles as he headed for the dung-heap. He whistled cheerily, oblivious to the rain dripping from his hat. He saw Sally carrying a bulging hay net and smiled. This was a marvellous way to start the day.